DAYLIGHT AGAIN

HELL or HIGH WATER: BOOK 3

SE JAKES

RIPTIDE
PUBLISHING

Riptide Publishing
PO Box 1537
Burnsville, NC 28714
www.riptidepublishing.com

Daylight Again (Hell or High Water, #3)

Cover art: L.C. Chase, http://lcchase.com/design.htm
Editor: Sarah Frantz
Layout: L.C. Chase, http://lcchase.com/design.htm

ISBN: 978-1-62649-141-0

First edition
May, 2014

Also available in ebook:
ISBN: 978-1-62649-140-3

DAYLIGHT AGAIN

HELL or HIGH WATER: BOOK 3

SE JAKES

For the survivors.

There are two kinds of light—the glow that illuminates, and the glare that obscures.
—James Thurber

We burn daylight.
—William Shakespeare, *Romeo and Juliet*

TABLE OF CONTENTS

CHAPTER ONE

The second his eyes opened in the dark, Prophet knew exactly what was happening.

As he watched, the darkness of his apartment coalesced into pure slabs of concrete. The windows and the bed and everything in the room disappeared until it was simply a cell. And he was locked inside.

The sheets were twisted. He was on his belly on the mattress, pinned. He knew his arms and legs were free, repeated that in his mind, but it didn't matter. The flashback rolled through, capturing everything in its undertow.

He surrendered for the moment. There was no escaping it anyway, no matter how hard he fought.

"Fuck me," he whispered, the words echoing off the walls.

He'd said exactly that when he'd woken in this cell almost eleven years ago and realized he'd been saved from a terrorist only to be immediately re-imprisoned by the CIA. He'd psyched himself up for struggling through another ring of hell. After all, the CIA hadn't been his idea of the cavalry.

This particular flashback was one of the rarer ones, but it'd been threatening all goddamned day, the way it always did after seeing the eye doc. Prophet had hoped that working out harder than normal would bring on a more peaceful sleep, but apparently his demons decided to come out to play.

The same sick feeling rolled in his stomach now like it had then when he'd looked over his shoulder and blinked at the men in black BDUs standing over him. He'd been chained, facedown, to the cold concrete. He heard the hiss of the hose as they sprayed him with cold water, and even though he knew this reliving of what happened wasn't real, his skin sparked with freezing spikes like fine needles.

But he'd been numb at that point too, refusing to believe that John was gone, that Hal was dead, that the entire mission was a total goatfuck. He also didn't know anything about the other guys on his team, and he refused to ask, because asking equaled putting them in the crosshairs. Then again, no one was asking him anything yet anyway. They were just trying to break him down.

The smell of fear, anger, and despair mixed with sweat and blood was overwhelming. He ached in places he was always surprised could ache. The water rolled off his skin, soaked his BDU pants, and his dog tags dug into his chest, dragged on the concrete when he shifted his body.

When Prophet was first captured by Azar, the terrorist had taken the tags off. Someone from the CIA had gone to the painstaking trouble to find them and put them back on him.

It would be the last time he wore them.

Come on . . . wake up. This isn't fucking real.

And yet, when he looked over his shoulder, he saw Lansing coming into the cell. Locking the door behind him. Reaching up to flick off the camera feed and the hallway lights. It was really quiet. Much quieter than it had been over the course of the last four days, and yes, Prophet had forced himself to keep count of minutes and hours so he could keep track of how long the CIA had kept him in this hellhole, how long it'd been since the Humvee John had been driving was hit. How long it'd been since Prophet had been forced to kill Hal so he—and all his specialized knowledge of triggers for nuclear bombs—didn't fall into the terrorists' hands.

"Where's John?" Lansing asked him.

Prophet turned away, put his forehead on the floor, refusing to have another go-round at this. "I want a JAG."

"You don't get to make the demands." Lansing was leaning over him, then kneeling, grinding Prophet's own knees into the concrete floor. His ankles were already chained to the floor, spread so he couldn't kill anyone with his legs.

As he worked Prophet's tattered BDU pants down, Lansing sneered, "Did you and your lover plan this?"

It wasn't anything Prophet hadn't already heard over the last several days while in the CIA's care—obviously Lansing thought he and John had something to do with Azar. Couple that with the fact that there were no bodies on the scene, not John's or Azar's or Hal's, and Prophet—and John—looked guilty as fuck.

Azar was dead—*that*, Prophet could confirm without the shadow of a doubt. But John . . .

Prophet glanced over his shoulder. "I didn't plan on getting captured. Personally, I think it was a setup," he said casually. "How much did you know about the mission again?"

"You goddamned piece of shit," Lansing snarled. Because this had been Lansing's mission from start to finish.

Prophet hadn't moved, wasn't giving Lansing the satisfaction of fighting. When he heard Lansing pulling his own pants down, Prophet finally looked over his shoulder impassively. "You gonna be able to get it up?"

Lansing slammed his face to the concrete and took him. Prophet didn't know how long it lasted. Lansing kept up a steady stream of threats as he violated him, telling Prophet all the ways he planned on screwing him.

"Anyone new in your life? Gone. I'll hunt down your team members like dogs and kill them when I lay eyes on them if I find you've met with them. I'll fuck with your family, with every new partner—on the job or off. You fucked with the most important job of my career, and you'll pay until you bring me John."

Prophet hadn't given the bastard the opportunity to follow through on those threats, although Lansing managed to keep his hold over him anyway. Prophet shifted partners like the wind, kept contact with his teammates to a minimum . . . and there'd been no one new in his life beyond one-night stands. Until Tom. Now, on his bed, in his apartment, Prophet screwed his eyes shut and told himself that this wasn't happening, that any minute now he'd be free.

That he'd *never* let Lansing near Tom.

At that thought, Prophet nearly hyperventilated. Cursed. Prayed.

And finally, Lansing pulled out without coming—and fuck, at least he'd worn a condom—and since Prophet refused to speak or fight back, and since Lansing hadn't been able to come, Prophet felt like he was in the lead, but he hadn't exactly gotten in the last word. Because Lansing had still fucking violated him.

Until Prophet almost killed him several hours later during the interrogation, and that *had* been caught on video, then circulated through the CIA offices making Prophet infamous . . . and making it impossible for Lansing to kill him off once and for all.

That video made Prophet a wanted man—and in CIA-speak, wanted equaled highly desired operative.

And Prophet had never said anything to anyone about what Lansing had done to him in that cell. But it was always there, between them. Because to Lansing, what Prophet had done to him in that interrogation room was far worse, and fuck, Prophet could live with that.

Or at least he convinced himself he could, until nights like this.

Once Lansing's weight was off him, it was only a matter of time before Prophet could talk himself out of the flashback. *Come on, Prophet . . . not real . . . open your fucking eyes and look around . . .*

Open your eyes and look around while you still can. Because when you can't . . .

"Asshole," he cursed himself. He forced his head up, blinked, waited until the cell turned back into his room. He moved his arms. Sat up. He was in sweats, not tattered BDU pants. No tags around his neck, and he was shivering violently. He went to grab a blanket from the end of the bed and saw the figure sitting on the windowsill, staring out into the darkness.

It was the flashback that kept on giving. "Get the fuck out of here," Prophet growled.

"I'm not the one who keeps bringing me here, Proph," John said.

John Morse, his best friend, first love, SEAL teammate. The man he'd been captured with. The man supposedly shot by a terrorist because Prophet wouldn't answer questions. The man who now may or may not be the leader of a terrorist cell himself.

The man whose disappearance was responsible for changing the course of Prophet's life, for better or worse.

A man who Prophet couldn't help but believe was alive, until he was shown hard proof otherwise. So far, he'd seen nothing but John's ghost visiting him, which only proved that he had PTSD, not that John was dead.

But fuck, the guy seemed as real as Prophet. Dressed in desert BDUs, like he'd been the last time Prophet had seen him. Tanned. Pensive. Staring at Prophet.

"You keep bringing me here."

"Fuck that. Maybe I need to perform an exorcism."

"That's not going to help you."

Prophet sighed tiredly. "What is, genius?"

"Walking away. Letting it go," John told him. "This is going to kill you."

Prophet turned his back on John. "So let it."

"Fucking stubborn. It's too late for me. It's not for you. Don't, Proph. Just . . . for what we had. Don't."

Prophet turned around, prepared to throw the first thing he picked up at the apparition, then realized he was alone.

You were always alone. As he heard the open and close of a window, he rubbed his eyes like they were fully responsible for the hallucination.

When he stared where John had been sitting, he also heard the jangle of a doorknob, a sound so low and yet magnified to an unholy echo in his mind, that it took him several seconds to realize the room wasn't turning into a cell again.

He sat there, trying to pick apart the sounds . . . one coming from outside the bedroom window, the other coming from inside the apartment, the creak of a door, the slam of something outside the window . . .

He swore and got out of bed. Ran his hands along his bookcase and his dresser, reassuring himself that this was his room. He turned and looked out the window.

No sign of John. And still, he was shaking.

Something was going to happen. Ever since Tommy came into his life, bearing that video of him and Lansing—a harbinger—he'd known.

Again, he heard a jangle. Maybe he was on high alert from the flashback, but he didn't think so—if someone was actually there, they'd purposely bypassed the motion sensors. He was up and moving toward the door, but he was still shaky, like he was swimming through molasses.

When he got to the entranceway, he was thrown off-balance, tackled, but caught before being slammed to the floor and rolled so he landed on . . .

Tommy.

Tommy, who rolled him again fast, pinning Prophet underneath him, grabbing Prophet's wrists and holding them on the ground above his head. Tommy, who kissed him before he could curse or think, an all-consuming, punishing grind of a kiss that promised Prophet exactly the fuck he was in for.

God, he liked those kinds of promises. Needed Tommy to hold him down and make things okay, because he would. But he didn't stop struggling though, because hell, he wasn't going to lose his touch, wouldn't make it easy on the fucker who'd decided to go Houdini and bypass all the security cams, just because.

But even as he surged up, Tom dug in, using his body's position to hold Prophet to the ground, his knees pressing Prophet's thighs together.

"You're going to want me to open my legs," Prophet murmured against his cheek once Tom broke the kiss and was concentrating on biting Prophet's earlobe.

"And you'll do it for me," Tom drawled, his breath warm against Prophet's cheek, his hips a slow, steady rock, forcing their clothed cocks to rub together. "Jesus, that's good."

"Fucker," Prophet grunted, Tom's heavy weight grounding him. "You've been practicing."

"Practicing fighting you or fucking you?" Tom held Prophet's wrists immobile with one hand and reached to pull his sweats down with the other.

"You tell me." But Tom had always been good at both the fucking and the fighting. The things Prophet wanted to teach him were beyond that.

Tom's sweeping gaze was predatory at best, and Prophet shuddered under its intensity. "Well, since you're already the one pinned, we've got that covered. And since your pants are down . . ." Tom's hand slid along Prophet's inner thigh, hot and demanding, pressing a knuckle against his hole, and he fought a groan. "Yeah. It's going to be my cock soon enough."

Prophet's legs opened wider, pushing against the barrier of Tom's legs.

"Yeah, that's right . . . let me in," Tom urged, and Prophet wanted to tell him to fuck off, but he couldn't. Not when Tom entered him with a finger. A few twists to open him, coupled with several swipes of his prostate, and Prophet was pushing his hips up to meet Tom's motions. "Good. That's what I want to see."

"Fuck your good," Prophet growled, but his voice was too raw and gave away exactly what he was feeling.

Tom added another finger, turned them until Prophet groaned his surrender. The sensation of Tom's fingertips brushing his gland made him shudder. He kept his hands above his head, didn't try to break Tom's grip. He'd have rug burn on his ass by the end of this, and he didn't care. Tom was here. Home. Safe.

Now, so was he.

"Go ahead—ride them," Tom encouraged, and Prophet rocked his hips in time with the rhythm, letting Tommy fill him, tease him, and generally drive him fucking nuts.

Tom practically crooned, "So good when you obey and take what I give you. Going to bite you, fuck you. Make you scream my name, for starters. Gonna make you forget everything but me . . . so much I want to do to you."

"Yeah, do it," Prophet panted before he could stop himself. "Please, Tommy . . . need this. You don't understand . . ."

But even if Tom couldn't understand the why, he did understand. He bit Prophet's shoulder, then pushed up and eased down his own jeans, kicking them off. He'd taken his boots off before he'd rolled Prophet, which meant Tom'd definitely planned this.

If he'd come in earlier, when Prophet couldn't get out of the flashback . . .

Tom bit his nipple and he jumped. Tom's version of an order to stay with him. One that Prophet was more than glad to obey. He glanced at the barbell piercings laddering up Tom's cock—more impressive when Tom was as hard as he was now. Prophet wrapped a leg around Tom's calf as Tom eased his thighs wider, ready to make Tom fuck him now.

"Oh, you're not taking control," Tom told him. Before Prophet could respond, Tom rolled him half onto his side, while he remained behind Prophet's ass, propping one of Prophet's thighs onto his, preparing to enter him while Prophet grabbed uselessly at the rug. "Don't you come yet."

It took everything he had not to when the hard and fast slide of Tom's cock took his breath away, and when Tom jerked against his prostate, he gladly lost the battle, shooting all over his belly and chest, groaning, contracting around Tom's cock. Then Tom was cursing, and Prophet knew he was struggling not to come too.

Tom slapped his ass hard. Twice.

"Couldn't help it," Prophet groaned, his cheek rubbing against the rug. "And I'll do it again. If you'd hurry."

"Asshole. Jerked off . . . twice . . . on the flight . . . so I could do this," Tom managed finally.

"You lubed up before you came in here?" Tom was throbbing inside of him as his own cock stayed half-hard.

"I'm a good planner." Tom rocked his hips against Prophet, his balls touching Prophet's ass. Prophet ground against him, like he could get the man deeper, but Tom chuckled and pulled back, obviously planning a hot, slow ride.

All of Tommy's focus was on him. His hands alternately held Prophet down and then caressed his skin, then held him down again. The touches were proprietary. Possessive. They'd leave some marks. That was usually Tom's kink, but right about now, Prophet was understanding the benefits of feeling Tom long after they were finished with their grind.

This was part recoupling, part reassurance that time apart didn't lessen anything between them. Tom reasserting that he wasn't going anywhere . . . and Prophet accepting it. His fingers wound into the plush carpet, his breathing harsh, his cock impossibly hard even though he didn't think he'd come again soon.

His balls obviously didn't get the message. They tightened against his body, and Tom reached his hand around, rubbing his palm against the cum on Prophet's stomach, using it to jack Prophet's cock slowly, so goddamned frustratingly slowly. Prophet watched the head of his cock disappear into Tom's broad, tanned hand as his body threatened to jackknife and spill.

He forced himself under control, needing this to last. Giving himself over, letting Tom take what he wanted . . . this was the kind of helplessness Prophet wanted to handle. Tom was ramrod hard inside of him, his strokes powerful, and Prophet's whole body throbbed.

"Jesus . . . Tom . . . this is *reallyfuckinggood*," Prophet breathed in a rush of words.

"Really fucking good, baby," Tom echoed, smiling, the way he always did when Prophet was losing control.

Prophet had lost it a long goddamned time ago when it came to Tom, but he'd be damned if he'd admit it. Out loud.

Again.

"Tommy . . ."

And then Tom murmured, "Lije," in his ear, his voice raspy and desperate, and Prophet shuddered, suddenly as desperate as Tom sounded.

Of course, Tom noticed. And that's when he began fucking Prophet in earnest, saying his name like a cross between a chant and a prayer, and Prophet was damned sure no one had made it sound better. No one had ever shortened it like that, but back in New Orleans, Tom had taken it and made it his own, using it every time they fucked. Like he was proving he knew Prophet, reminding Prophet that he'd let Tom in and there was no backing out now.

Prophet couldn't say anything. It wasn't for lack of trying, but anything that came out was pretty fucking incomprehensible. He was a ball of sensation, his entire being focused on being impaled by Tommy, owned by him for these moments. He was on his side, with Tom between his legs, bending one of Prophet's legs forward against his belly, which let him drive his cock deeper . . . without Prophet being able to do a damned thing about it. One of his arms was half-trapped under his own body, the other trying to gain some purchase, but he gave up and let his face push against the rug as Tom just completely claimed him.

"Tommy!" he cried out as his orgasm rushed through him with an intensity he hadn't expected so soon on the heels of his first climax. It nearly paralyzed him for several seconds, his muscles stiffening as he jerked helplessly on Tom's cock.

"Lije . . . yeah, that's it, baby . . . God, fuck . . ." And then Tom came, spurred on by Prophet's climax, dragged along for the ride. Prophet could feel him pulsing through the condom.

They had to get rid of those, and soon. *Soon.*

He made a mental note to tell that to Tom as the man half collapsed on him for a few moments. He reached up, ran a hand through Tom's sweat-soaked hair, yanking him down hard for a kiss. Tom's tongue claimed his mouth, his way of telling Prophet that it wasn't over, not until Tom said so.

And no, he wasn't stopping. The rest of it was a blur, with Tom pulling out, turning Prophet onto his back, taking his time licking, sucking, not leaving any of Prophet's skin untouched. And Prophet was patient enough to allow it, the haze of orgasms softening him for the moment.

That didn't mean he wouldn't come again. Which he did, a hot, nearly dry orgasm with his cock in Tommy's mouth. That one pushed him over the edge, left him a strung-out, groaning mess, so full of sensation he didn't know what the hell to do. So he lay there, spread out on the rug like a sacrifice, everything forgotten except Tom.

CHAPTER TWO ◉

Tom's body was finally sated and decidedly lazy as he stared up at Prophet from between his legs. "Didn't you jerk off while I was gone?"

Prophet's laugh was a low rumble of contentedness, his gray eyes closer to blue than their usual storm-colored slate. "Twice a day, yeah."

"Still a teenager in so many ways."

"Got that right, old man."

He climbed up Prophet's body and pinned him again, with Proph offering zero resistance. "Keep pushing. You won't have a voice left."

Prophet laughed weakly. "I'll risk it." He looked so comfortable, boneless, Tom knew that unless he carried Prophet to bed, they were sleeping right here where he'd brought Prophet down with his tackle.

They played this game every time he came back after being away or working a lot. It'd started out as a joke, then a bet, and finally, a source of pride for Tom.

Prophet had been shaking when Tom tackled him, but he knew Prophet wouldn't admit he'd recently had a flashback. Tom wouldn't push him, but he'd witnessed them enough. But if he'd stopped to coddle the man? Yeah, he would've had his ass handed to him, and not in a good way.

He reached up and grabbed the blanket off the couch. And a pillow. They shared it, curling on the carpet in the dark.

Tom'd only been gone for two weeks, but that was the longest he'd been away from Prophet since New Orleans. If there was other news, something that'd triggered Prophet's flashback, Tom didn't want to know tonight. "We gonna stay down here all night?"

"Says the man who fucking rolled me in my own doorway."

"You said to make yourself at home."

Prophet snorted, but ran a hand through Tom's hair at the same time. Four months out of the bayou, four months of Tom living with Prophet, but neither of them said anything about making it a permanent thing. Tom had gotten kicked out of his place unexpectedly, Prophet had taken him to his place, and that was the end of the discussion.

Four days after he'd moved in, Tom had left for an EE mission. He'd come back to find that Prophet had unpacked his sad twelve or so boxes, his stuff intermingled with Prophet's.

The sudden ease with which it had been done had hit him harder than he'd thought possible. Prophet put up a hell of a fight, but when he surrendered it was so completely, unmistakably beautiful. Actions spoke louder than anything Prophet could ever say. Even though both of them knew it was simply the calm before the inevitable storm their lives would become—could become, at any moment—they had an unspoken agreement to make the most of this normalcy. Probably the closest either of them'd ever had, Tom figured. And while it made each of them slightly antsy in their own way, for the most part it worked, and it worked well.

Prophet turned on his side to stare at Tom. "I like the nickname."

Tom had noticed, but it was the first time Prophet'd actually brought it up. He'd learned Prophet's real name months ago, but didn't use it outside of sex. He kissed Prophet's collarbone, then flicked his gaze up to Prophet's eyes. "It's not as simple as Elijah is a Prophet. You get those same feelings I do. You predict shit."

"Not like you, Tommy. Just seems that way. I notice things before other people, so it just looks all spooky and voodoo-like."

Tom brushed his knuckles over Prophet's cheek. "I like it. Suits you."

Prophet's face flushed. No smart-assed answer came back. Just a hint of an almost-shy smile and a change of subject. "Your trip okay?"

"Until the blizzard."

"A dusting," Prophet scoffed.

"It's a foot at least."

"I've offered to build a swamp out back to make you feel more at home."

Winter in upstate New York had been brutal so far. After four days' delay and rerouting, he was finally home. And no place had felt like an actual home to him in a really long time. "Already there," he told Prophet.

"Did you do your paperwork?"

"Cope told me he'd file it."

Prophet tucked an arm behind his head. "Impatient?"

"If you're just figuring that out . . ."

Cope had clapped him on the shoulder when they'd touched down, telling him, "Go on, get out of here. Loreth's picking me up later on, so I'll do the debriefing with Phil."

Tom had accepted that offer, mainly because the mission had been a simple one, as the last three had been. Short-term bodyguarding assignments of high-profile executives, completely routine, not an ounce of trouble, unless he counted the executive's mistress showing up when the executive was hooking up with a new chick.

After he and Cope defused the situation, the executive had ended up having a threesome with the two chicks.

Now, Prophet stretched, and Tom traced his ribs with a finger. He was leaner than Tom had seen in a while—he'd upped his workouts like he was a prizefighter in training. Since John Morse was involved, Tom supposed it was the same thing. It's why he was also training every chance he got.

Prophet wasn't dealing with this alone.

"It's not the same without you at EE. Everyone says so." Tom hadn't been sure he'd wanted to bring this up at all, but since he'd gone there. . . "He wants you back there."

"Cope?"

"Don't play dumb. You know I'm talking about Phil."

Prophet frowned. "I don't want to think about any Marines during my afterglow."

"Come on . . . let's go to bed." Tom half dragged Prophet up, luring him to the bedroom with promises of more orgasms. Of course, Prophet fell asleep almost as soon as his head hit the pillow. Tom went to grab something to eat and came back to bed with a turkey sandwich and chips. He put the plate on the night table, and his eye caught on a shadow in the corner of the room by the window. He moved toward it, bent down, and scooped up some sand.

He held it in his palm, remembering he'd seen sand around the box Prophet kept on his dresser. Maybe Proph had been going through some things. He stood, went to the box, and gently brushed the sand from his palm back to its rightful place.

CHAPTER THREE ⊙

P rophet grabbed his phone after a single ring. He'd been buried under Tom, who now shifted and muttered but didn't fully wake up. Prophet had gotten used to these middle-of-the-night calls, usually from Mal or King, passing along intel or checking in.

But it was Zack, his first CO, who launched right in after Prophet's "What's up?"

"I need your help, Proph. Dean's in trouble."

Prophet stared out the window in the dark. Fat snowflakes drifted by, the pavement below already coated and quiet, and Tom's breath was warm against his chest. *This* was real. "Tell me everything."

LT did. And after he'd laid out the problem, Prophet said, "I'll be there in twenty-four hours."

After he hung up, he lay in the dark for a few minutes.

He'd dreamed about LT two nights ago. And a couple of times last week. He'd told himself it was because he was talking to his old team constantly these days, instead of just quick checking-in texts, because they were getting too close to an old wound that had never been allowed to heal.

But something about spending time with Tommy—and his voodoo shit—made Prophet realize that his own instincts had strengthened over the past year. And sometimes, things in Prophet's life came up that coincided so goddamned eerily that he was sure someone up above was fucking with him.

He'd also started noticing how much past he had—and was learning that unpacking it was the only way to have some peace. So he'd started by letting Tom in. Part of that was the physical unpacking of the boxes Tom'd been dragging around with him—forcing him to settle. Because Prophet wasn't the only one with commitment issues.

Still, unpacking Tom had been more for Tom than for him, because in Prophet's eyes, the man had already moved in everywhere: Prophet's place. His room. His heart. And Prophet knew when it was time to give up the ghost. It was too late to save himself.

For Tom's bodyguarding, missions, they'd settled into a routine. Tom would get called in with Cope and he'd go; Prophet would threaten Cope with severe bodily harm if anything happened to Tom; Cope would tell him to fuck off; and then to deal with Tommy being gone, Prophet would throw himself into the planning of the biggest mission of his life. Because the trap was elaborate, and Prophet needed to ensure that it was far sturdier than the house of cards it appeared to be.

At one point, Tom came back with another tattoo hidden under the bracelet he'd worn since his and Prophet's first mission together. A tattoo that was almost an exact replica of the bracelet.

"So no one can take it off me again," he'd said in response to Prophet's unasked question. Because when Tom had been jailed in New Orleans, he'd been forced to take it off, and he'd then waited until Prophet could put it back on him.

The superstitious voodoo bastard.

But Prophet had to admit it made him smile when Tom wasn't looking. And once he'd discovered it, he'd taken the time to trace it with his tongue and nip it with his teeth, marking Tom hard, wanting to give tangible proof to his feelings.

When Tom found out about the other shit—his eyes, everything else he was hiding—he might run, but Prophet resigned himself to the fact that his heart could get ripped out. Again. And it would be worse this time. Way worse, because Prophet knew more, felt more, loved harder.

Tom heard the change of cadence in Prophet's voice immediately. Even half-asleep, he knew the difference between usual news received and trouble—and Prophet's tone meant the latter.

He slid out of bed, headed toward the living room where Prophet was sitting on the windowsill, staring out, unmoving. He didn't glance in Tom's direction, but there's no way he didn't know Tom was there.

Instead of attempting to figure anything out, he went to the kitchen to put on coffee. Because they'd need it. And he'd just poured the mugs and put the eight tons of sugar and lots of milk into Prophet's coffee, when Prophet came up next to him. As he reached for the mug, he put his cheek against Tom's bare shoulder, rubbed his scratchy stubble against Tom's skin. He did that often, in different spots, with his cheek or with a bite, all of it marking Tom. Tom didn't think Proph even knew he was doing it.

He took a sip of his own coffee, penned in against the counter by Prophet's body, his chest pressing against Tom's back. Over the past several weeks, he'd gotten very little sleep, but he was on full alert now.

Prophet finally said, "I've got to go to Djibouti."

"That's a requirement now?"

Prophet snorted, then moved away so Tom could turn and face him.

"No. It's a favor for my old CO. His brother, also a former SEAL, has been living and working there for years. And he's been kidnapped. LT's already on his way with the ransom." He paused, then added, "And no, this isn't John-related."

"You're sure?"

"LT retired before that last mission. Dean was out before John and I enlisted." Prophet's phone gave the distinctive beep of a text message. He punched a few keys, then looked up at Tom. "Will you come with me?"

The man was so serious, like he thought Tom would actually think about saying no. Like Tom wouldn't have insisted on going, whether invited or not.

But being asked like this? It was fucking everything. "When do we leave?"

Prophet gave a small smile, almost shy, before he ducked his head to text more. "Two hours."

"If this *was* about John, the answer would've been the same."

"I know."

The coffee had cooled enough for Tom to finish his mug in several quick gulps before pouring another mug. "I'm going to grab a quick shower."

"I'll join you. But check in with Phil first, yeah?" Proph didn't look up from his phone.

"Yeah. All right to mention this?"

Prophet glanced up at him. "Phil knows the guy. So yeah."

"Won't he wonder why LT didn't call him instead?"

Prophet glanced up at him steadily. "No."

Okay then. Tom went to the hallway to retrieve his bag from where he'd thrown it earlier before he'd tackled Prophet. As he waited for Phil to answer, he picked up the blanket and pillows from the floor, put them on the couch, then carried his bag to the bedroom to switch out clothes.

"Go," Phil barked. His usual greeting. Granted, at five in the morning it was rougher than normal.

"It's Tom. I'm going out of town with Prophet for a job."

There was a long pause. "Who's in trouble?"

"Some guy named Dean, brother of Proph's old CO?"

Phil muttered several strings of curses, then ordered, "Talk him out of going."

Wow, no love lost there. "Seriously, Phil?"

"Do I sound like I'm joking? You have influence over him. Use it."

For a brief second, Tom understood how bulls must feel when a cape was dangled in front of them—a flash of red clouded his vision, and he wanted to smash the phone against the wall. He took a deep breath and told Phil through clenched teeth, "We're going."

Phil cursed. "At least make sure LT doesn't ask Prophet for anything more after you get Dean out. You think you can do that much for him, Tom?"

Phil hung up then, obviously not requiring an answer, which was good, because he wouldn't have liked what Tom wanted to say. Phil, like Prophet, expected Tom to follow orders without question, and even though Phil had asked Tom to bring Prophet back into the fold, he still kept Prophet's secrets close to his vest.

Prophet had quit EE nearly nine months earlier, and from the looks of things, he had no intention of going back. No matter how badly Phil wanted him to. And Tom had only agreed to remain working at EE in order to get more training, so he'd be a better partner to Prophet, no matter what they decided to do, work-wise, once all this John crap was finished.

Whether Prophet's quitting EE was for better or for worse remained to be seen, but Tom never worried about stuff like that. The specifics didn't matter—following the path was what did. Everything that happened was part of his life with Prophet—a path, the next step. Tom refused to miss a moment of it.

At this point, Tom's return to EE after all was said and done was probably on shaky ground as well.

He moved into the shower, the water cool to fully wake him up. Whatever was happening with Mal and Cillian on the John Morse front was being handled well enough that LT's brother could take precedence for the moment.

At times, it almost hurt to watch Prophet's loyalty in action. Obviously, Phil thought so too.

A few minutes later, Prophet slipped into the large, glass-door-enclosed shower. He was already in planning mode, Tom could see, because he absently grabbed for the soap and missed. Three times. And then started rubbing his chest with his hand, until Tom moved his hand, made the water warmer, and soaped him up.

This—the showering together, the taking care of Prophet when his head was someplace else—was familiar. Routine. Tom liked to think of the shower as his way of bringing Prophet back down to earth. And when he was like this, Tom didn't treat him gently—the way he rubbed Prophet down with the soap was brisk, a different kind of foreplay. And even though Tom understood how Prophet got when he was planning, the subtle pullback still brought him back to the time when Prophet hadn't let him in.

"Phil's good with me taking the time," Tom semi-lied as he rinsed Prophet's hair.

Prophet snorted. "He wants you to tail me, get me the fuck away from LT as fast as possible, and talk me into going back." Prophet opened his eyes. "And no, I didn't spy on you. But come on, it didn't take much to figure out. Especially when your jobs are so short and easy."

Tom bristled. "Easy?"

"It's not like you're fighting your way through an international incident," Prophet pointed out. "You haven't even been able to use a flashbang or a grenade. It's not a mission until that happens."

And yes, Prophet was still an asshole. It was almost comforting.

Almost. "So don't fucking bring me then. Unless I'm just coming to carry your bags."

"Is that all you can do?"

Tom sighed. "You're deliberately pushing my buttons. Any particular reason?"

"Yes." A warm, flat palm landed on Tom's chest. "Just fucking accept it, Tommy."

"That you're a dick before a mission?"

"Yeah." Prophet's eyes flashed, a warning signal that Tom had seen before.

Dealing with Prophet wasn't entirely unlike dealing with a live grenade or a Claymore mine. You had to know when to ease off the pressure and when to stay firmly planted and unmoving so you didn't die in the explosion.

Then again, Tom supposed that Prophet would say that dealing with Tom wasn't all that different. "That's good. I wouldn't recognize you otherwise."

Prophet snorted and just like that, they were on an even keel again.

CHAPTER FOUR ◉

As they bypassed security in favor of the passenger entrance for private jets, Tom asked, "Is this your favor?"

Prophet shook his head. "All LT's. We're not flying in close to where we need to be, though. We're going to have to drive a good way in, to avoid being spotted."

"I'm guessing you'll give me all the details on the flight."

"After you sleep," Prophet agreed. "Because you've clocked, what, maybe twenty-four hours over the past six days combined?"

He wasn't wrong, but Tom fought the urge to point out that Prophet didn't sleep much either. Instead, he nodded, because keeping the peace was easier. And to be fair, he had a lot to learn from Prophet, no matter how you sliced it. A lot to learn, and he was more than willing to learn it. Because as teachers went, he couldn't do better than Prophet.

They headed to the tarmac where the private planes were kept. He'd take this over coach any damned day, not the least because he could keep some of his own weapons on him.

Prophet apparently had an arsenal. He clinked when he walked and had two large bags slung carelessly over his shoulder as he moved easily through the crowds. They thinned as they got closer, and Tom was grateful to not be one of the harried-looking suits they were passing. Once they boarded the small plane, the captain came out and gave Prophet a semi-tackle hug. "Man, it's good to see you."

Prophet smiled. "Mitch, this is Tom. Mitch and I did a few joint missions when he was in."

A Navy pilot. That made sense.

Another wiry man poked his head out. "Hey, Prophet."

"How's it going, Jin?"

"We're good. Be ready in a few," Jin assured him. "We're just checking to make sure that we're prepared for any and all eventualities."

He said that last part casually. Too casually. It was something Prophet had said before as well, and Tom glanced at Prophet, who raised his brows innocently when Tom said, "That doesn't sound like a normal part of airline travel."

Mitch clapped Prophet on the shoulder. "No worries, Tom. We've done this before. Sometimes landing's a little tricky since we're not officially registering the flight, but with the extra precautions, we'll be fine."

Mitch walked out of the plane, and Tom told Prophet, "It's you, isn't it?"

"Me? You're the one who causes the problems on our flights, Voodoo."

"You let me think it was me. But maybe, the whole goddamned time it was really you." Tom thought back to the flights they'd taken together. A near–heart attack victim on one. Another, a stalled engine—while they were taxiing down the runway. And then the drunken passenger who'd had to be subdued on the flight they'd been moved to . . .

Jin slipped by them. "Everything happens when Prophet's around. Wheels come off—they don't deflate, mind you. They come off. And we lose landing gear off the wings. Ducks walk onto the plane. You know, shit like that."

"Ducks?" Tom asked, and Prophet gave a put-upon sigh.

"That wasn't me and you know it," Prophet told Jin. "I don't know how the duck got in there."

Tom groaned. All this time, he'd thought *he* was the issue, when in reality, he was working with one of those walking, talking disasters, an angel of death in the flesh. "So basically, when this plane drops out of the sky . . ."

"Blame him," Jin said, jerking a finger a Prophet. They all paused to watch a guy dump parachutes by the entranceway before saluting and leaving. "Those are just in case."

"He's kidding, right?" Tom turned to Jin. "You're kidding, right?"

"Sadly, no. But don't worry—we've only had to do it twice." Prophet steered him to their seats, a set of four grouped in a square pattern. He went to the window seat and pulled Tom to sit next to him, so they could put their feet up on the seats across from them.

"You know I've never actually jumped out of a plane," Tom pointed out. "Not since the academy, anyway."

"What are they teaching you boys?" Prophet asked. "No matter. You can just clip yourself to me. I had to do it for the last guy too."

"No wonder no one wanted to be your partner."

Prophet snorted. "You'd fucking love it. Don't tell me that you're not ready to vault out the emergency exit once we hit the right altitude."

In truth, that was exactly what Tom wanted. But he muttered, "Asshole," at Prophet anyway, leaned back, and closed his eyes as Mitch called out, "Takeoff in four," at them.

Tom snapped his seat belt on and put his earbuds in. Turned up his music to drown out his own thoughts during takeoff, which was smooth and without incident. As they reached cruising altitude, the Fasten Seatbelts sign turned off. Both Tom and Prophet clicked theirs off, and when they did, the plane dipped sharply to the right, so much so that Tom slammed against Prophet, who had to grab Tom's seat arm to keep them both from falling out of their seats.

Cackling from the cockpit traveled through the speakers.

"That's not funny, Mitch," Prophet called.

"You have to make your own fun around here," Mitch called back.

"You're all goddamned crazy," Tom announced.

"Co-sign," Jin said as he walked by and tossed Tom a pillow. He succumbed to the sleep Prophet practically forced on him and woke eight hours later much more clearheaded.

"Hey, Sleeping Beauty—you hungry?" Prophet asked.

Tom ran his hands through his hair. "I could eat, yeah. Something semi-healthy."

"Any food on this plane?" Prophet asked loudly.

"You know where to find it," Jin called. "I'm not a stewardess."

"They like to be called flight attendants," Prophet corrected before stalking to the galley. There was a lot of rifling and some banging around, and finally he came back with donuts, soda, and a bagel that he tossed to Tom. "You said something healthy."

"This is healthy to you?"

"Very. Especially without butter." Prophet nodded sagely. He left again and came back with coffee for both of them, and they ate as Prophet pulled up maps on the laptop and began to trace out routes. He'd obviously been going over this for hours, in his mind and on paper.

"I'm guessing you know who's got him and why?" Tom finally asked.

Prophet nodded grimly. "Rebels. Money. Kind of their new income stream. They know the government won't intervene unless the guy's someone big. And they figure the family will pay anything."

Tom shifted, his booted feet hitting Prophet's as they got comfortable again. "Do they know he's former military?"

"I'm guessing that's pretty well hidden. But LT and Dean's family is really wealthy. And that's not something Dean can really hide, since his family funded his foundations. He's the face of the foundations, does a lot of speaking engagements. And he spends as much time as he can actually working in the clinics." Prophet blew on his coffee and took a few sips. "Perfect. Just the right amount of sugar. Yours too—try it."

Tom stared at his cup, which was basically sugar with a little coffee. "So Dean's a target. Bodyguards? Why not use EE?"

Prophet shook his head. "Dean and LT like to use guys who've just gotten out."

"And so *they* fell down on the job?" Yeah, heads should be rolling.

Prophet waved his hand—the one holding the donut—the sugar starting to take obvious effect. "One was killed and the other was taken with Dean. Once the rebels made up their mind to take Dean, there's not much they could've done. From what I know, it was a big group and they threatened the entire community, and after the first shooting, Dean went quietly. The rebels left the rest of the hospital and facilities alone."

Tom nodded, handed Prophet his coffee, which Prophet drank half of immediately. "You said LT's been contacted for ransom."

"Yeah. He's coming in on another flight, directly into Djibouti. So they can track him and the money he's bringing. And we're bringing up the rear." Prophet chewed thoughtfully, but his body was practically vibrating. How he'd spend another hour, never mind at least four more on this plane, was beyond Tom.

They were landing in the middle of the night, which could actually attract more attention, but Prophet had a plan. He also had aerial views of the place Dean was being kept. As the hours passed, Tom studied them while Prophet pointed out paths. They discussed weapons. Strategies. Different MOs. The what-ifs.

"LT's going to try to lead this, and I can't let him," Prophet warned at one point.

"Because he's too close to it?"

"He's also been out of the game awhile," Prophet explained. "He's going to be a bear about it. Not the good kind."

Tom raised his brows. "Didn't know you were into that."

"Like I told you, I'm full of surprises."

Tom rolled his eyes. "I'll give you a surprise," he murmured.

"I count on that." Prophet turned serious then. "Are you worried?"

"Yes."

"Good. Me too." Prophet leaned back, eyes closed, and immediately fell asleep. It amazed Tom how trained he was to do that, how he barely needed any sleep. No matter how many times his mentor, Ollie, had tried to show him, Tom had issues with shoving himself into a deep sleep. Prophet had offered to help, but so far he'd declined.

So he studied the map on Google Earth, then pulled back to trace a broader route from the airport to the hotel. From there, they'd head out to LT's.

Prophet hadn't told him much about LT, beyond the fact that he and Dean had a great deal of family money, and that it was public record. They all knew that paying the kidnappers was a slippery slope, setting up the possibility for a second kidnapping for a higher amount.

Prophet had also mentioned that Dean had only had two bodyguards with him. Tom hadn't questioned it because, at this point, it was too late for twenty-twenty hindsight. But no way two bodyguards were enough, and if the family was wealthy, spending money on bodyguards shouldn't have been an issue. Sometimes, even having extra muscle for show was enough to dissuade this kind of kidnapping. But this was shit that certainly LT would've known too.

He wondered briefly if that kind of cavalier planning was one of Phil's issues with LT, or how much deeper the problem went.

"I can hear you thinking." Prophet's voice was rough from sleep. He stretched, then instead of asking Tom to move, basically walked over him. When he came back, he was carrying coffee for both of them. Instead of letting Prophet climb over him again, Tom was ready to move; but Prophet was too fast, handing him the hot cup of coffee, which forced him to balance it, while Prophet vaulted over him.

Of course, Tom could've moved to sit across from Prophet, avoiding the issue entirely, but, much like the "break into the apartment and get rolled" game, this was one of those Tom enjoyed playing. Even if it meant a near scalding. "So you met Dean through LT?"

"Yeah. After Dean got out, though. It was the end of my first year in."

He took a sip and found that Prophet had actually made the coffee the way Tom liked it this time. Because just when you could kill the guy... "Did Dean know John?"

"No, never met him." Prophet glanced at the Google Earth images Tom had been studying. "Deal with this in the FBI?"

"Several." It took a light hand and a lot of judgment calls to figure out how savvy the kidnappers were.

"Ever have it go bad?"

"Once," he admitted. "But not for the woman who was kidnapped."

"A partner?"

"Yeah."

Prophet nodded. "Did you warn him?"

"Yeah."

Prophet dragged his gaze along Tom's arm, to the bracelet that hid the tattoo. "I'm not that partner, Tommy."

"You going to remind me of that every time?"

"I think I probably need to. Haven't you gotten the whole 'worried you're going to kill your partner' shit out of your system yet?"

"You're such an asshole," Tom muttered.

"And yet it surprises you every time. Good for our relationship, right?"

"I don't know whether to punch you or kiss you."

"A combination of both is usually the best," Prophet advised. "Might want to wait until later, though."

They were about to start their descent, according to Mitch's call over the loudspeaker. But Tom gave Prophet a quick, hard slam with his fist to Prophet's biceps before grabbing his face and yanking him close . . . and kissing the shit out of him. He pinned Prophet against the seat, ground against him . . . both knowing they didn't have much time before they'd need to be officially seat-belted.

A hard, hot grind, and both of them yanked their pants down. He caught their cocks in his hand and stroked them together. Prophet reached down and tweaked one of Tom's piercings and that was enough to make him shoot. Prophet was right behind him, shuddering, murmuring into Tom's mouth, since they hadn't stopped kissing at all.

Tom only pulled back slightly to breathe—they remained, foreheads together, panting. Smiling.

And he decided that yes, Prophet's surprises could actually be good for him.

CHAPTER FIVE ⊙

A s they got closer to the ground, Prophet suddenly got more agitated. He buckled in, but he was leaning forward, alternately looking out the window and toward the exit, like if the plane didn't land fast enough, he was just going to exit anyway. The second the wheels hit solid ground, he unbuckled and started over Tom, even though the plane was bouncing a little along the makeshift runway, and since there was no tarmac, it never got any smoother. He didn't stop, not even after Mitch yelled at him several times to sit the fuck down, and Tom wondered if maybe the two of them had somehow switched tempers, since Prophet growled at Mitch to "Back the fuck off."

And Mitch did.

Tom collected their papers and as many bags as he could, because Prophet was out on the grass-covered edges of the runway already, gun in hand, checking over the truck that'd been left there for them. Tom waited for Prophet to give the all clear, not wanting him to get any more pissed than he already was.

Finally, Prophet waved him over. When Tom got to the truck, Proph opened the doors to the backseat, telling him, "I'll grab the rest of our gear. Don't want to leave this unattended after I checked it over."

And Tom agreed, because even though they were twenty feet from the plane, he knew what Prophet could've done with those twenty feet. He loaded their bags onto his shoulders and looked around—the area was deserted but it had definitely been used as an impromptu landing strip many times over.

"Lot of journalists land here," Prophet explained, handing him the keys as they loaded up, waved good-bye to Mitch and Jin, and got into the car. Tom set up the address in his phone and let that guide him along the roads, as Prophet tucked his weapons under the seats.

"So we're journalists?"

Prophet nodded, handed him a small portfolio that he knew would contain documentation of his new identity, probably a stamped passport with a new last name. He tucked it into his back pocket and handed Prophet his regular ID information. Prophet tucked it away in his bag so they'd lose all traces of themselves in favor of the new identities.

"Any voodoo feelings, Cajun?" Prophet asked him suddenly.

And yeah, there were definitely some, but Tom couldn't pick them apart from the general heightened awareness that a mission like this brought with it. He shrugged and concentrated on the roads instead.

After driving for less than an hour, he pulled into the entrance of the small, gated hotel that was most definitely more of a tourist place than not, thanks to the beaches. It was also a terrorist hotbed because of its proximity to water without any major barriers in and out of the country.

He parked, and they unpacked their gear, not wanting to leave any of it. It didn't look like much, if you didn't know what you were looking for.

"You check in for us, okay? It's under your badge name." Prophet was more than a little distracted—he'd pulled out his phone and stopped along the side of the lobby.

"Got it." Tom showed the clerk behind the desk his new ID, and the guy didn't seem to care. Tom was sure a thousand journalists had passed through here.

He took the keys when they were offered, but before he could turn around, he heard Prophet's voice—loud, not a yell, but a definite command that rumbled through Tom and made his hackles go up at the same time.

"Show yourself, motherfucker."

Tom turned around to see Prophet standing in the middle of the lobby, his back to the front desk—and to Tom—as he scanned the area in front of him. And there was no one there, but that didn't stop Prophet from growling, "*You're* trailing me? They've got you slumming?"

There was no one else there, besides them and the clerk, who was watching Prophet as though he was crazy.

Which ... yeah. But Tom's senses had been reeling all day, and he'd thought maybe it was from the flight or their upcoming mission, because in general, Prophet turned him inside-fucking-out, but no ... "Proph—"

But Prophet didn't acknowledge Tom. "Come on, you son of a bitch. Show some balls for once in your miserable life."

Finally, Prophet moved slightly, turned halfway so Tom could see his profile, and then he stopped. Stared straight ahead toward a grouping of palm trees that shaded the entrance to the long hallway. His arms were at his sides, his hands relaxed instead of fisted, and he was shaking them out slightly. It was a gesture Tom knew all too well.

Prophet was readying for a fight. Expecting one.

A stocky man dressed in khakis stepped out from seemingly nowhere. Tom wasn't sure who he'd been expecting. Maybe Cillian?

But definitely not the guy from the video, the man Prophet had almost killed with a table he'd been cuffed to. Tom had watched that video enough times that he'd know this asshole in the dark.

His hands fisted as he forced himself not to just blast in and fuck the guy up. But it was only a matter of time.

"Prophet," the guy said.

"About time you showed yourself, Lansing. They pay you for this shit?"

Lansing smiled. "You know you're my special project."

Something about the way Lansing said that made Tom's skin crawl, but he remained stock-still. Waiting. Watching. Prophet was way too calm—Lansing had to know that.

Why the fuck *was* Prophet so calm?

"What do you want from me this time?" Prophet asked Lansing.

"There's no reason for you to have left the States."

"I don't have a restricted passport," Prophet shot back.

Lansing's eyes shifted, slid over Tom. "You brought your partner in crime," he said quietly. "You're slipping, Prophet."

Prophet smiled, and Tom knew in that instant that Prophet had made sure Lansing could find him. The fucker. Asking Tom about his voodoo feelings had been a goddamned test, and if he wasn't ready to rip Lansing's head off already, Prophet's would've definitely been coming off first.

Prophet shrugged. Smirked. "You've been a step behind for the past ten years. You finally get a foothold and you assume I haven't let you in purposely."

A shadow flitted across Lansing's expression, so briefly that Tom might not have caught it. But Tom smelled fear, and it wasn't his or Prophet's.

Prophet had planned this, had lured Lansing here. Whatever the reasoning, Tom was pretty sure Prophet hadn't planned to kill the bastard in the lobby. But that was the problem with old enemies—you never knew how you'd react when confronted by them. Prophet usually had the most control of anyone Tom knew, but Tom wasn't surprised when Prophet lunged so fast and viciously that he brought Lansing to the ground, mainly from sheer surprise.

But Lansing wasn't going down easy. He wasn't evenly matched against Prophet—although most CIA operatives had to be in damned good shape—but he had the same sheer, unmitigated rage running through Prophet as well, and they'd both stopped hiding it.

Tom's stomach clenched. But he wasn't stepping in to stop it, unless Prophet needed help. Prophet needed to fight this one—and Tom understood fighting.

From what Tom had seen in the video, Prophet had taken Lansing out in front of his team. Held him hostage, almost killed him, and smiled about it. So for Lansing, like Prophet, this was all personal, and he had no qualms about showing it. Tom's hands fisted as he watched Prophet and Lansing rolling around, the sound of fists hitting flesh, grunts and curses echoing in the air.

Tom glanced back to see the clerk, still behind the desk, but inching toward something in a cabinet behind him, no doubt a gun or a security button. Tom whipped around and pulled his weapon. "Back the fuck up. Did you call security?"

The clerk shook his head, eyes wide.

"I'm not going to hurt you. I want you to forget you saw any of this." Tom took out a roll of cash and walked forward, handing it to the man. "Clear?"

"Very."

"Good. Where's the security footage of the lobby?"

The clerk pointed.

"Is security watching the feed?"

"No, they patrol. I watch the feed and radio them." He pointed to the cabinet. "That's where the equipment is. And the walkie-talkie. It's been a slow night—I didn't take it out after I came back from dinner."

"That saved your life. Get into that closet now."

"But—"

"You'll be fine. Someone will come let you out. Just don't make any noise for the next half hour. Not a sound. And that money stays yours. Now give me your keys."

The clerk nodded vigorously, handed over the small ring, and went willingly into the closet. Tom locked it and then shoved a chair under the doorknob, all the while the background music of the fight let him know things were still going strong.

He tried two keys on the cabinet, but the third one was the charm to give him access to the surveillance cams. He rewound and erased the footage of him and Prophet through to the present moment and then he disabled the cameras.

When he straightened, he realized how quiet it had become, and moved quickly around the desk to see Prophet standing over Lansing.

"He's not dead," Prophet said. But he looked like he wanted to change that immediately and was fighting with himself not to do so.

He was at Prophet's side in seconds, a hand on his shoulder, forcing him to drag his gaze to Tom's eyes. "No more."

"I can't leave him like this." Prophet's words were ground out as he kept looking between Lansing, who was splayed out with Prophet's foot on his back, and Tom.

Tom heard the answer in his own voice when he told Prophet, "You're not going to do anything. I will. You go to LT. Now."

Prophet stared at him steadily. "Like I'm not already implicated?"

"Not like I'm going to be. I'll meet you." Tom knew that if Prophet was ever going to do this, to let Tom truly help him, to trust him like an equal, now was the time.

Prophet stared at him. "You're pissed."

"Damn straight I'm pissed. You set me up."

"You're fucking kidding me, right, T? I don't want you anywhere near him."

"What did you think you were going to do with him then?"

"Get the truth out of him, once and for all. I was going to send *you* along to LT's."

"Just reverse it and we'll stick to that plan."

"Why?"

Tom ran his fingers gently on Prophet's bruised cheekbone like he could heal it. "He's taken too much from you already."

"He has. And I won't let him take more. I'm not letting you do whatever it is—"

Tom put a hand on Prophet's shoulder, clapping down hard. "Leave, Prophet. Grab the fucking gear and get the hell out of here. No more discussion. I'm taking care of it."

Prophet drew in a sharp breath and seemed to almost come to. He looked down at Lansing and back up at Tom. "How long are you going to be?"

"Several hours behind you. Maybe more."

Prophet nodded. Opened his mouth to say something, but Tom said, "Go, Proph. Now."

And Prophet did, shouldering his bags and walking stiffly out of the lobby and toward the car.

Tom slung Lansing over one shoulder, his bag over the other, and headed for the stairs. He'd taken the keys to a lower level room nowhere near where he'd registered. He'd like to move to a different hotel, because he didn't know if Lansing was alone. But the guy had been beaten badly and for the past fifteen minutes no one had come to his rescue.

Tom would make sure no one did.

"You're just another pawn in their game," Lansing told him calmly.

Another fifteen minutes had passed. Tom had been getting a pitcher of water ready to throw at Lansing to wake his ass up. Now, he turned and stared at the stocky blond man who was watching him intently.

The fact that he'd taken Prophet's beating and still roused without help made Tom wary. He hadn't taken any chances, tying Lansing tightly and keeping all weapons or anything that could be used as one away from him. But Lansing was obviously resilient and he needed to remember that.

He'd swept the room for bugs. Turned on the TV. They were on the upper level, facing the beach. The ocean was the perfect white noise–machine, and would hopefully drown out Lansing's screams if Tom dragged him onto the balcony later.

Later. For now . . . "The CIA reports claim that John Morse was KIA."

Lansing snorted. "That's what Prophet told you."

"The CIA said there's a body." Cillian had actually told Prophet this, but the CIA had never confirmed or denied it.

"That's what Prophet told you. I wouldn't be here if there'd been any bodies at all."

"So your own agency's lying to you?"

"Or whoever gave you that intel was."

Touché, since it was Cillian they were talking about. "Prophet told you he killed Azar."

"And there's no body. So he admits to an unauthorized kill—"

"To save his own goddamned life."

"He could've disarmed him, brought him in for questioning. But he didn't. And suddenly, Azar is missing."

"You really think Prophet's in on this with John?"

Lansing smiled. "I really do. You're under his spell. Just like John was. Did you ever stop to consider that John's not the one calling the shots? That your *partner's* pulling all the strings, the way he always has. The way he always does?"

"Tell me more."

Lansing's smile twisted. "You have no idea what you're asking."

Tom backhanded Lansing without warning, hard enough to bounce the chair to the ground. After several moments, Lansing ground out, "I will fucking kill you, Tom Boudreaux. I made that promise to Prophet, years ago. I promised to make his goddamned life a living hell, and I'm going to follow through with it. And you're first on that list."

Tom yanked Lansing—and the chair—upright, then hit him again, this time aiming for the diaphragm and the ribs, hitting both with a one-two punch, hard enough to temporarily stun the man speechless. When he spoke again, his voice was low and monotone. "You want me to pass out . . . because you're afraid you're going to learn things about Elijah Drews that you don't want to. Think you're the first partner he's slept with? The first partner he's gotten to help cover his tracks? Think again."

Tom crossed his arms and studied the man so intent on destroying Prophet. And then he walked behind Lansing and reached for one of the man's fingers.

"If you value your life, Tom—"

Lansing didn't finish—he howled when Tom snapped two of his fingers in quick succession, then demanded, "Can you prove John helped Azar plan the attack on his own team?"

Lansing stared at him, his eyes glazed. "Yes."

"And you can't prove that Prophet was."

"The CIA's let me work this for years. That's enough proof."

"So why torture Prophet and let him loose?"

"So I can follow him. Eventually, he'll lead me to John. He's already gotten me close. I'm sure you'd think that was just coincidence."

Tom itched to backhand him, but no, he wouldn't give Lansing the satisfaction of knowing that last jab stung. "You know, you keep talking about Prophet, but I can't seem to get a straight answer from the CIA. You tell Prophet that John's dead. Then you accuse John of running a terrorist organization. With Prophet. And yet you leave Prophet loose. None of that makes sense."

"You only know the bits and pieces he throws out to you. Did you ever stop to think he's using you to do his dirty work? You and all of EE and his SEAL team?" Lansing smirked. "Ask Prophet how his old team's managing so well with no real source of income for the past eleven years."

"I'm sure they've got their ways. But you're making my point—eleven years. You've met Prophet—patience isn't his strong suit."

Lansing sneered at him like he was a fool. "Think with your head, not your dick. Prophet's patient when it counts. So is Morse. Two sides of the same coin. Prophet looks like a concerned friend. You all go in to try to kill John—you end up killing other terrorists."

"I thought killing terrorists was top priority?" Tom asked.

"Bringing terrorists in is top priority," Lansing corrected. "Prophet and John need to get rid of Sadiq—he's the only one standing in their way now. And then they're the only ones who have the intel they need to do what Sadiq and the others couldn't."

Lansing attempted to shift in his chair and Tom watched him carefully, walking around to make sure the bindings weren't loosening, that he hadn't somehow procured a weapon. Lansing looked over his shoulder then, asking, "Don't you know that Prophet's collected specialists over the years? Claims he's protecting them. Do you really think one person should have that much power?"

Tom hadn't thought about it like that. "Isn't that better than those specialists being at the mercy of the CIA?"

"He's got you so turned around," Lansing spat.

Blood streamed from his nose. His lip was split in three places.

But his eyes still glowed with determination.

He really believes in what he's doing . . .

Fucking prick.

Lansing studied Tom for a long moment. "You didn't know he was hiding specialists, did you?"

Tom had known about Gary and his family, yes. But he hadn't known there were others that Prophet was still watching over. It made sense—those weren't jobs that finished after a month. Definitely not something Prophet would just abandon, given his loyalty, the never-ending sense of duty that hung like a weight around his neck. And it also made sense that Prophet couldn't tell him about those specialists. That would compromise them, their families, and Tom.

He stared at Lansing, his mind spinning. There was no real new information, but that didn't matter. Having the CIA talk about John being alive . . .

Christ. What the hell had happened on that mission? What had happened in the hours and the days and the weeks before Prophet and John and Hal got into that Humvee?

"Why are you the one here with me, Tom?" Lansing stared at him, like he was studying him, and Tom didn't like it.

"To keep you alive." Tom spoke firmly—believing it.

"No, that's not it. You're not protecting Prophet as much as you're suspicious of him. You want to know. If you didn't, you wouldn't be here now. You'd still be playing lapdog, following him around the country when it suits him. Taking jobs at EE when he has things to do you can't know about."

"I'm waiting to hear about proof."

Lansing gave a harsh laugh. "When people are killed, that's when you'll have all the proof you need. There's so much you don't know. So much you're afraid to ask about. He tells you just enough to believe in him, to have faith in him. To fall in love with him. You're not the first, you know. The other one is living on the run, playing with terrorists, hunted, while Prophet runs around a free man." Lansing spit to the side. "Sounds implausible, right? You know what he's capable of. At least you think you do, but you've never really, truly seen Prophet in action. Multiply what you know by a million and you might be getting warmer on how incredibly violent he is. Prophet's spent his life surviving by any means possible. His missions of mercy conveniently line up with terrorist attacks around the globe. And you're helping him. Ready to kill a CIA agent."

Tom smiled with an ease he didn't feel, and a pride he did. "You're just pissed you couldn't break him."

"Can you, Tom?"

Fucking son of a bitch. Had Tom ever wanted that? "Suppose I do believe you, Lansing—then what?"

"If I was living with a major terrorist, I know what I'd do," Lansing said. "One shot, and it's over. John can't be doing all of this alone."

Tom blinked. Then he turned as calmly as he could and retrieved his laptop, powered it up and pulled up the video he'd watched so many times he'd memorized it.

Lansing stared at the screen, his expression hard, then turned away.

"Did you send me this?" Tom demanded, grabbing the back of Lansing's head and forcing him to look at the video of him interrogating Prophet.

"No," Lansing spat. "I destroyed that fucking thing."

Tom bared his teeth with a smile. "Another fuckup on your end."

Lansing simply said, "*I* didn't send it to you. Prophet's the only one who has a copy of that video."

No way had Prophet faked his reaction to Tom having been sent a copy of the video. Tom would bet his life on it.

But still, something was nagging at Tom, and he hated Lansing for it.

Lansing tilted his head to the side and winced. His voice was heavy when he asked, "Did Prophet tell you that I've taken everything away from him? Did he warn you that you'd be next?"

Tom slammed him across the face. "Does it fucking look like I'm next?"

That woke the man up, got Lansing smiling through his bloody teeth. "Does it bother you that I fucked your boyfriend first?"

Something in the brutal way Lansing spoke made Tom go still.

"That's right. Prophet screwed me, so I screwed him. He never reported it though, which makes me think that on some level he really liked it."

Tom could barely see through the white-hot rage. There was no reason not to kill this fucker—none. He'd go to jail if need be, but thankfully, he'd had the presence of mind to tape this entire conversation.

Lansing was too good to not think otherwise.

"I'm leaving you alive so Prophet can have the pleasure." Tom was surprised at how controlled his voice sounded. "But that doesn't mean I'm through with you yet."

"Remember that the anger you've got now should all be directed at him, not me. One day soon, you'll know I was right."

CHAPTER SIX ⊙

Prophet was running on pure adrenaline fumes as he drove the three hours toward LT's hotel. After the first half hour, his hands began to shake fiercely, and it took everything not to pull over, or to turn back and grab Tommy.

God, he'd put the man in a shit position. And even though Prophet had thought he'd be able to interrogate Lansing, he couldn't have. Not the way Tom would be able to.

Whatever else Tom learned along the way? He was meant to learn.

If Prophet knew Tom—and he did, really fucking well—Tom's interrogation would buy them forty-eight hours free from Lansing.

What if he kills Lansing?

It wasn't that Prophet would give a shit about Lansing, but he didn't want that on Tom's conscience, dogging him for the rest of his life.

Then again, even though Tom's eyes had been turbulent, the rest of his façade had been calm. Really in control. He'd come a long way in nine months. They both had, although Prophet thought he was actually going backward.

He hadn't turned the radio on, and when he didn't hear the jangle of dog tags, he automatically looked around the car's floor for them. To most, the sound they made wouldn't register, but to him, every clink was a thudding echo.

It took him a few seconds to remember that he wasn't in his Blazer, but in an old Land Rover.

Tom had noticed the tags—Prophet knew that. Hell, maybe he'd even picked them up and looked at them when he borrowed the car. Maybe he'd looked through the glove compartment and found the old registration that showed his name and John's. But maybe he hadn't.

At this point, Prophet kept all of it like it was some kind of spell, a way to lure John back out into the open.

The past months had a slowed-down feeling, a relentless pattern to them, as if they all—he and Tommy, Mal, Ren and King and Hook—knew they were simply biding their time, their lives were on a collision course with change. Again. In the past, that couldn't have come fast enough. At this point, knowing what that end might entail caused them all to slow their roll, just slightly.

"Latest intel isn't good," Ren had reported last night to Prophet in his typical understated drawl. Ren's *not good* meant things were close to DEFCON 1. Apparently, there was chatter, and while that was nothing new, this was some significant shit concerning Sadiq. And so yes, Prophet had known with as much certainty as possible that Lansing would follow him. Because Lansing believed he and John were in on this together—so any significant chatter about John being anywhere in Africa, coupled with Prophet leaving the country, would catch Lansing's interest.

And ironically, Prophet was here to help LT, who'd gotten him involved in rescuing and guarding specialists in the first place.

"Hold it together, Tommy," he said out loud, willing Tom to listen, even though he wasn't there—and for far more than the sake of the damned plan. He was well aware that their relationship would be affected by what Tom was doing right now . . . by what Prophet had kept from him. Because Lansing was going to lay shit out that sounded seductively true. And he needed Tom not to falter in his trust. If Tom did, Prophet would be forced to keep him out of the plan to stop John once and for all.

When he got to LT's hotel, and texted him so he didn't get shot making his entrance, LT greeted him with, "You're early."

"Want me to sleep outside?" Prophet couldn't keep the irritation out of his voice.

"You said you were bringing help."

"And you said you wouldn't let Dean do this anymore without several bodyguards just for him and more for the surrounding area."

LT's expression hardened. "You think I don't feel guilty enough?"

"I don't know what the hell you feel," Prophet muttered.

Hours later, his knuckles bruised, Tom left Lansing tied to the sink in the locked bathroom, gagged and bloodied. He might be able to get out of the bathroom in a few hours, but it would take him days before he could do anything other than get to safety. The broken ribs alone would ensure that.

Sometimes, the pent-up violence living inside him could do a world of good. The fact that he'd stopped Prophet from unleashing his own violence . . . the fact that Tom had controlled himself enough to pull back, well, he'd learned.

He'd also learned that the CIA wired their trucks, even the rented ones. So he drove Lansing's about ten miles up the road, to another hotel, so it looked like maybe he was following Prophet somewhere. From there, Tom borrowed another truck and with his weapons tucked in around him, made the several hours' drive to LT's hotel.

Their rental car from the airport wasn't here, but he assumed Proph had gotten rid of it. He parked several structures down and walked through the dusk. Two quick knocks and Prophet was opening the door, letting him in, checking him over and cursing.

"I'm okay," he said. Prophet shook his head, but didn't disagree. He put a hand to Tom's cheek, pressed his lips together, so Tom assured him, "We're okay."

Finally, Prophet nodded. From behind him, Tom heard the clearing of a throat, but Prophet didn't drop his hand, not even when someone said, "You must be Tom."

Tom turned, and Prophet's hand finally dropped. "And you're LT."

LT was about fifty. Still in good shape—probably could give guys half his age a beating and barely break a sweat. His hair was more silver than black, his eyes were dark and serious, and he was dressed like a man on vacation, not someone about to bring a suitcase of ransom money to kidnappers.

Tom held his hand out to shake. LT went to grip it, but turned it over instead, glanced between Tom's knuckles and his face. "I can see why Prophet likes you."

Prophet snorted. "Subtle, LT."

"Any updates?" Tom asked.

Prophet studied his face carefully. Frowned.

And then LT broke in. "They called again—want to move up the meeting time. Didn't give me a choice. Glad Prophet showed early. Gave us time to plan."

Tom didn't say anything. He waited until Prophet motioned him over to the table with his computer. When he sat next to Prophet, he said, "Anything we're doing differently?"

Prophet seemed to understand that Tom was not talking about Lansing right now. Instead, he answered Tom. "I think this house they're sending LT to is a fake." He pointed to a smaller structure barely visible in the photograph Prophet had to have taken himself at some point today. "So they're having him deliver to the wrong house . . ."

"Have they given proof of life?"

"Yes—through late this afternoon," Prophet confirmed.

"Okay, so LT goes to the wrong house with the money and then . . . what? They take the money and kill him?"

"I'm thinking either that or keep him and up the ante."

"And Dean?"

"Keep him and hope his lawyers pay . . . or they kill him and keep LT." Prophet sighed. "Of course, this is all dependent on how antsy these guys get. They're not as organized here as South America. They want the fast buck, and they're not against kidnapping the same guy twice to try to get more money. According to LT, Dean was paying these guys—they shook down the clinic, so he paid them monthly. For protection, they'd insisted. And then, when they wanted double and triple the amount, Dean refused. We need to get in there soon."

He wasn't arguing with Prophet's gut. Mainly because his was singing the same tune. "Do they know LT was also former military?"

"I'm guessing, but I can't be sure. Just follow my lead," Prophet murmured to him, then, louder, "Okay, LT, listen. Tom and I are going to go in first. You follow behind—give us half an hour. Park where we planned. And then you'll bring the suitcase in while we watch."

"Don't you think it's better if I go with you?" LT asked.

"I need you here in case they call and change anything," Prophet said, and yes, apparently LT was buying that. It was actually completely reasonable.

What Prophet and Tom planned on doing, on the other hand? Completely fucking nuts, and it got Tom's blood pumping. He waited until LT went into the other room to start getting ready before he asked, "You trusting me . . . letting me in. Is this about Lansing?"

"It's about us. You took him on for me."

"I didn't do anything I didn't want to. Ever since I first saw that video, I wanted to kill him. I didn't know why, but I just fucking did."

"But you held back."

"I'm learning self-control."

Prophet gave a wry smile. "Don't practice any of that shit tonight."

"I know what I'm doing."

"I know, Tom." Prophet paused, his expression tight. "You don't trust me, tell me now, before we go out there."

"Guilty conscience, Proph?"

"I'm a realist."

"And I'm not stupid. Didn't think Lansing would sing your praises."

"You think I don't know what Lansing tried to tell you?" Prophet demanded. "That I'm collecting specialists and hiding them away from everyone for my own gain?" He shook his head, his lips pressed together tightly, before he lifted his finger and pointed at Tom. "If I was worried, why would I leave you with him?"

"Come on, Prophet—I'm not stupid. I don't believe a lot of what he says."

Prophet narrowed his eyes. "Fuck you, Tom. Fuck you hard." And then those eyes flashed, dark storm clouds settling into the slate gray. "It wasn't your fight."

"I know. I took it on. No regrets. You?" Tom challenged.

"Only that I thought I was stronger than that."

CHAPTER SEVEN ⊙

Against his better judgment, Tom rode shotgun so he could wrap his cut-up knuckles to prevent infection and tried his best not to watch the road. Prophet drove the truck as close to the meeting place as he could possibly get without being seen. Luckily, they were parked on higher ground, which meant the truck would be tough to spot.

He and Prophet, on the other hand? Sitting ducks. Which is why they'd take the longer route down and around to get to the back of the house. The truck was for the escape, which would be a straight run up the hill for one of them—with Dean and his bodyguard—while the other covered them.

Prophet had informed him that he'd be doing the covering while Tom took the hostages up the hill, but conceded when pressed that sometimes, things happened and you had to be flexible.

Tom had simply rolled his eyes and nodded, in no mood for the Special Forces lecture.

Together, they half slid, half commando-crawled down the hill. Tom hadn't spotted any guards actively watching the hills, but that didn't mean there weren't cameras trained on them from the inside.

"Time?" Prophet asked quietly.

"We've got fifteen minutes until LT gets here," Tom confirmed.

"Ten. He's always early," Prophet corrected.

"Looks like there's no one in the big house."

"Gotta be a trap. Door's gotta be rigged."

Tom shifted the binoculars to get a glimpse of the small house. He got lucky with a tiny window on the ground floor that was cracked open several inches. "I see four men, walking around."

"Hang on," Prophet said, and Tom watched him use the heat-sensing equipment. "Okay, got two more guys upstairs. All of them moving as well . . . except for two more heat spots in another room that aren't moving at all. Shit."

"Gotta be them, Proph," Tom said.

"And we've got to be prepared to carry them out of there."

"I was never not prepared for that—you always say to be prepared for every eventuality." Prophet nodded approvingly. "We've got to go in now."

"Roger that." Binoculars down, weapons up, hidden flat on the ground. They moved stealthily until they were maybe fifteen feet from the back of the small house.

Prophet reiterated the plan. "I'm going to take them out. Distract the fuck out of them. You grab Dean and his bodyguard and go to the truck. Set the flashbang off behind you."

That last part was new. "Won't that fuck you over?" Tom asked.

"I'll be fine. And if the bodyguard's in decent shape, I'll keep him with me."

"And if Dean's all right?"

Prophet stared at him for a long moment, then said, "Just get him to the truck, even if he's all right."

Tom could only afford to wonder briefly why he wouldn't let Dean, the former SEAL, help if he wasn't injured, figured it had to do with his family money and other threats. "Consider it done. I'll also deal with LT until you get there."

"If I'm not there within fifteen minutes, you go back to the hotel without me. And then I'll meet you at the second hotel."

"Proph . . ."

"I'd do this with Mal or King or Ren or Hook," Prophet told him. "You don't want special treatment."

He didn't. And Prophet was ready to prove himself in control again. Tom trusted him. "Fine. But let's take out the two on the second floor with the rifle first. Fewer to deal with."

"Yeah, I like that. Same time?"

Tom nodded. He adjusted his scope, and Prophet did the same next to him. "You take the one on the right."

Tom got him in the crosshairs. It seemed like forever, and once he pulled the trigger it was as if the world moved in slow motion. The window shattered quietly, the men went down, and Prophet wasted no time in launching the next part of the attack, which consisted of Molotov cocktails arcing perfectly into the front windows, driving the kidnappers to the back, away from where the prisoners were being kept, since the front actually faced the jungle paths. Prophet pointed, motioned with a hand signal for Tom to go in behind.

Tom did, running under the smoke and haze to the second floor. He saw Prophet approach the thin, dark-haired man on the floor, and then a black man in camouflage was helping Prophet to drag the dark-haired man up.

"Dean and Reggie," Prophet said, pointing and then swinging to cover them as Tom cut in, ready to get Dean out. Reggie was propping Dean up, and Dean's legs kept buckling. Tom propped Dean's free side, held a rag over Dean's mouth and nose to keep him from inhaling the smoke, since it was all the guy could do to hang on to him and Reggie, until they got clear of the house.

Which they did, clearing the stairs, the front door, and half the distance to the jungle area before Prophet stopped and looked at Reggie. "You up for a sweep?"

"I'm your man," Reggie said. "Dean, you'll be okay."

Dean coughed, then nodded. He held out his free hand and Reggie pressed something into his palm before heading back toward the house with Prophet.

"Dean, I'm Tom. I'm taking you to safety—your brother will be there too, okay?" He glanced over in time to see Dean close his eyes and nod.

Tom was ready to throw him over his shoulder and haul ass out of the line of fire—because even though the kidnappers were momentarily stunned didn't meant Tom would take chances. Impatience burned through him—Prophet's must be catching. And then Dean's hand shot out as if he was throwing what now appeared to be a thick, wooden stick Reggie handed him, but a long walking stick emerged instead. The kind a blind person would use to tap in front of him in order not to trip over anything.

Tom allowed himself another look at Dean's face—bruised and covered in soot from the fire. His eyes were unfocused, but they weren't glassy or faded, the way Tom had in seen people who'd been blind from birth.

The blindness was a recent injury then, and why the hell would Prophet keep this intel from him? Although Tom could easily see the former SEAL training in Dean once he got moving, the man was still dehydrated and shaken and trusted Tom more than the stick.

"We're almost there," Tom told Dean without stopping. "Up the hill and the truck's beyond it. A good vantage point to make sure no one's coming after us."

"There were six men in there with us," Dean huffed.

"We took out the two upstairs with sniper rifles before we bombed the downstairs," Tom said. "And two more died in the initial firebombing."

Two left. Prophet could handle that with both hands tied behind his back. Still, that was no reason to not be vigilant. Especially because Dean was weak and putting a good deal of his weight on Tom.

Tom led him forward into the dark jungle brush, not stopping when he heard the sound of gunfire behind him. Reinforcements. It was far enough away not to impact them . . .

"Half a mile out," Dean said quietly. "Enough time to get away."
Unless Prophet decided to hang around and blow them up.

"Truck's in sight." Tom still bore most of Dean's weight as he hustled them up the remaining several yards. "So's your brother."

"Great," Dean drawled.

LT was fucking furious, but at least he'd had the good sense not to jump into the fray. It looked like he would've started yelling right away if Dean hadn't half collapsed against the truck. With LT's help, they got him into the back seat, and Tom ran a glucose IV.

LT kept patting Dean's cheeks to keep him awake him.

"He's okay. Exhausted. Dehydrated. Probably has a little smoke inhalation," Tom catalogued after the IV was running. For Dean, sleeping through the rest of this wasn't the worst thing in the world. "Stop fucking hitting his face, all right?"

"Don't you tell me what to do, boy."

Boy? Okay, one of those. And since Prophet wasn't there yet, the fucker was going to attempt to make Tom his punching bag. Even when Dean roused and advised him to "shut the fuck up, bro," LT was just warming up his rant, all the anger and fear from the last days pouring out without thought, his voice drowning out the gunshots and mini-explosions below. He continued to rail about Tom's total irresponsibility and the importance of following plans and following orders.

It got so bad that Tom walked away from the truck so Dean could get some peace. Of course, LT followed him, grinding out, "I don't know who the fuck you are or why Prophet trusted you with my brother..."

"I'm a former federal fucking agent. I worked for a sheriff's department, and I'm a private contractor with EE, Ltd. So I think I'm more than qualified to lead a man to safety."

"You could've killed him. Prophet's always been a goddamned cowboy, but he'd never leave me out of a plan. This had to be your doing."

"It worked," Tom said succinctly. "Shut your mouth, or lower your goddamned voice, LT. And get in the goddamned truck."

LT stabbed a finger in his face. "This isn't over."

Tom grabbed the man's hand and twisted it away. "Put your hand near my face again and you'll fucking lose it. Trust me on that. Now go sit down and see how your brother is doing before I shut you the fuck up myself."

LT jerked his hand away and went into the back of the truck with Dean. Tom waited on the hill for Prophet, willing the man to get his ass in gear so he didn't have to leave without him.

When Prophet went back into the danger zone with Reggie, cradling the M249 SAW—a lovely big motherfucking machine gun—like a baby, he knew he was losing control, even as he knew he appeared more in control than ever. He also knew both were necessary, and he was more than grateful Tom was there to catch him in the end. Because Lansing had unraveled him, and seeing Dean's face during the rescue had nearly undone him completely.

As he took out an incoming Jeep of kidnappers who must've seen the flames and come in for backup—and they had no chance against the SAW, with its seven hundred rounds of raw power per minute—he realized he was so fucking angry at Dean. He hated seeing the fear etched into the man's face, and there was no better place to take out his aggression than on the bastards trying to kill him.

As gunfire cracked the night in staccato bursts, Reggie stood at his back, covering him.

There was nothing wrong with fear. But Christ, Dean had gone beyond harnessing it to just flat-out scared beyond reason. Too scared to save himself, or to try to.

When Prophet first burst in, he'd sworn that for a split second Dean had seemed pissed. That he hadn't wanted to be saved.

Or maybe that's just you, projecting.

But no. Prophet knew better. It's not like they hadn't noticed they were being rescued. When he'd gone in, head down, mouth covered, Dean had just been sitting there, waiting. And Reggie had been desperately trying to yank him up.

And sure, fire was unpredictable, but it was better than bullets. Reggie had known that—and so had Dean on some level. The smoke was meant to be a shield.

And when he'd urged, "Dean, come on—it's Prophet," Dean had turned sharply to him—sharply and angrily—and even in those brief moments, it was apparent Prophet hadn't imagined the death wish Dean harbored.

Mainly because he held the same one at times.

He had to face the fact that Tommy and his voodoo might already know the truth about his eyes, that he might be waiting for Prophet to spill. God, it'd be so much fucking easier if Tom would just tell him he knew.

Sometimes, Prophet wanted easy. And this motherfucking machine gun? This was easy.

Major retaliation was a way to ensure no one would make the mistake of kidnapping Dean—or harming his community—again. It could also totally backfire and make the rebels seek revenge. But Prophet was ready to take that chance.

He was going to burn it all goddamned down. With Reggie's help, he threw the dead bodies back into the burning house. There'd be nothing left of this fucker when he was done.

CHAPTER EIGHT ⊙

I t was only when Tom saw Prophet's quick flash of light signal that he knew they were close. He'd had the truck idling, waiting for Prophet and Reggie to haul ass. As soon as they were in, he pulled through the footpath, away from the house. LT followed alone in his own truck.

He used the parking lights only—and his instincts—and Proph watched the road like a hawk. When he got to the main road, he stopped so Prophet could get out to check for visible ambushes or roadblocks.

Prophet got back in. "We're clear. You see a roadblock, you speed up." He pulled out a sawed-off machine gun from under the seat and glanced in Tom's direction. "Good?"

"Good," Tom echoed, then pulled out and got on the road. He turned the lights on and sped along the road as fast as the terrain would allow. He knew from working with Cope that the roads were unpredictable at best, moving from asphalt to rocky dirt with no warning. It was the dry season, so most of the roads had suffered through flooding and settled back in over the last months, but there were still craters that could take out any vehicles.

The new locale was several hours away from the scene of the kidnapping. Tom and Prophet utilized their press badges to check in, leaving the other men in the trucks. They weren't able to drive right up to their new place, had to go through the lobby of the tourist hotel. And while they didn't exactly blend in well at the moment, the rebels weren't going to risk coming there to grab them. Not with all the armed soldiers around, paid to guard the hotel guests. And they hadn't been followed.

Tom got out and Reggie was already helping to grab the gear, and that's when he saw that Reggie only had one arm. In the earlier confusion, Tom hadn't seen the metal, hook-like device attached to a prosthetic.

Reggie waved it. "So much better than a pretty-looking hand. I'll take this metal shit any day of the week. I throw a hell of a punch."

"Yeah, you're a real brawler," Dean drawled, obviously feeling better. He was halfway out of the truck, his stick down.

But Tom didn't want to take chances. "Hey, Dean, let me help you in case you're still weak."

He took the IV bag down and held it as Dean stared in his direction. Tom expected resistance but got none. Instead, Dean grabbed Tom's arm to finish exiting the truck and paused. Moved his hand from gripping Tom's forearm and felt for Tom's bracelet. Touched it. Looked toward Tom and smiled. "Yeah, okay, that makes sense now."

Tom didn't question it, just took a step toward the building. Dean tapped the stick in front of him, although it made no noise when it hit the ground. Dean was a man used to moving silently.

"I'm still a little shaky," Dean admitted finally.

"You're doing much better. But I'll keep the IV in for a while longer," Tom informed him. "Some food will help too."

"Thanks. Sounds really good."

Tom stayed close, but Dean didn't ask him for any further help as they walked.

When they got through the lobby, Tom guided him in the general direction of the luxury "tent"—a large, three-bedroom, free-standing structure that LT had rented.

Before he went inside though, Dean turned until he was facing the beach several hundred yards away.

"I love the smell of the ocean," he told Tom. "And I love it here. I'm sure that's hard for you to understand."

"Not really, no. You need more protection, though."

Dean bristled, and Tom saw the resemblance between brothers. "You don't know anything about it."

"I know that I risked my life to save your ass," Tom countered.

Dean smiled. "It's nice to be spoken to like I'm an asshole. You wouldn't believe how nicely people treat me, just because I'm blind. And it's annoying because, generally, I am an asshole."

"I'm not disagreeing." Tom paused. "Did you talk Prophet into doing the jobs he does?"

"I didn't talk him out of them," Dean admitted. "I strongly encouraged him to do what he was meant to, because he could get hurt at any time. He was so good, Tom. Still is. At the time, I thought that he shouldn't waste that talent when there were people to help."

Tom stared at him. "And how do you feel about that now?"

Dean shrugged. "I realize that it sounded good—and that I did mean it then. But I was pissed off at myself, at the world. I told him what *I'd* want to hear. And Prophet *was* perfect for those jobs. He still is."

"Christ," Tom muttered.

"Prophet knew exactly why I preached what I did. He's not stupid—never was. But the guy who gave me that bracelet first told me I needed to pass it on to someone who could do some good in the world. And to take it back if that didn't happen."

So Dean had given it to Prophet. At some point, John had worn it . . . but either John had given it back or Prophet had taken it back. Tom would never—and Prophet hadn't asked, simply nodded approvingly over the tattoo and moving the bracelet back over the ink. Both were now a symbol of their trust in each other, and a way to make Tom believe in himself during a time when he didn't. A time when he didn't think he ever could.

As far as Tom was concerned, the bracelet was just a symbol of Prophet's magic. If Dean had been able to give that to Prophet during a time in his life when he'd needed it, then maybe he could forgive the guy for being an asshole. "Thanks for telling me that."

"Don't go all nice on me now," Dean warned.

"Don't worry—I'll make up for it with your brother."

"Speaking of." Dean pointed to where LT was waiting in the doorway. "That's my cue to leave."

The brothers paused for a moment, LT touching Dean's face, leaning in to hug him. Tom turned away and stared at the ocean until LT came up next to him.

The gruff man stuck his hands in his pockets, rocked on his heels, obviously uncomfortable with the apology he was no doubt here to make. Finally, he ground out, "Prophet told me it was all him."

Tom glanced at him. "Maybe he told you that to try to save my ass."

LT frowned, obviously not reading the sarcasm—or blatantly ignoring it. "Yeah, I thought about that. But no. Still, the fact that you took the blame for him, no hesitation . . ."

"Makes me the kind of guy you like?" Tom made sure LT couldn't miss the sarcasm in his tone this time.

LT stared at him steadily, the circles under his eyes deeper than they'd been even an hour before. "Next time I won't bother apologizing."

Tom turned to face him, ignoring the growled warning of LT's tone. "Is that what that was? Maybe you're apologizing for the wrong thing."

LT squared off to him as well. "Yeah? What's that?"

"Prophet met you early on. Said you helped put him on the path he took." Tom paused, then emphasized every word, imagining each one a knife twisting. "You were the one who talked Prophet into doing those jobs."

LT's eyes were a pale blue, but the man behind them wasn't as flinty as they were, at least not any longer. "Do you expect me to apologize? He's the perfect person for them."

"Whether he was or not—"

"Is, Tom. *Is.*"

"No. Fuck that." Tom got in LT's face, consequences and old friendships be damned. "You leave him the fuck alone. I won't let you pull him back into shit. He's still paying, all right? That won't end, even when all the shit that came with it does."

"I'm just glad he got away from that EE bullshit. He hid there, wasting away. I'm glad he stopped making that mistake. He's good at the jobs I pushed him into—just like he was good tonight."

"Tonight, you were ready to kill him for taking chances," Tom reminded him. "And what about what's good for Prophet?"

"He had a talent. I made sure he used it."

Tom stared at him steadily. "Did you make sure your brother used it too?"

"You have no right to come in here and question things you had nothing to do with." LT's voice raised, and a few of the guests who'd been cutting through a path several yards away glanced over. Tom simply waved and smiled, and they went on their way. And then he turned his attention back to LT.

Tom liked Dean a lot. LT . . . not at all. "I think you talked guys into doing what you'd never do yourself."

LT looked shaken—that Tom said it or that he'd been caught, Tom would never be sure. Because he got up and left LT outside and went into the front room where Prophet was waiting.

CHAPTER NINE ◉

He found Prophet in the living room section of their place, sitting on the back of the couch, staring into space. He'd changed out of the camouflage on the road, like Tom, and now he only wore khaki shorts, his shirt thrown on the floor. There was dirt and mud and red dust all over his skin, and he looked like hell, but his reverie broke easily when he saw Tom.

"Everything okay?" he asked.

"I'll be happy to be away from LT. Guy's a fucking dick." Prophet snorted but didn't argue. "Dean's cool."

He grabbed some water, took a drink from the bottle, and passed it to Prophet, who he was sure hadn't hydrated or eaten anything since last night. "You need to eat."

Prophet passed the bottle back. "I ordered food. They'll bring it here within the next few minutes."

"Good."

Prophet reached out and touched the bracelet. Smiled. Then moved it aside to rub the tattoo. "You know Dean gave this to me, right?"

"He made a vague reference to it."

"The guy who gave it to Dean told him to pass it along. And the guy before that too. It's supposed to stop when it gets to the right person."

Tom raised a brow. "So that's me?"

"I don't think anyone else got a tattoo of it, so I'm thinking you win."

Tom gave a brief smile. There was still the Lansing crap between them, but he was happy to push it off in favor of keeping watch on the three men in the other rooms. "Are you okay?"

"Not really, no." Prophet pushed a hand through his hair but didn't elaborate. Tom supposed he didn't need to. "You did good out there."

"It was a good plan."

Prophet nodded. And then the food came, and all the men came together briefly to eat. The table was quiet, but since LT didn't open his mouth except to shove food into it, it remained peaceful. Dean looked better, but exhausted, and he and Reggie went back to their room, carrying their drinks with them. LT bowed out too, taking a third helping of food with him.

Prophet continued eating and Tom sat back, full and comfortable. When Prophet finished, he went to check on the others, and came back after a few minutes. "They're out."

Tom flicked on the monitors. He hadn't wanted to invade their privacy while they'd been awake, but now, in order to give them some space, it was necessary to keep an eye on the doors.

He and Prophet would remain out here, closest to the main door, putting Dean and Reggie in the middle room. Prophet had rigged something to the windows, both outside and in. LT was camped out in the back room, with a monitor on his brother's room as well.

Tomorrow, the other three men were going back to the States for a while, via LT's private plane. LT had decreed it earlier, and Dean'd looked like he'd wanted to argue but hadn't.

"He says he's not giving up his work here," Prophet told Tom now.

"What did you tell him?"

"I just listened. He knows the risks."

"And what, you're willing to jump in and save his ass every time someone makes a grab for him?"

"I mentioned to him that I wasn't," Prophet said.

Tom sighed. "I think he needs better bodyguards."

Prophet winced a little, then turned away.

"Ah, come on, Proph. I get what he's doing. I think it's great. But obviously, Reggie . . ."

"What? A guy with two arms could've saved them from twenty soldiers?" Prophet demanded.

"You're the only one I know who could've done it, possibly with your hands tied." It wasn't a reference to Azar and Sadiq, but of course, Tom went there briefly, glancing at Prophet's wrists. Prophet's hands fisted and he shook his head, turned away to stare out the window. "Reggie could stay on. Dean could still employ bodyguards who are—"

"Fucked up?"

"Disabled," Tom corrected.

"Right. But the non-disabled guys should do all the work. The disabled guys are just for show."

"I don't get it—this guy's important enough for you to race down here and save him, not because of who he is, not because anyone orders you to, but because he's your friend. And now you don't want to give him every chance you can to ensure this never happens again?" Tom threw up his hands, unable to hide his exasperation at the more stubborn than normal resistance. "I'm being realistic. Typically, that's your job."

Prophet stared up at the ceiling before glancing at Tom. "You know that Dean took out ten of the soldiers himself, right?"

"I heard. I'm glad he can defend himself. But the remaining ten still captured him, which proves he needs backup."

"Because he's blind."

Tom took Prophet's hands in his across the table, then ran his palms over Prophet's forearms. "We've all got weak spots. Things we need to be careful of."

"Is this going to turn into some kind of inspirational talk? Because I'll throw you out the motherfucking window."

"You could try," Tom said. "And for the record, I don't consider anything about you weak. But everyone needs backup, Proph. Everyone."

Prophet stared at him a beat too long, then looked away. A ball of nerves found its way back into the pit of Tom's stomach, but there wasn't much he could do about it.

It was so quiet—soft music played in Dean and Reggie's room through the monitor, the ocean's hum in the distance, but that was it.

"They're not together, right?" Tom asked now.

"Not like that, no."

"Reggie feels guilty."

"They both do," Prophet said. "I talked with LT earlier. He picked up another group of full-time bodyguards—he's going to train them, along with Dean."

"So they're compromising."

"Yeah, with LT being lead bodyguard. I want to say, that's what family does, but if you know my family, I don't mean blood relatives."

Tom snorted. "Uh, yeah, I think I understand that."

Prophet reached a hand up—at first Tom thought Prophet meant to push him away, but then Prophet's hand splayed along the side of his neck and jaw, tugging Tom in for a kiss. It held the usual flare of heat, but there was a lot between them tonight. Lansing. The men in the other rooms. The fact that they were all still in danger.

Prophet pulled back with a soft groan. "Sorry."

"Don't be. Not about that. Ever."

CHAPTER TEN ⊙

T he flight time was just before 0400. Prophet roused Tom and
they drove LT, Dean, and Reggie to the closest airstrip and
waited until the plane took off.

"Sure you guys don't need a ride home?" LT asked Prophet.

"We're good, thanks," Prophet had said.

Once the roar of the plane was gone, Prophet put the truck back
into gear, and Tom was lulled to sleep within the first five minutes.

When Prophet nudged him gently, Tom opened his eyes and
blinked at the structure in front of him.

"Come on, Tommy," Prophet said. "I've got the bags."

Tom slid out of the truck and stretched, then followed Prophet
inside the luxury rooms. They were still in a hotel, and they couldn't
have gone far, but the change of scenery was welcome.

Prophet dropped the bags behind Tom and locked the door. Tom
was already moving toward the large picture window that led out to a
big covered deck overlooking the parks.

He saw elephants and zebras. No snipers were coming in from
the back.

Prophet motioned. "You like it?"

Tom nodded, unable to look away from the animals. "It's gorgeous.
Makes you forget all the other crap. I'm guessing that's the point?"

Prophet put a hand on his shoulder. "It's time to start enjoying
shit."

"I thought that was *always* your motto."

"It is," he conceded. "But my mind sometimes fucks it all up."
And since he rarely talked about his flashbacks, only once since Tom
woke him from one, that was a big step. "You've seen me have more
flashbacks, since New Orleans."

Tom stuck his hands in his pockets, still staring straight ahead, figuring that would make it easier for Prophet to take what he was about to tell him. "I stop a lot of them from getting *to* flashback status."

There was a pause—a little too long, telling Tom that Prophet really didn't have any idea. Finally, Prophet spoke, simply asking, "How?"

"Usually, I lure you into having sex. Half the time, you probably think it's a dream, but it's a better dream than what you usually deal with."

"Yeah. Much," Prophet agreed as Tom turned to face him, staring into those remarkably calm gray eyes. "Guess I give you a run for your money."

"You make it up to me."

"Figured we'd stay an extra day, if that's all right with you."

"Yeah, that works," Tom said quietly, still half-asleep. This time between night and morning was always like a hazy dream for him, and even once they were back inside their place, with the doors locked, all alone, Tom wasn't on solid ground.

Once Prophet tugged him close though, he was. Tom nuzzled his cheek, murmured, "You've definitely smelled better."

"You'll take me anyway."

"Damned straight."

Neither of them had worried about showering last night, and they'd sat together quietly instead, taking turns on watch since they'd both been too restless to sleep much . . . too worried that talking would bring them to the conversation they hadn't been ready to have.

Tom guessed they still weren't, since he was the one leading Prophet into the shower. Neither of them took off their clothes before stepping under the spray. Tiredly, they began stripping one another, pretty much holding each other up while Tom lathered them both up.

Prophet loved this. He'd never admit it, not with words, but Tom's hands in his hair made him want to submit, made him want to beg Tom to fuck him. But Prophet was still punishing himself for the fuckup with Lansing, so no, they couldn't sink into sex until they talked about this.

No matter what his dick was telling him.

Tom seemed to silently agree—even though he was hard, he didn't make any kind of move beyond actually washing Prophet. Because there was angry sex—and that was hot. But this would be beyond that, resentful and questioning, trying to pretend they could fuck away this particular problem. There was no room for that kind of distraction now.

Prophet ran a hand through Tom's wet hair after he turned the shower off. He got them both towels and they dried off and dressed pretty quickly. A light rain had started, like it did most days. When it cleared, it would leave behind plenty of sun.

He sat heavily on one of the couches—Tom settling into the chair next to it—and tried to figure out how exactly to explain this. Mainly because he wasn't sure what the hell had happened himself.

Fucking liar—you froze.

Not exactly, but basically the equivalent of it. Because all Prophet had needed to do was take Lansing out. One bullet, a well-placed couple of fingers, even a ballpoint pen to the carotid.

Fuck.

He hated that Lansing had that hold on him, hated that he hadn't realized it until he'd been face-to-face with the guy for the first time in eleven years.

When he'd fucking lost it. Simply killing Lansing suddenly hadn't been good enough. He'd needed to slam the agent, in a way that he hadn't been able to the last time they'd been in the same room. Because death by table wasn't nearly as satisfying as his own fingers around the man's throat.

Because Lansing didn't believe him. Didn't believe in him. And Prophet had been nothing but loyal.

But if Prophet was going to be accused of being a killer, then he'd be a goddamned killer, and prove Lansing right.

Before he could figure out where to start, Tom jumped right in, asking, "You really figured, 'Hey, I'll just kill Lansing and then get on with the rescue'? Like it wouldn't have any fucking repercussions?"

Well, then, that was as good a place as any. "I'm good at what I do, Tom."

Tom leaned forward, almost urgently. "I'm not talking about hiding bodies, *Prophet*. I'm talking about the punch of emotional repercussions. Or didn't you expect those, man of steel?"

Prophet opened his mouth, then closed it. Ground out, "No, I didn't."

"What the fuck is wrong with you?" Tom stood then. Prophet was glad he'd waited to unleash this anger until after the rescue, but judging by the tension in Tom's body, he wasn't about to rein himself in or tiptoe around this any longer.

"So fucking much," Prophet muttered, turned away. But Tom was on him, slamming his shoulder back, forcing Prophet to face him. A dangerous fucking move considering everything Prophet had been through, but he did move his hand away as if he realized that.

"You were going to kill him? And then what?" Tom sounded so reasonable, standing waiting an answer with a patience Prophet knew neither of them had.

"I was going to do it quietly. You wouldn't even have known."

"Right. That plan really worked."

"I don't need the sarcasm."

"Too fucking bad. You're getting it."

"I lost it, okay."

Tom stared at him, so obviously angry and disappointed, but no more than Prophet was at himself. Tom reached out, grabbed the front of Prophet's shirt, bunching the fabric in his fist, and pulled him up off the couch so they were only inches apart.

Prophet didn't resist. Hell, he owed Tom a punch, at the very least.

But Tom wrapped his arms tightly around him. Threaded a hand into his hair, rubbed his scalp. Comforted him. "You gotta let me in, Proph. All the goddamned way. Or one of us is going to get hurt."

"Fuck." It was getting to the *all or nothing* stage. Beyond it. He buried his face against Tom's neck, let Tom's hands run over him.

"I can't help ease your burden if I don't know what it is."

"Throwing my words back at me."

"Been waiting for the opportunity. They're good words." Tom's hands continued to soothe him. "It was hard not killing him. For everything he did to you."

"I trained for torture."

Tom pulled Prophet's head back, cupped his chin. "No one trains for that."

Prophet sighed. He'd pushed the rape down so far because that was the only way he knew to keep it from hurting him. Turned out it was too late to avoid that.

"You don't have to be strong all the time with me, Proph. You can let it go."

"I know, T. I do."

"It's just not easy." Tom got it. Got him the way John had, except the major difference was that Tom cared. Tom gave back, in all the ways that John wouldn't—or couldn't.

John wasn't a psychopath, but he'd definitely gotten the short stick when it came to feelings—and the total lack of empathy when there should've definitely been at least a flicker sometimes floored Prophet, making him wonder if all of John's feelings had been faked. In many ways, John was his father's son. "I'll try, Tommy. Fuck, I'm sorry. I should've warned you . . ."

"Better this way," Tom said. "Suppose he never came? Suppose we got stopped? I had plausible deniability."

"And now? You've tortured a CIA agent."

"He deserved it." Tom's eyes went cold, his voice an angry pitch. "I wanted to kill him for you."

"I know," Prophet said hoarsely.

"Come here." Prophet let Tom tug him close and run his hands along Prophet's back, his neck, his head.

Prophet, in turn, bowed his head to Tom's shoulder. "I wanted to keep you innocent."

"I know," Tom said. "But you're about thirty-something years too late. Because I'm not—never was."

"You were. Thing is, you still are. You don't let it ruin you."

"Neither do you, Proph. You just don't let yourself see it."

With that, Prophet's head jerked up. He wanted to tell Tom, right then and there, about his eyes, but the words choked in his throat. Instead, he kissed Tom, a crushing, rudely intimate kiss that Tom immediately reacted to by jerking Prophet's hips closer.

And then Prophet was vibrating.

"Your phone," Tom pointed out gently.

Prophet looked into the man's eyes, wanting to just get lost there. "It's Ren—I left him a message earlier, told him it was urgent. I'd ignore it if I could."

"I know." It was actually Tom who disengaged and grabbed the phone for Prophet. While Prophet talked, he also let Tom fuss over some of the contusions on his back and calves, because he had nothing to hide in that phone call. And when he hung up, Tom asked, "Things okay?"

"I'll know tomorrow, and then I'll tell you. But for today . . ."

"We still have shit to talk about."

"Yeah." God, he wasn't getting out of this.

"What did he do to you, Proph?" Tommy pressed gently, but Prophet could tell that he already knew. Lansing had probably been more than happy to insinuate it, and Tom was far from stupid. Add to that the voodoo thing and Prophet didn't bother evading.

"What he told you."

Tom nodded, his expression tight. "He raped you."

Prophet ran his hand through his hair, suddenly feeling way too goddamned vulnerable for this conversation. Mainly because Tommy was looking like he'd snap Lansing's neck if he walked into the room. "You sure you didn't kill him?"

Tom bent down, his hands on either side of Prophet's chair, locking him in place. "I wanted to. I really fucking wanted to. Especially when he taunted me with what he'd done to you."

Prophet stared into Tommy's eyes and saw understanding behind the anger. "Yeah, well, it's been on my to-do list for a while too."

"We've got to finish this. Soon."

"I know." The fact that Tom would kill for him . . . well, Prophet always knew that, but to see clear evidence of it made Prophet's throat tighten. He reached up to cup Tom's chin and bring his face close. "Thank you."

"Are you sorry I know? Because I can't unknow it."

"I've never told anyone. I told myself it didn't matter, that he didn't hurt me. That I'd never let him. And I didn't, not really. But . . ."

"You're having flashbacks about it now."

"Sometimes, yeah. Maybe it was an early-warning system. Which worries me."

"Why's that?"

"Because I'm seeing John more often too." It was good to confess shit like this and not have Tom think he was crazy. "Sleep's becoming impossible."

Tom closed his eyes for a second, then pushed back. He went into his bag and pulled out his Kindle, then reached out and grabbed Prophet's hand and led him outside and over to the large chaise under the canopy. Prophet sank down into the pillows, lying on his back. Tom pulled off his shirt and lay down next to him. Facing him. Prophet turned onto his side too.

"You going to be able to sleep?" Tom asked him.

"I'd like to."

"Go ahead." He held up his e-reader. "Plenty to keep me busy."

"Anything on there that will give you ideas?" Prophet asked hopefully.

"Guess you'll have to sleep to find out."

"You're going to stay up and watch over me while I sleep?"

Tom gazed at him. "Yeah, I am. Is that a problem?"

"It fucking should be," Prophet grumbled as he closed his eyes. "Fucking should be. But it's not."

CHAPTER ELEVEN ◉

Hours later, after the sun had set and lights dotted the perimeter of the game park below, Prophet stirred. Tom had only left him long enough to go inside to answer the door and grab some drinks he'd ordered—strong, fruity drinks that would probably knock Prophet on his ass. Prophet rarely drank—Tom didn't drink much either, but somehow, Prophet was really a lightweight.

Prophet stared at the red drink with its umbrellas and big straw. "You're trying to get me drunk."

"Yes," Tom agreed. He put his Kindle aside. "But I did order dinner—it should be here soon. So I don't think you're an easy date."

"Yeah, you do." As if to prove it, Prophet motioned to Tom's hand, which was resting on Prophet's crotch. "Manhandling me in my sleep?"

"You slept well, didn't you?"

"Not the point." Prophet downed half the drink and smiled. "You really do think I'm easy."

"If the umbrella drink fits the lightweight," Tom murmured.

Prophet smiled and finished the rest of his drink. "These are fucking awesome. You need to learn how to make them."

"I'll get right on that, boss."

"You can call me that for the rest of the night."

Before Tom could scoff at that, Prophet grabbed him, pulled him to his feet, leaving them chest to chest for just a moment. Until Prophet pushed him against the stone and wood railing, and Tom had forgotten how good it felt to have Prophet manhandle him. Because the guy was damned strong. As much as Tom trained and practiced, as violent as he could get, Prophet would always be stronger. And Tom had to admit that he liked that. Probably as much as Prophet did.

Prophet's hands went under Tom's shirt, stroking the bare skin of his stomach for a few seconds before yanking the T-shirt over his head. For a second, Tom thought Prophet was going to tie him, to tangle his arms in the soft cotton, but he didn't.

And when Tom tossed it aside, Prophet bit his shoulder, and Tom hissed. Prophet simultaneously soothed the sting with his tongue and traced the skull tattoo on Tom's biceps with callused fingertips that felt like bursts of electricity.

His free hand went to the front of Tom's shorts, cupping his achingly hard cock through the fabric. Then his hand went down the front, and he yanked the shorts down past Tom's thighs. Tom shifted, shook them to the ground and kicked out of them as Prophet ran two fingers along the outside of his cock, up and down. It was at once too much and not enough, and Tom pushed his hips at him impatiently.

In response, Prophet's hand left the skull and went to Tom's ass, trailing in between his cheeks, pressing his hole with a dry finger. Saying, *Mine* the way Tom had told him not all that long ago.

Tom could only concede with a nod and a long groan that escaped, echoing into the night.

"Say it," Prophet commanded, his voice not overly loud but unmistakably forceful.

Tom had been gripping the wooden rail behind him, letting Prophet have his way, but in response, he dragged a hand across Prophet's cargo-clad ass and raised his brows.

Prophet's smile was nearly immediate, like he couldn't deny it, or anything at this point. Maybe it was the alcohol, but that would only make the admitting easier. It wouldn't make Prophet lie.

It was another game they'd played for the last few months that wasn't *just* a game, but Jesus, the thought that he owned Prophet's ass and the fact that Prophet wanted to own his? Got him every fucking time.

"Yeah, yours, Tommy. You know that." Prophet eased the tip of his finger inside Tom, and Tom jolted, his balls tightening and heat flooding his body.

"Yours, Proph . . . yes," he managed, and Prophet immediately circled his fingers around the base of Tom's cock, stopping any impeding orgasm for the moment.

"Not yet," he said firmly.

"Yeah." His voice already sounded spacey . . . he was ready to give himself over, to do anything. Except . . . "Proph . . . food'll be here soon."

"Uh-huh." Prophet didn't seem concerned as his finger worked Tom open, his mouth landing on Tom's nipple, tugging the ring with his teeth.

"Fuck."

"Yes." Prophet's fingers started strumming over the row of ladder piercings, spinning them gently, just letting Tom know he appreciated them.

"Want you on your knees for me, Tommy."

Tom didn't protest, watched as Prophet grabbed the lounge cushions and threw them on the ground around them, and then sank to his knees in front of him. Prophet's hand immediately sifted through his hair, then gripped, hard, but didn't force his head forward.

Oh God, yeah, that made Tom bare his teeth with pleasure. His stomach tightened with the anticipation and in response, he leaned in and kissed Prophet's stomach, then bit and sucked a line down the hot skin—leaving a trail of dark red marks behind. Prophet groaned, rubbed his cock against Tom's neck.

Without warning, Tom licked the head of Prophet's cock, tasting the leaking pre-cum, leaving him wet.

"Yeah, Tommy, get me ready," Prophet breathed, his eyes glazing.

Tom speared his tongue into the small hole, gripped Prophet's hips at the same time so Prophet couldn't get away. He knew how easily that could throw Prophet over the edge, and he loved being able to do that. So he ignored Prophet's hard tug on his hair, the moans of not-so-protesting protest.

"Jesus, you'll pay for that," Prophet promised.

Good. He swallowed Prophet's cock, taking as much as he could down his throat, guided by Prophet's rough hold on his hair. For a long moment, Prophet went completely still, stiffening like he was either about to come, or was doing his damnedest to stave off an orgasm. Tom didn't move, until Prophet slowly pulled him off his cock.

"Jesus." Prophet released Tom's hair and sank to his knees in front of Tom, kissed him, then murmured, "Turn around—on all fours."

Tom did, shifting around and putting his palms on the cushions, settling his thighs apart.

"Yeah, spread your legs wider," Prophet encouraged as he ground his cock against Tom's ass, then pulled back to spread it, to lick his hole, to thrust his tongue inside of him. Tom's mournful cry echoed over the balcony to the walkways below . . .

Shit. He glanced at his watch. "Prophet . . . they'll be here any second . . . I left the door unlocked . . ."

"Then you'll have to make me come faster," Prophet said reasonably. Tom heard the rustle of a condom wrapper, the snap of the lube bottle, and then Prophet's fingers were slicking him up, preparing him.

Finally, Prophet put a hand on his hip as he drove his cock inside of Tom, filling him halfway in a fast thrust, then pausing. "So fucking hot, Tommy."

Tom's body flushed. Prophet's hand rubbed along his spine, checking in, making sure he was all right. And he was, so he pushed back, more because he also needed to come badly than because of the threat of being caught. On his knees, he rocked against Prophet's cock, each time taking Prophet inside of him to the hilt. As he worked faster, he heard Prophet's strangled moan.

And then Prophet grabbed his hips, holding him steady. Reached around to stroke Tom's cock, but didn't let Tom move.

"Prophet, Christ . . ." He bit the words out, not giving a shit if anyone walked in. His skin was hot and tight—too tight and his ass burned the way he craved.

Prophet would torture him unless he pushed, so Tom flexed his ass around Prophet's cock, and he heard Prophet gasp in surprise.

Prophet loosened his grip on Tom's hips, allowing him to continue contracting and push back, harder. In turn, Prophet stroked his cock harder, and Tom saw stars as he started to climax, hot cum spilling onto Prophet's hand. And Prophet finally lost it, cursing and crying out *Tommy* as he came.

Tom was still recovering when Prophet practically picked him up, put him on the chaise, and covered him with a blanket. He yanked up his own shorts and waved inside, to where Tom guessed room service was setting up their dinner.

"That's fine—we'll be in shortly. And no, you don't need to stay for anything. Thanks." Prophet called, then sat down next to Tom.

"You could be a PSA against drinking."

"Against drinking and fucking? Ah, Tommy, you got exactly what you wanted." Prophet furrowed his brow. "Did you order more drinks with dinner? Otherwise I'll catch the waiter . . ."

He was up and heading inside and all Tom could do was groan after Prophet's laughter.

Prophet did end up getting several more drinks. They were scattered around him like an offering as he played with an umbrella, both of them full on dinner and tired from good sex. "It's been a long ride."

"Yeah, it has." Tom knew he wasn't talking about the sex. "I'm ready for whatever happens next."

Prophet looked serious when he said, "I need you to know you don't have to go with me." He held up his hands when Tom narrowed his eyes. "Not because I think you can't handle it. Because maybe you're going to resent me for pulling you in. We've gotten through a lot of shit already, Tommy. A lot. Maybe more than we're supposed to. Maybe we've reached our limit."

"Still trying to protect me."

"Always."

"I'm going to chance it. Figure the universe already put us through hell. I think we're meant to come out the other side together."

Prophet rolled his eyes. "Romantic fucking voodoo Cajun shit."

"That's lovely. Anyway, what would we do with all our free time?"

"We could go run a goat farm," Prophet suggested.

"You watch way too much *Spartacus*."

"You only watch *those* scenes," Prophet pointed out.

"I skim the rest. You think they're fucking in real life?"

"If they're not, they should be." Prophet lay back on the sand, arms behind his head so he could stare at the stars. "You know, Dean's accident happened when he was captured. Right as he got captured actually, thanks to an explosion at a checkpoint. After they had their specialist safe and sound and they were less than three miles from their destination. He said that they made the mistake of thinking they'd hit the easy part of their mission. It's what LT always talked about during boot camp, that when things seem the calmest, the absolute best, that's when you need to be on your guard and worry the most. Because fate always wants to jump in and fuck you up."

"I'm not arguing with you. Is that why you brought me along, though? To keep an eye on me?"

"Isn't that why you would've insisted on coming in the first place—to keep an eye on me?"

"Yes."

"I wouldn't ask you if I didn't think you'd be able to do the job," Prophet said after a beat. "I don't give jobs as charity. You did good, T, getting him out. I'd have let him try to do too much on his own. That would've fucked things up."

"Ah, Proph." Tom paused. "You did have a nightmare last night."

"And here I thought maybe I dreamed it," Prophet muttered sarcastically.

Tom had grabbed hold of him and stroked his hair, pressed his body against Prophet's to stop the nightmare from becoming full-blown. Prophet had opened his eyes, whispered "Tommy," and then fallen back asleep.

"Well, you definitely had a good dream after that."

Prophet narrowed his eyes. "How do you . . .? Fuck me. You blew me. That was a real orgasm."

"You're welcome."

Prophet grunted and finished the last half of an umbrella drink. Tom had lost track—maybe it was Prophet's third—but the food was helping to even out the man's buzz.

He turned his head to Prophet, who remained staring up at the stars. He'd brought blankets and the food out there, and now, neither of them wanted to move. Occasionally, the silence was punctuated with music from the main part of the hotel and the sounds of an elephant trumpeting. "You know, even though I'm still pissed at Phil for what he did to you, he was right about LT."

"They have a long and not-so-wonderful history of bumping heads when they were stationed together. Marines don't play well with others. Phil was no exception."

"You're really sticking up for LT?"

"No," Prophet scoffed. "He's a complete fucking dick. But you needed to be to train guys like me."

Tom supposed that was true, to some extent. "You're not going back to EE, are you?"

"I can't see it happening," Prophet said honestly, then shifted and turned to face Tom, propping his head on his arm. "I haven't broken into your records yet. How'd you end up at EE anyway?"

Tom rolled his eyes. "Like that information would be there."

"Phil takes notes on everything. He does it in shorthand because he thinks I can't understand it."

"You're a fucking menace." Prophet looked pleased. "I met Phil when I was still in the FBI. Phil had just retired from the Marines and he'd started EE. I remember there was some grumbling that he was trying to pull agents, but really, I think that was from the people he didn't try to pull, you know?"

"I believe that."

"You weren't with EE from the beginning, were you?"

Prophet ran a hand through his hair, pushing it off his forehead. "No. I met him when I worked a joint mission with Force Recon. We kept in touch. Always useful to have a Marine on your side."

"That it is." Tom reached back and grabbed his beer, took a long drink of the warm brew. Because all drinks here were warm. Always. "I was brand-new when I met him. I'd been recruited for the Bureau out of college because I'd gotten a full ride, and I guess they notice shit like that."

Prophet didn't seem surprised. "For what?"

"Academics. But I played varsity sports too."

"The total package." It would've sounded snotty coming from anyone but Prophet.

"And when I was in college, I got in trouble for hacking. Just a little. I guess they notice shit like that too, because at first, the Bureau used me for its Cyber program, but I did well on the physical tests. And sitting behind a desk wasn't my thing." He paused. "You know why I left the FBI."

"Right—you think you killed all your partners."

Tom spit his beer out, wiped his chin, and glared at Prophet.

"What? You do think that."

"I'm never letting you drink again. You're horrible enough when you're not drinking."

Oddly enough, or maybe not so oddly, Prophet appeared to take that last line as a compliment. "Okay, so you fucked up, left the Feds and . . . decided to save your high-water parish."

"Red River Parish," Tom said.

"Like that's not the same thing? Did you not see the high water?"

"For fuck's sake." Tom closed his eyes, shook his head, and opened them again to find Prophet laughing silently. "You're a child."

"Really, I'm listening."

"Fine. Phil came to town, looking for one of his Marines. He'd heard the guy had disappeared into the bayous and gone a little crazy." Tom remembered the guy well. "He wasn't from around there. He used to tell people he moved there because it reminded him of the jungles. At night, he'd have these blackouts, and he'd start shooting at nothing—blanks, at least—but it was still dangerous."

Prophet winced but didn't interrupt.

"Phil wanted to get the guy help—his name was Stanley, but Phil said his nickname was Bullets. So when he started firing again, I got Phil out there, and Phil played his CO again, and I helped Phil drive him to the hospital and get him help. Phil gave me his number and told me that when I got tired of wasting my goddamned time, to give him a call. It took another few months, because I wanted to see the election through. Fucking glutton for punishment, I know. And then I packed up and went to the training place for EE. Figured I could save the world, just like you."

"I wanted to blow shit up," Prophet corrected, but Tom didn't buy it, not for a second.

"And now look at us."

"I guess we're both just big fucking saps." Prophet picked up his drink and gave a cheers to Tom's bottle. "You'll have to get over being pissed at Phil to keep working at EE. Too much resentment's going to fuck you up."

"I don't have to work at EE. I don't even know if I want to."

"What would you do, then?"

Tom sighed. "I've been thinking about that."

"Come up with anything?" Prophet asked. "Because you draw on me every chance you get."

"Not every chance," Tom said. "Speaking of…" He made a motion for Prophet to turn over, and Prophet didn't argue. Tom grabbed a pen and began to work on Prophet's shoulder. "I told you that your skin was made for ink."

Prophet snorted. "*You* have a body made for tattoos."

Tom smiled, thinking about the way Prophet traced them with his tongue or his fingers. "Is that why you spend so much time on them?"

"Damn straight." Prophet looked over his shoulder. "So you're thinking of opening a tattoo shop, right?"

"Something like that," Tom said. "Still rolling it around in my mind. Not ready to talk about it."

"Fair enough."

"What've you been thinking about?"

"Honestly? I can't see beyond this John thing."

Tom pressed a kiss to the back of his neck. "Soon."

Prophet rolled over a little but Tom remained on his hip, pinning him to the chaise. "Suppose there's no epiphany after it's over?"

Prophet smiled lazily at Tom. "I'll give you epiphanies as often as you need them."

Tom smiled back, charmed. He cherished these rare, unguarded moments from Prophet. For Prophet to feel protected enough with him was the real victory here. And that was happening more and more lately.

Prophet tugged at his arm. "What time is it?"

"It's tomorrow," Tom stretched, more relaxed than he'd been in forever.

"How do you feel about Amsterdam?"

"You gonna tell me how I feel about it, *bébé*?"

"I think you'll feel just fine," Prophet practically growled. "But there's a lot going on. I didn't think all this would happen at the same time."

"That's okay, Proph."

"I know you're ready. I know I keep asking you if you're okay and how fucking annoying that must be. But that's because *I'm* not okay. *I'm* not ready."

Tom stroked a hand through Prophet's hair at that confession. "I know."

"Part of me hates that you know me so well."

"And the other part?"

Prophet gave a faint grin, then said quietly, "Loves it," like if he said it too loudly, fate might swoop in and snatch this moment, the word, out from under them.

Tom stilled. He didn't need the words, never really had. Like Prophet, he valued actions, but to actually hear that one word out of Prophet's mouth . . . it was all Tom needed. "I'll take those odds."

"Yeah?"

"Definitely." He bent down and kissed Prophet, realized he was shaking a little. Jesus. *Loves it* echoed inside his brain, and it was on the tip of his tongue to say it back. It was always there, and he showed it to Prophet a thousand different damned ways. But to give voice to it . . .

He wouldn't say it back now. This was Prophet's moment, and even though he'd always thought he'd be the one to say it first, it didn't matter. This was better. Right.

Prophet wrapped an arm around him, pulling Tom down on top of him, and pressed his face against Tom's chest as Tom said, "We'll get through this."

"No choice."

"You're the one who told me there's always a choice," Tom reminded him.

"For this, that's the choice. No matter how badly I want to back away from this whole thing, I can't. There's too much at stake. Too much at risk."

"Then we'll do it. Together. No matter what, Proph. You don't try to send me away."

"Definitely not in Amsterdam."

"We're going to have to talk about this further," Tom told him.

"Talk later." Prophet kissed the side of his neck. "Fuck, then sleep, then fuck again, then pack."

"Good itinerary."

Tom woke under the sun's warmth to Prophet pacing and cursing. He was staring at his phone while he did so.

"I'm seriously going to tackle you if you don't stop," he warned.

Prophet turned. "You're going to have to book us a flight."

"Like a real flight? With real people?"

Prophet sighed. "Yeah. I don't want to call in a favor for this one, so we'll have to chance it. And trust me, I've tried to find a way around it. Short of chartering a fishing boat—"

"No fucking way am I doing that with you." Tom sat up, suddenly completely wide-awake. "Did you order breakfast?"

"I can swim," Prophet protested. "And steer a boat."

"As well as you drive?"

"Just book a flight under our real passports, all right? And I'll order breakfast." Prophet groused and rubbed his bare stomach, Tom's bites still there, glowing against his tanned skin. "First flight you can get. Since Lansing's MIA, the timing's too good to pass up."

"Pass up what?"

"We're going to have a meeting with the team."

Tom booked the tickets, with Prophet hanging over his shoulder, micromanaging while he ordered breakfast.

"First class? Big spender?" Prophet said after he hung up, clapping him on the shoulder.

"Your credit card, big daddy," Tom told him.

"Asshole," Prophet muttered, and Tom laughed.

CHAPTER TWELVE ◉

After showering and packing, they got to the airport and onto a flight that was strangely on time and free of issues. Neither man mentioned it, and Tom figured that Prophet was as much of a superstitious bastard as he was.

Once they landed in Germany, after two connecting flights—the last one being fraught with issues as if making up for the first one, including missing their connection to Amsterdam, Prophet told him, "I can't get on another goddamned plane anyway. Plus, it's just one more way we can be traced. Let's drive."

Stuffing himself into the car, Tom muttered, "This is more uncomfortable than the plane. And it's going to take forever."

"You've got somewhere to be?"

Tom glanced over at Prophet and frowned. Then smiled a little. "I like the way you think."

Prophet sniffed. "Try not to sound so surprised at how smart I am, okay?"

Speaking of smart, Prophet had made him take the piercings out before they traveled. They'd gotten rid of weapons, knowing they'd be able to pick some up wherever they landed. And now, pulled off the side of the road, Tom let Prophet help him put the piercings back in.

Tom hissed with each one. "Jesus, should've gotten a room for this."

Prophet grinned. "We only have forty-eight hours. No time for that."

Once Tom's piercings were back in place, they got on the road. To his credit, Prophet stayed awake the entire time. He even offered to drive but Tom already had taken his life in his hands with Prophet and his angel-of-death plane rides, not to mention Prophet's driving in Africa and . . . everywhere else. He figured the odds were better this way.

"What's a BFFL?" Prophet asked as Tom got back in the car after a quick food break.

Tom glanced over to see Prophet staring down at his phone. "You'd better not be talking to Cillian."

"It's Remy. Telling me about some chick who's his BFFL."

Tom put the car into gear and pulled into the street. "Best friend for life."

"How do you know this shit?" Prophet muttered. "Wait a second—who's your BFFL?"

"His name begins with E."

"Hmmm, all right. You're not just saying that because I took you in off the streets, right?"

"Why you gotta make me sound like a hooker, *bébé*?" Tom drawled, because he loved the way Prophet's eyes got that lazy-lidded, turned-on look when he did so.

"Not fair. BFFL's aren't supposed to use your weaknesses against you."

"Maybe I don't consider you wanting me a weakness."

Prophet gave a nod in concession to that, then sobered. "I'm worried about that kid."

"Yeah, me too. I'm glad he checks in every day." Tom heard from Remy a lot, but not as much as Prophet did. There had been a bond there from the first time they'd met. "Where is he?"

"At one of his friend's. Says he's staying at Della's this weekend. His mom's going out of town." Prophet cursed, even though both men knew that ultimately, her not spending time with Remy strengthened their case. The PI Prophet had hired was doing a bang-up job of getting the dirt on Remy's mom. The now sixteen-year-old couldn't stay there much longer. It had been tolerable while Etienne was alive but now . . .

"We going to visit him when we get back?" Tom asked.

"Tickets are already booked."

"How's my aunt doing?"

Prophet cut him a side glance. "Same as she was when you spoke to her."

"Actually, I spoke to Roger . . ." Prophet groaned, put his arm over his forehead. "Nice of you to fix the roof while you were there."

"I had some free time."

"Uh-huh."

"You should be glad I went there," Prophet warned. "Because there was other stuff I could've done."

There was an hour between checking into their hotel and the meeting time. Prophet was just happy to be out of any moving object, and insisted they walk there.

They did so hand in hand.

He took the texts from Remy in the middle of all this shit as a good sign. There were a hell of a lot of responsibilities coming their way. And for a little while, the fantasy of pulling up stakes and just leaving, forgetting about John and what he'd done, not using what little time he had left chasing an obsession, had seemed like the perfect solution.

None of his former teammates would fault him for it—he knew that already. There'd been a hell of a long road behind them.

But they also needed to look past it all, to be reminded of what was waiting for them on the other side.

Now, Prophet motioned with his chin toward the gay club with a long line and the promise of fun and sin inside.

"This is where you guys are meeting?" Tom asked with a small grin.

"Yep."

"This is Mal's idea, right?"

"And Ren's too. King and Hook stopped arguing a long time ago. It's actually a pretty good plan." Prophet shrugged, took Tom's hand again, but didn't make a move to go inside. "King and Ren are coming in tonight. Mal's already here."

"Because of your favorite spook?"

"He's not mine, Tommy." Prophet stood with him along the mouth of the adjacent alleyway, scanning the crowds. Tom kept watch behind them, and if he felt any voodoo vibes, he didn't say anything.

They were both keeping an eye out for Lansing, who was potentially a far bigger threat than Cillian at the moment.

"Would Lansing send agents if he couldn't get here himself?" Tom asked finally.

"He usually sends his underlings to follow us. Me, at least. Because as long as we're all on separate ends of the earth, we're less dangerous. He doesn't want us hunting John, wants us to believe John is dead. So finding John is part of this. Finding out Lansing's stake in it is another. He's as much the enemy as Sadiq at this point. But typically my tails aren't going to follow me into a club. Too noisy to hear, too crowded for surveillance, and a lot of people to get lost around. Plus, they think I'm going in to pick up guys."

"So Lansing doesn't have the others followed?"

"Not the way he does me," Prophet said. "He's got their passports monitored, so they'll only use them when they want Lansing to know where they're going. Usually, they'll go to a decoy location on their own passport and then leave on their fake ones."

"And Lansing thinks they don't?"

"Lansing thinks they're too worried about being tossed in jail. He doesn't realize that those are *his* fucking fears, not ours," Prophet said through gritted teeth. "So I'm the liability."

"Except it's been forty-eight hours and we haven't been tracked by him or anyone from the CIA."

"That we know of."

"You'd know," Tom said firmly, and yeah, he would. Still . . .

"Maybe that's strategic on his part. He could be planning to arrest us all."

"Let him try," Tom said, his expression hard.

CHAPTER THIRTEEN ◉

Tom let Prophet lead him to a table in the center of the madness, cushioned between the dance floor and the go-go dancers' platform. When they sat, no one could see them, which was entirely the point.

Mal was already at the table, drinking a giant, red umbrella drink. It had six straws, and Prophet clapped him on the shoulder before taking a sip. Mal looked as ready to kill as ever, like a biker with his black leather jacket, hand tattoos, and sardonic dark eyes.

Tom slid into the chair against the dancers' platform, figuring he'd be the one to keep an eye out while these guys discussed their plans. The go-go dancers were trying to get his attention. Every once in a while, he'd glance up at them and nod. In response, they'd shake their asses faster. Tonight, they wore white boots and white wings. And jockstraps.

Mal signed something and Prophet laughed, then turned to Tom to translate.

"I don't want to know," Tom said.

"Plan's in place—spoke to Kasey this morning, so your 'sister's' on board," Prophet said.

"There's more than one of him?" Tom muttered.

Prophet snorted while Mal glared. "Long story—I'll fill you in. And moving right along . . ."

Prophet signed quickly as Mal watched intently, occasionally glancing at Tom. Had to be the Lansing story. And although Tom wondered why Prophet wasn't waiting for the others so he didn't have to repeat the story, he supposed it didn't matter.

"We're not being followed. Not by Lansing," Prophet said.

Mal, in turn, studied Tom like he didn't trust him as far as he could throw him. And knowing Mal, he'd probably try. Then he signed to Prophet, who translated.

"He says that Cillian's got informants who claim to have contact with John. Now we've just got to figure out if that's true."

Tom looked at Mal. "You never believed he was dead?" He didn't have to yell over the music—both these men were pretty well versed in reading lips.

Prophet translated as Mal signed. *Wouldn't believe someone was dead unless I was the one to kill them and I got to gut the body. And it's been awhile since I had a body to gut. How tall are you?*

"Sick motherfucker," Tom muttered.

Mal stared at him with his *You're just figuring that out?* look. No translation needed on that. And then he smiled as Prophet said, "*That was never a secret.*"

Prophet turned back to Mal. "You've been with Cillian the whole time?"

Mal nodded. *Except for two nights ago. I lost him for about twelve hours.*

"You *lost* him."

CIA was on my ass. Had to shake them. But Cillian turned up again for a meeting with an informant.

"Find out where he was," Prophet instructed. "And where are the rest of those assholes?"

Like that was their calling card, they appeared silently, two of them sitting on either side of Tom and a third standing behind Mal, surrounding Tom before he fully realized it. There were introductions, although Tom figured that they'd no doubt put him through a vetting process already and knew all about him.

That pissed him off slightly. As if Prophet sensed that—or hell, maybe it showed on his face—he gave Tom a look. One that Tom knew well. It meant, *I've got your back.*

So Tom relaxed, as much as he could, given all the circumstances, and watched the group dynamics, pictured these men in happier days—on the battlefield, in the mess hall, on leave. They were simply easy with one another and these weren't easy men. There was King, with his ever-present dark skullcap and blue-green eyes that almost looked see-through, along with his promised shadow, Ren, a stocky blond with piercing green eyes and a palpable energy buzzing around him. Tom got the feeling that if Ren really wanted to, he could lead all the people out of this club and off a cliff, and they would gladly go, drinking, laughing, dancing the entire time. As evidenced by the fact that Ren himself was happily on a table, drinking. Dancing. Laughing.

"Way to be covert, babe," was all King mouthed, but no one seemed too worried, as Ren was mainly blocked in by the go-go dancers.

Ren laughed, did a shot, and danced with a drag queen while King surveyed the situation as if it happened on a daily basis. Which it might.

Hook was easily six foot six. And lanky. Reddish-brown hair and dark brown eyes. He seemed the least lethal, which Tom translated to mean he was the most.

"We've got an hour at most," Prophet said.

The men talked in the kind of shorthand born from knowing one another for years. Tom knew there was a plan forming, and he grasped bits of it, but the edges were still fuzzy for him. He knew Prophet would explain it later, but he wanted to get this. Needed to understand so he could help.

He gained the most points with Mal—or maybe lost them—when he spotted Cillian before Mal did. He mouthed the spook's name, and Mal straightened, glared—but whether it was aimed at Tom or Cillian, he couldn't tell.

With two signs at the men that Tom didn't really get, Mal was gone. When Tom looked up, so was Cillian.

"Could've fucking predicted that," Hook growled.

"There are a million of these clubs," King pointed out, "and Mal specifically said Cillian's never come here." But they quickly moved on since it turned out that King had more intel, thanks to Mal. King had been following several of Cillian's sources, and he thought he'd discovered a lead on another specialist, buried by the CIA but being actively sought by Sadiq.

"Final piece of the puzzle," King added. He showed them a picture on his phone. Then another and another, and Tom realized that it was all the same man in different disguises.

"Hal used to wear all different kinds of disguises—new identities every time they move, which is about once every three months in the first few years," Prophet confirmed for him before asking King, "Do we have him?"

"We will."

"And then what?" Tom asked.

"We leverage him," King said. And there were too many possibilities there for Tom to ponder, but in his gut he knew that the specialist was the carrot to lure Sadiq—and John—closer.

Prophet nodded, his expression guarded. "Hey, T, keep your head down and check on Mal? He's not on the dance floor or at the bar."

Prophet was trusting him not to let Cillian see him, and hell, it was good practice. Ren came along too, but he veered off to keep company with the man Cillian had come into the bar with—and to pick his pocket while dancing with him. But there was no immediate sign of Mal or Cillian.

Soon the only place left to check was the back room. As he walked in, men brushed against him, propositioning him with every step, and he knew he couldn't stay here alone for very long without the bouncers tossing him. His cock hardened, just with the smell of sex, and he wondered how fast he could get Prophet back here . . .

When he got into the main area, he blinked into the darkness and checked out shapes. Some were easily dismissed by height and build. In the corner, he spotted two tall men, one pinning the other to the wall.

Mal.

And Cillian.

Mal *fucking* Cillian.

Okay, yeah, accounted for.

And they were just finishing up. As Mal hitched his pants up, Tom walked out and waited along the hallway so he wouldn't be spotted. Mal walked past first, followed by Cillian several moments later. The spook headed to the bar, and Tom was about to thread his way back toward the go-go dancers when he heard shouting and watched a massive brawl break out in the space of a few moments.

When he looked toward the table where the team had been sitting, he saw Ren. Swinging a chair over his head.

Great. *Really covert, guys.* He sighed, and then he dove headlong into the fight because what else was there to do?

God, Prophet fucking loved a good bar fight—hadn't had one in a while. He sent tables and chairs flying, was more cautious with actual people, but hell, anyone who came at him got a good, sharp right hook.

Ren had, of course, started the fight when Mal gave the signal that Cillian was heading toward the bar. Now, Prophet and Tom were the only ones from their group left inside the bar, and Tom ambled over to him while he waited by the dancers' platform that was mostly unharmed. As were the dancers.

"You all right?" Tom asked.

Prophet nodded, noting that Tom looked entirely too pleased with himself. "That felt good."

Tom shook his head.

"What? I needed to release some tension." Prophet stretched his neck. "I definitely don't get to do that often enough."

"There are other ways to relieve tension, Proph."

"I know that. And now I'm going to try one of them."

He grabbed Tom and yanked him close, rubbing his rough-stubbled cheek against Tom's, knowing full well Tom loved the scratch and burn. "You fought too, Cajun."

"Self-defense, pure and simple," he protested. "And I saw Mal and Cillian. We were clear before the fight."

"And after. Saw Cillian leave with the majority of the crowds," Prophet confirmed. "Where were they?"

"Closer to the back." Tom waved a hand casually in that direction. "Shouldn't we leave?"

"Not till we get the all clear."

He pulled Tommy onto the dance floor, wrapping around him, burying his face in Tommy's neck. Tom did the same as they swayed. Partly so they wouldn't be spotted, but mainly because it was really nice to be able to hold Tom like this.

"Want to fuck you right here," Prophet murmured. "Get on my knees, suck you. Then turn you around, hold you against the pillar and take you in front of everyone."

Tom groaned against Prophet's ear.

"Ah, you like that idea," Prophet shifted his glance to another couple, made sure Tom noticed they were stroking each other.

"Fuck," Tom muttered. "We need to go to clubs more often."

"Right," Prophet teased. "Because we don't have enough sex." But really, sex with Tommy was everything. It was where and how he'd gotten the best possible education on everything Tommy—and he was well aware that Tom had gotten the same information on him. Until you really knew what someone was like in bed, you didn't really know them at all.

"Never enough," Tom informed him seriously. "And maybe *I'd* push you onto *your* knees. Then down on the ground. Spread you and fuck you in front of everyone."

Prophet hissed a breath, bared his throat slightly. "You'd make me perform?"

"You'd fucking love it, Proph."

Fuck yeah, he would. "When this is all over . . . that."

"Yeah, that," Tom echoed.

When the slow song ended, Prophet's phone buzzed with the all clear, and he reluctantly led Tommy off the dance floor and out onto the street. When they got back into their hotel room, Tom turned and asked, "Is there any way out of this?"

"Barring John getting killed by a random bus when he crosses the street? No."

"So we pray for random buses," Tom said seriously.

CHAPTER FOURTEEN ◉

P rophet hadn't pushed him on where Mal and Cillian had been, and yeah, Tom would never have thought he'd find them fucking either, so why would Prophet?

And really, telling Prophet that Mal and Cillian were fucking wouldn't end well . . . but as psychotic as Mal was, he'd never have gotten this far if he wasn't good at his job.

He tried not to smirk though, at the thought of having something on the asshole. And also because Cillian was involved with someone else's cock besides Prophet's now.

"What exactly do Mal's favors entail?" he asked suddenly.

"Where'd that come from?" Prophet asked.

"Because you've avoided the question every other time I've asked it."

Prophet shrugged. "Really depends on the circumstances. Let's just say, his type of club usually involves more whips and chains than go-go dancers."

"Jesus, he's a fucking psycho, Prophet. He likes pain. He's out of control. He's—" Tom stopped dead. Grabbed the side of the dresser for support. He stared up at Prophet, stricken. "He's me."

Prophet pressed his lips together, like he was trying not to smile. And not succeeding.

"Tell me," Tom urged. "Tell me it's not true."

"You guys have . . . some stuff in common," Prophet admitted.

"And you knew!" Tom said accusingly, pointing at him. "You knew and you let me go on about what an asshole he is."

"To be fair, I let Mal go on about you being an asshole too," Prophet said reasonably.

"Was he this miserable when he came to the same conclusion I did?" Tom heard the hope in his voice as he asked, and Prophet shook his head.

"He's still in complete denial."

Maybe there was hope. No more piercings. Normal sex. And hey, it's not like he went out every day and beat people up for the hell of it . . .

Except when he needed to protect Prophet.

Or for the mission.

Or . . .

Yeah. He sat on the bed, rested his head in his hands. He heard Prophet trying really hard not to laugh as he said, "It could be a lot worse."

"How?"

When there was silence for a long time, he looked up.

"I'm thinking. Something will come to me," Prophet promised.

"Forget it. Just . . ." He stared at Prophet.

"What?"

"As long as I'm psycho, might as well have some fun with it," Tom reasoned.

"Hold that thought, Tommy. I have one call to make." Prophet started toward the bedroom, calling over his shoulder, "But shit, I've got to shower first—someone dumped glitter all over me," before heading into the bathroom.

Tom snorted, then looked down and noticed a lot of that glitter had rubbed off on him. He'd wait until he heard the water running and join him. And in the meantime . . .

He whirled around and caught King by throat, pinning him to the wall.

"Impressive," King said, his voice hoarse. "Prophet's teaching you well."

"That's something I learned on my own." Tom reluctantly released his grip. Mainly because he didn't love the suspicious vibe he was getting off the man tonight. King had snuck up on him before, but tonight was actually the first time watching the man interact with Prophet. Speaking of. "Prophet's in the shower."

King rubbed his throat. "I'm here to talk to you, Tom."

"So talk."

King narrowed his eyes. "He's going to be too worried about you to be effective."

"Fuck off, King. I've worked with Prophet before. He's the one I discuss this with, not you."

"He's not thinking clearly."

"And you are?" Tom shot back. "Honestly, out of all of us, *I'm* the only one thinking clearly. You're all way too close to this for comfort."

"Sadiq tried to kill you too," King pointed out.

Tom kept his voice cool when he said, "Collateral damage—we both know that. So I'm the best goddamned thing to happen to your team."

King studied him. "You prepared to die for this?"

"King, I'm not a fucking wet-behind-the-ears FNG. You can't scare me like that. But to answer your question, yeah, I've been prepared to die for as long as I can remember. Some days, I even prayed for it."

King held his hands up in silent surrender.

"Don't fuck with me, King," he hissed. "I'm in this. I'm more invested than you'll ever know. I get what I'm walking into. And I'm willing to keep walking. But I'm done justifying my existence."

He turned his back on King, because it was important for him to let King know that as far as Tom was concerned, he trusted King.

When he heard a door open, he turned back around and found Prophet standing in the doorway, the window half-opened where King had made his escape.

Judging by the half-troubled look on Prophet's face, he'd heard it all. "For all the shit you've got going on with Mal, I've never heard you do that."

Tom shrugged. "Mal would never say that to me."

Prophet tilted his head. "Why's that?"

"As fucked as it is, Mal and I get each other. We're the same fucking person. He doesn't need to question my motives—he knows them intimately."

Prophet smiled.

"And how long have you known that, too?" Tom demanded.

"Long time."

"So what the hell is King's issue?"

"He'd like to remain alive. He's never worked with you. And he's going into one of the most important jobs of his life."

Tom sighed. "Is he going to get past it?"

"You didn't give him a choice."

Prophet woke before Tom did, and he knew exactly what was happening. Before he woke Tom up, he rifled through his bag, pulled out Tom's meds, and grabbed some ice to wrap in a towel.

He also soaked a washcloth in alcohol. He figured that something had to help, and he'd try anything.

Tom's migraines were few and far between, but yeah, Prophet should've predicted this one, especially after King's visit.

"Tommy, can you take your medicine?" he asked quietly, and Tom opened his eyes, blinked, stared, then muttered, "Shit."

He struggled to sit up, grabbing at Prophet to help. Prophet fixed the pillows behind him, got the meds into him, and worked the ice and alcohol compress. He also used some of the pressure point massage he'd learned specifically for this purpose.

After forty minutes, Tom relaxed, although the meds had made him flushed and uncomfortable. Prophet took a handful of the small cubes and placed them on Tommy's chest. The man's skin was on fire and when Prophet touched him, he jolted, nipples tightening, and grabbed Prophet's wrist.

Prophet let Tom hold him, but he took one of the cubes and dragged it to a nipple, circling it first around the piercing, then putting it directly onto the already taut tip. Tommy was staring at him, but Prophet was too busy concentrating on his work. He blew on the nipple, and Tommy moaned.

And that might be the best thing he'd ever heard. He did the same thing again, circled the nipple, touched the peak, blew, and then he leaned in and bit it before sucking on it, playing with the barbell under his tongue and between his teeth.

Tommy flailed, caught his shoulders for purchase, and groaned. Dug his fingers into Prophet's hair, sending a jolt of incredible, searing hot straight to Prophet's cock. Jutted his hips against Prophet's cock like he had no control over himself.

Which he didn't. Tommy was melting for him. Prophet loved the taste of his skin, his nipple hard under the scrape of his teeth, loved making this man crazy. And Tommy was begging, but for what, Prophet knew Tom had no idea.

Tom's breath was choppy, and even though his body temperature had cooled, his cock was hard as it'd ever been. His eyes were still closed though, features relaxed.

"Any better, baby?" Prophet asked.

"Will be."

Prophet didn't fight when Tom rolled him onto his back. Let Tommy grab his hands, bring his arms over his head. He was already shirtless, groaned when Tom bit then sucked at *his* nipple. Prophet needed this, and he always let Tom run roughshod over him when he was in pain.

Tom pushed Prophet's pants down, then his own. This would be quick and dirty, the way they both liked it. He grabbed for the lube, but instead of readying Prophet, he readied himself, covered and lubed Prophet. Prophet watched, his breathing fast, and finally, Tom lowered himself onto Prophet's cock.

Prophet pushed up on his elbows. Tom helped him up and they rocked against each other, Tom holding onto Prophet's shoulders as they took each other.

Prophet looked up for a second, said, "Come on, Tommy . . . come now."

And he did, shot and groaned and looking surprised, like his body couldn't help but follow Prophet's orders. That caused a chain reaction in Prophet, and he grabbed for Tom's hips, held him down tightly on his cock as his hips bucked up wildly. He cried out Tom's name—*Tommy*—and Tommy smiled at that before collapsing on top of him.

Prophet let Tom sleep in the next morning, ordered him breakfast, and got him settled with food and a good movie before he went to meet King.

Tom knew, of course, but he'd just snorted and said he'd much rather stay in bed.

As Prophet walked the block to the diner, he mused on the fact that Lansing hadn't been seen or heard from. How there were no lackeys around—he and his team could spot them a mile away.

And as odd as it was to worry when they had it too good, Prophet knew that nothing was ever as good as it seemed. Now, he slid into the booth in the back across from King. "You're pushing it."

King could interpret that one of two ways, but he went with, "Any word on Lansing?"

"Could be a major problem," Ren said from the booth behind him.

Prophet didn't turn, just said, "Christ, Ren, you two ever going to cut the cord?"

"You and Tom first."

Prophet stared at Mal, who sat behind King and gave Ren the finger in Prophet's honor. His eyes blurred for a second. God, he was tired. He rubbed his eyes, but the blurriness got worse, and he tried to blink it away.

"You all right?" Ren slapped him on the shoulder.

"Getting old," Prophet muttered and Ren laughed.

"Never, Proph. You've got the fountain of youth hidden in your pants."

"What the fuck does that even mean?" Hook demanded, then held up a hand. "Never mind, I don't want to know."

"Means fucking keeps you young," King told Hook. "But you're married, so what do you know about sex, right?"

Hook threw the ice from his glass at all of them. The waitress yelled, Prophet blinked, and everything was clear again.

CHAPTER FIFTEEN ⊙

Prophet and Tom had dragged into Prophet's apartment at three in the morning. At 8 a.m., Prophet was in the doctor's office. He'd missed an appointment last week—routine—but after the incident in Amsterdam . . .

"Prophet?"

Prophet looked up at the doctor who'd just come into the examination room, looking concerned. "Hey, Dr. Salen. Sorry. I was just . . . somewhere else."

"You looked it. And you didn't hear my knock. Feeling okay?"

Prophet shrugged as the doctor leaned against the counter and crossed his arms. "I'm jet-lagged."

"Any other issues?"

More than you have prescriptions for. "Hard to tell." Because between flashbacks and Sadiq and Lansing and all the other shit . . . "I had something happen yesterday. Blurriness."

"Could be the result of a long trip with no sleep, which I'm guessing yours was." Dr. Salen motioned for him to sit up, and he brought the machine between them. Prophet opened his eyes as he was put through all the usual tests. They always worked like this—Prophet didn't ask questions during the exam, and Dr. Salen didn't talk at all.

When the exam was finished, Prophet sat back and waited while Dr. Salen wrote his notes.

Finally, Dr. Salen looked at him. "We talked about how it's hard to predict the progression of this disease, given its genetic component."

Prophet cut through the bullshit so Dr. Salen knew he could too. "My father's came up fast."

Dr. S nodded. "Things look worse—there's definite progression of the disease."

"And that means?"

"Could be five years until your vision goes. Two years. Could be tomorrow."

"So it's not just tiredness," Prophet said tightly.

"Based on what I've just seen, I don't think so, no." Dr. Salen didn't couch things, which was why Prophet liked him. Most of the time. Right now, not all that much. "You could stay at the intermediate stage for a long time."

Except his father had blown through it in months. So had his grandfather. But Dr. Salen already had his family history, so now, all Prophet could bring himself to say was, "Okay. So I'll be back in a month."

"Unless you have problems in between."

"Right, yes."

"Did you think about any of the resources we discussed?" Dr. Salen asked. "Best to implement them before they're necessary."

Prophet had. He'd taken initial Braille lessons, researched all the newest software. Thought about Seeing Eye dogs. Dean had given him a lot of resources.

But Prophet would have to stop denying and start working. "I've been using the blindfold."

"How's that going?"

"Fine."

Dr. Salen frowned at the lie. "I'll be back in a few minutes."

Prophet nodded, heard the door click behind him. The problem was, the darkness gave him panic attacks. And no matter how many times he told himself he wouldn't be in total darkness, he still heard Joe Drews's voice in his head.

"Bullshit. They don't know. Fucking bad at being a cripple. I'm not going to be worthless. Going out strong. That's how we do it."

Prophet hadn't wanted to do anything like his father. He'd tied the blindfold on, sat in the dark, and just tried to deal.

He had more situational awareness than most, because of his job. He could hear more, sense more, but having one of those senses completely cut off . . .

He took a deep, shuddered breath, the way he did when the blindfold was on. He closed his eyes and remained in the darkness.

The disease had been passed down through his family like a plague. His grandfather and father had killed themselves before it had gotten past this stage.

Prophet had simply refused to dwell on it. He couldn't fix it and whatever he couldn't fix, he ignored. He'd just gotten stronger, physically and mentally. And he'd made plans to continue working in this field, whether he could see or not.

But planning on being blind and being blind were two different things entirely. And he hadn't really grasped that shit until right fucking now.

It'll be better than this.

He opened his eyes.

It had to be.

He stood, ready to leave, despite the fact that he was supposed to wait for Dr. Salen, and in walked the reason he was, no doubt, told to wait.

"What the fuck? You moonlighting now?" Prophet asked, caught inches from the door.

"It's the only way to get in touch with you." Doc stared him down, pointing for Prophet to move back. Which he did, two steps. Doc sighed.

"You're following me?"

"Because you're avoiding my calls. You know I don't play that shit, Prophet."

No, Doc didn't. "What do you want? I'm not working for Phil anymore. And I've been busy."

"Fuck that not working for Phil shit. You're still my fucking patient and my friend, asshole. And yes, I've heard how *busy* you've been." Doc was a big man, and he was scary when he glowered. Which he was doing now.

"Fuck off," Prophet muttered, fully realizing he was taking his life in his hands and not caring.

Doc stared up at the ceiling, doing some muttering of his own before leveling his cool gaze on Prophet. "You're a selfish bastard."

"*I'm* selfish?"

"Yeah, and I'm going to tell you why, asshole. I know what you've been thinking."

Prophet shook his head, turned halfway, trying to figure out a way to bolt because he didn't need this shit. Not now, not ever. "Now you're a mind reader too. You and Tom could practice your voodoo together."

"I've known it since the moment I found out about your disease, Prophet. And I know what you've been thinking while you were sitting here."

Prophet stared at him steadily, trying to keep the venom out of his voice, because it was *Doc*, for Christsakes. Why the hell was the man doing this to him? "Want a medal?"

Doc's eyes flicked over him, flashing with an anger Prophet was more than familiar with. "I want you. To listen. To. Me. I won't let it happen."

"Can't stop me from going blind."

"I can stop you from killing yourself."

Prophet inhaled sharply. Wanted to come back at Doc with a smart answer about how Doc wasn't around twenty-four seven to stop him, but that would give realness to something he didn't want to admit to. So he shut his mouth, which was pretty much Doc's intention anyway.

Doc gave a nod in his direction. "You know, when my injury took me out of the SEALs, I wanted to take my toys and go home too. I fucking hated anyone with good knees. I didn't want to leave the teams. But I sulked for a while, until someone kicked my ass and reminded me that I had a bigger responsibility. That I couldn't hoard my knowledge."

Prophet rolled his eyes and let sarcasm drip from his words, even though Doc didn't deserve that. "Right—come work at EE so I can pretend I can do shit. Maybe I could answer phones."

"And maybe you could lead operatives home safely over the satellite comms—be their voice in the sky. Maybe you can still save lives. Maybe giving up right now is going to hurt every other operative who relies on you. Because how many calls do you end up getting when you're not on missions? Even when you are?"

Prophet thought about his clogged email and voice mail messages when he'd gone off the rails a few months earlier. Operatives had been calling—to check on him. To ask for help. To brainstorm. To see if Prophet could lend a hand. "People think they need me now. That'll change."

Doc sighed, put his fingers on the bridge of his nose, shorthand for *Prophet is trying every last bit of my patience*, and Prophet was too miserable to even be proud of that. "That shit's not going to stop. The only one who sees you as damaged is you—and you'd fucking think that with twenty-twenty vision. Because I know you have."

"You gonna take your own advice and get over Nico one of these days? It's only been what, seven years?"

Doc's jaw clenched and his expression went stony.

"Right. So we'll talk when *that* happens."

Prophet could tell that, if they weren't in someone else's office, Doc would've fucking rammed him through the wall. As it was, he'd be lucky if Doc didn't take him out to the parking lot and beat the shit out of him there, and Prophet would deserve it. Maybe that's what he wanted.

As if reading his mind, Doc grunted. "Me beating the piss out of you isn't going to make the fact that you're going blind any easier to take, you shithead."

Prophet took a page from Mal's playbook and shot him the finger.

Doc snorted. "What? You want to be left all alone? Is that it? So you'll have an excuse to take yourself out? Are you pushing Tom away, or do you have a new plan to get rid of him? Because if you want to kill yourself, save him some grief and do it now, before he's really invested in you."

"Fuck you," Prophet muttered, blinking hard, his throat tightening. *Stop it, Doc. Just fucking stop it*, he wanted to say, but the words choked on the way out.

"Come on. I'll give you the pills. An injection. It'll be painless. Quick. And exactly what you were trying to do with your missions."

"You're wrong."

"Really? Tell me how wrong."

Now *he* wanted to take *Doc* out to the parking lot and beat the shit out of *him*. But he didn't move an inch.

"Why the fuck are you doing this to me?" he finally managed to blurt out, and heard how raw and hollow his voice sounded. He had to get out of here, but Doc was standing in front of him, hands on his shoulders, and the fucker was built like a bull. Strong. Maybe stronger than Tommy.

"Finish your shit," Doc continued. "Find John. End this once and for all. And then open a new chapter."

"You're just doing this to make yourself feel better."

"I will fucking punch you, you disabled asshole."

Prophet threw his hands in the air. "I swear to Christ, that's abuse. You can't yell at a disabled person like that. You can't call a disabled person *disabled asshole*. That's just fucking wrong."

"Who says?"

"I do," Prophet said indignantly. Doc was biting back a smile. "And it's not funny."

Doc's voice was quiet, a little rough and choked when he said, "I know, Proph."

And that was enough for Prophet to admit, "I don't think I can do this." Although he had no real idea what *this* was. At this point, it translated into *everything*.

Doc tucked an arm around the back of Prophet's neck and Prophet buried his face in Doc's shoulder as Doc said, "It's not fair. I know it's not. But before you do anything else, you have to tell Tom."

"How do you know I haven't?"

"How do I know the sun rises in the morning?"

"Fucker," Prophet muttered against Doc's shoulder. "Disability-hater." Doc rubbed the back of his neck but didn't make a move to let him go. And Prophet was okay with that.

"Do you want me to tell him?" Doc asked finally.

"Yeah. But you can't." God, it was safe right here, with Doc. And Prophet wanted it to be this safe with Tommy . . . and it was, except for this issue. Which he hadn't given Tommy the chance to deal with.

"I can be there with you. I'll answer the questions he'll have, so you don't have to."

Prophet lifted his head. "Yeah, I get you're trying to make it easier on me, but fuck, it's not going to be at all. I can't pretend anything will help."

"Not pretending is the first step."

CHAPTER SIXTEEN ◉

T he flashback was quieter this time—just John, sitting in his usual spot, smoking a cigarette. Watching him while he remained in that half-sleep, half-waking stage.

"You knew it was going to happen, Proph," John drawled. "Not such a shock."

"Go fuck yourself," Prophet muttered.

"I've tried, but it's not nearly as fun as what we used to do."

Prophet turned away, turned his back on the guy in a way he hadn't been able to do in real life. "Maybe when I lose my sight I won't fucking see you anymore."

"You have bigger things than me to concentrate on," John continued. "Deal with your shit."

"That would be convenient for you."

"It would be. But that's not why I'm telling you."

It was quiet then. Prophet finally yanked himself out of the dream, and found himself sitting up on the edge of the bed, his back to the window. And he was shaking.

He cursed his weakness and swore he could still smell cigarette smoke. He was moving toward the window when his phone beeped with a text. And something told him to look at it, right fucking now.

Confirmed.

Prophet stared at the text, which could've been about anything. But it wasn't. It was telling him something he'd already known for years. It was the reason he'd gone UA all those years ago, roaming third-world countries, risking life and limb, throwing the CIA off his trail at every opportunity.

He knew they'd questioned King, Mal, Ren, and Hook extensively while he'd been gone. That the men had been in limbo, awaiting a possible court martial. That the CIA had dragged them in and then informed them they could only go free, or a reasonable facsimile thereof, once Prophet came home.

And that was the reason he did come home. Because those guys would've taken the brunt forever. And he couldn't have lived with that guilt.

He punched the numbers on the secured line and waited for all the men to hook in. Mal tuned in on Skype and Prophet lay there, surrounded by his team, looking at the spot John had lectured him from moments before.

"You alone?" King asked.

"For now, yeah," Prophet said, resentment building that King was still questioning Tom. He shoved it down where it belonged and turned to Mal. "How?"

Two of Cillian's informants had the same intel, Mal signed. *I traced it.*

"We've traced things before," Prophet said.

Mal's expression hardened. *I heard his voice, Proph. I fucking heard his voice. Twice.*

Prophet closed his eyes for a second and sighed. "We wasted a lot of time trying to prove something I've known since day one."

"No choice," King broke in.

"What else did you find out?" Prophet asked Mal.

Cillian's informants were on John's payroll. They met him. And they were tasked with killing Cillian.

"Does Cillian know this?" Prophet demanded.

Mal shook his head. *Not yet. I don't have plans to tell him. He's pretty well freaked out at the moment. And I'm not done with him yet.*

Ren jumped in. "Now we go get John. And we fucking kill him. Although I think we should torture him first."

While the others agreed, the way they always did, Prophet remained quiet. Normally he'd join in, because he didn't want to deal with them all silently judging him.

Although he was pretty damned sure they discussed this shit amongst themselves all the time.

"Prophet?" King asked.

"I'm here."

"You sure you're with us?" King probed. "I know it must be hard, hearing this about the guy you loved. Your best friend."

"Jam the knife in deeper, King," Prophet said quietly, and King exploded.

"After all this goddamned time, you still think he was forced, Proph? Come the fuck on. We've been coddling you, knowing you feel guilty about the guy you loved fucking us all over, but you have to open your eyes." King's brogue was strongest when he was angry, and Prophet hadn't ever had King this angry at him.

He avoided Mal's gaze, because he could feel Mal's fucking pity. He gave the guy the finger instead and told them all, "I never said I thought he was forced. And I never asked you to fucking coddle me. And I don't get why it matters to you—I never said we weren't going after him."

"Can we trust you to kill him if you're the first one to see him?" Hook asked.

"Yes," Prophet ground out without hesitation.

"You've always been a good liar, Proph," King said.

"Fuck all of you." He cut both of the lines at once, turned them off, and went into the living room. It was dark and quiet, and he thought about calling Tom, asking him to come home. But Phil let him get all that time off, and would let him leave at a moment's notice. Taking a few hours to do paperwork wasn't something Prophet would get in the middle of.

But fifteen minutes later, Tom went by the cameras, not trying to be stealthy. He came into the house and went right to Prophet, yanking his jacket off along the way.

For a long moment he stared at Prophet, and then he tugged him close, asking, "What happened?"

For a second, Prophet thought Doc had told him. Then he realized that he must've been giving off a *come home now* vibe . . . and obviously, message received. He buried his face against Tom's shoulder for a few more seconds before pulling back. "John's alive. Mal heard his voice. He's alive and well, and I'm going to have to kill him."

CHAPTER SEVENTEEN ◉

W hen Tom had gotten the hinky feeling, he'd known it was Prophet. It hadn't felt like immediate danger, but these days, who the fuck knew? Prophet had been gone when he'd woken up—a prior appointment he couldn't miss, the note said, and so Tom figured he'd go into EE and deal with leftover paperwork.

Luckily, he'd avoided Phil, who'd been taking the morning off. Because he had nothing new to report to the man except he'd told LT off.

Which Phil might give him a promotion for.

Now, looking at the storm warring in Prophet's eyes, he knew he was right to be here.

"John's alive. And it's what you've believed all this time," Tom said quietly, because what else was there to say? What else could Prophet hope for—that John had died that day Azar was supposed to have shot him? How different would things have been? And what a fucking thing to have to wish for.

"It's what I wanted to believe," Prophet corrected.

"Because you didn't think the man you knew would do this. You were convinced there had to be another reason." He led Prophet to the couch, sat next to him.

"Just because Lansing told you that, doesn't mean it's true."

"I know. But John's been alive all this time. And if he's sending Sadiq after you . . . it doesn't make sense. He's had eleven years, and you're not exactly living off the grid, which means he can find you easily enough. He's had plenty of time to kill you, Proph. He didn't. So something's going on with him. He might not be the man you knew entirely but . . ."

Prophet acknowledged that with a glance at Tom before he turned his gaze toward the window. "Thanks for not thinking I'm in some kind of denial."

"Does your team think that?"

"Yeah. They're fucking pissed at me right now. I told them I'd kill him. They don't believe that. But goddamned, if I couldn't, I wouldn't lie. It's too important." His voice was tight, his shoulders stiff.

"Ah, Proph. Suppose . . ." Tom's question remained unasked, hanging between them, but Prophet obviously knew what he was trying to say, because he turned to him and said, "I'll kill him if it needs to be done."

"But you're hoping it doesn't need that?"

"I don't think it's possible."

"Proph, what do you think happened to John, really and truly? Do you think he sold you out and went with Azar?"

Prophet stared at Tom as though making a decision, his expression tight. Finally, he admitted, "I think it started out as a highly classified mission, a way to put a US military man into a terrorist organization so he could work his way up the ranks."

"So John might have been working undercover, all this time?"

"It's the kind of job I would've been tapped for," Prophet said quietly.

"So why weren't you?"

Prophet shrugged, so Tom didn't push him. "Does your team think that too?"

"It was one of the theories, sure. But there had to be a way to do this without fucking all of us over. And if there wasn't . . ." Prophet stopped, his eyes flashing with anger. "So I thought, maybe he was forced. He had no choice—maybe he took the job so I wouldn't have to. Because I never would've survived that kind of shit. I don't have that kind of death wish."

"So when he disappeared?"

"I thought . . . yeah, I thought maybe he took the job. I also thought that maybe the CIA killed him, let him be killed, to show me that I shouldn't say no to things. A punishment. And after what happened with Lansing—the way they kept me and questioned me—I figured they were following through on that threat. And then, when

I was being jerked around about there being no bodies, and I realized it was going to haunt me and my team forever, I knew I needed to try to figure it out."

"And Lansing still doesn't consider that John might've been following actual orders?"

"They would've been in direct opposition to Lansing's, so I'm guessing not. And why would he, when he's got a lot of us to blame instead. If you just look at what happened dispassionately, you might come to the same conclusions."

Tom hated that Prophet might be right about that. "Why didn't you say something to Lansing anyway? Maybe he would've believed you, maybe not, but he'd have investigated it."

"Back then . . . I didn't want to do anything to hurt John. I didn't know what the fuck'd happened. Christ, I couldn't get the ringing out of my ears for months. I didn't give a shit what Lansing believed or didn't believe." He paused, drew in a shaky breath. "And telling Lansing wouldn't have mattered. John's good, Tommy. Better than I am, because he doesn't have much of a conscience or a use for people."

That must have been a hard truth to have to admit about a man Prophet had once loved . . . a man who'd supposedly loved Prophet.

"You can't tell me that kind of mission's just forced on Special Forces operators, no matter how good you are. There's got to be tacit agreement."

Prophet sighed. Nodded.

"I want to hate him, Proph."

"Go ahead. Some days, I do. A lot of days, actually. I know better than anyone that there's no real way to save him. He's gone, Tommy. No matter what the reasons are, no matter the actual outcome, John died the day he left Azar's. And he knows it."

"So why go after him?"

"I'll go after him because, if he's turned, he's got to be stopped." Prophet bared his teeth. "I'll go after him to see him, one last goddamned time, and tell him that he used us, in the worst possible way. That he's still using us, holding us hostage to a mission we never agreed to. No matter what way you look at it, it doesn't matter—it was always a suicide mission for him, and he tried to take us with him. Granted, all of the missions he and I went on were, but this was beyond the pale."

"Why, Proph? Why take those on? Because you were young and untouchable?"

Prophet shifted uncomfortably, like he wanted to tell Tom something important. But all he said was, "Maybe that was part of it. Another was wanting to do a job that most other people couldn't do. I had choices to make, Tom, and I made them the best way I knew how. And now they're all coming back to fuck me over."

Tom nodded.

"I know you believe in signs," Prophet continued. "It's like this is taking me back to the very beginning, where it all started. A conversation with LT and Dean changed my life—the whole direction. Changed John's too."

Tom traced Prophet's forearm—muscled, with a soft dusting of light, crisp hairs. No sign at all of the trauma he'd endured, the inherent weakness he lived with. "Why are you really going after John?"

"A lot of reasons, T. But it all comes down to the fact that we don't leave any man behind. For better or worse. And I left him behind. I'm responsible."

Tom nodded. "I'd do the same."

"I know."

"And you know I would never betray you like that."

Prophet nodded, but his eyes were faraway.

Tom took Prophet by the shoulders. "Never," he repeated firmly. "I know you thought John would never, but . . . ah, shit, Proph."

Prophet blew out a stiff breath. "Yeah."

So now he finally had a clear picture of what Prophet's team had been doing over the years. While they were tracking John, they were also making sure John couldn't get the help he needed through the specialists the CIA had hidden. Because if someone from the CIA was working with John and letting him use the specialists, well, fuck that and their idea of collateral damage. And if the CIA wasn't handing over specialists, Prophet knew his team could give them a better shot at hiding successfully than anyone. Hook watched over the specialists while Ren and King rescued and moved them as necessary. In between, they tried to gain as much intel on new terror threats.

"Eleven years, Proph. What the fuck's he been doing?"

Prophet reached into the bookcase where the photo albums of his childhood were shelved. He pulled out a folder from inside of one of them. "This."

It was thick with clippings. That made sense. He'd never put it into a computer because this would surely incriminate Prophet as being in league with John. And it was buttressed by pictures of Prophet's family, mainly from when Prophet was a preteen.

"Can I look through this?" he asked.

"Knock yourself out."

He paged through the file, watching the puzzle pieces add up, the final product a frightening a web of terror that stretched across Europe and the Middle East, a plan years in the making, and so carefully mapped out it made Tom's hairs stand on end. Because he knew that these men had been collecting the bits and pieces of chatter regarding Sadiq—who they rightly assumed would ultimately tie to John. And Prophet and his team had turned them over and over until they came up with the bigger picture.

It was exactly what Lansing told him.

Prophet's spent his life surviving by any means possible. His missions of mercy conveniently line up with terrorist attacks around the globe.

Lansing never stopped to consider that Prophet had just been following John's suspected trail of terror.

And from what Tom could understand, based on articles and maps and fuzzy black-and-white surveillance photos that were in chronological order, he was seeing the remnants of practice rounds—small acts of terror where no one had come forward to take credit. But then the last portion pointed to two key cities in the US, one on each coast . . . and the threats that Homeland Security had picked up on chatter. And those were eerily similar to the patterns that Sadiq and John had used on a smaller scale over the years. And Prophet had it all here, mapped out. "Jesus, Prophet. This is . . ."

"Incriminating to me?" Prophet said tiredly. "I flew into those places after those incidents happened—sometimes within twelve hours, sometimes forty-eight, but hell, it's not like anyone had my itinerary. It could look like I was covering my tracks instead of hunting down John. And trying to make sure there weren't any specialists or families of specialists who needed help in the aftermath."

"Well, you've said that Lansing wants you loose so he can track John through you, all while you took the brunt of Lansing's punishment."

"I don't think I took the brunt of it. I was allowed to stay in the States. To work. The team lives like exiled refugees."

"Again, purposely, to ensure they could make contact with John more easily than if they were in the States, right?" Tom asked.

"Maybe. Or maybe because Lansing's a generally power-hungry asshole."

"Hal was his recruit?"

"Yes. And he wanted someone with more experience than me to guard him."

"So why did you end up on that mission?"

Prophet shook his head a little. "LT's rec."

Tom cursed inwardly. "You did your job. John was point—it was up to him to get you and Hal where you were going safely." Tom stared at him. "Ever think that Lansing set you all up?"

"All the goddamned time. But . . ."

"What?" Tom pressed.

"There was a lot of fury in that rape. That kind of anger . . . it can't be faked. I'd know." Prophet looked over at the clippings, his expression hard but his voice raw from emotion and lack of sleep. "Lansing definitely believes I'm a traitor."

He squeezed Prophet's hand. "You need sleep."

"I . . ."

"I'll wake you if you have one," Tom promised.

Prophet swallowed hard.

"You need sleep. Because I need you."

Prophet tightened his grip on Tom's hand and fell asleep with his head on Tom's thigh, and Tom paged through the clippings (again) that made up the last eleven years of Prophet's life.

CHAPTER EIGHTEEN ◉

wo nights and several flashbacks later, Tom approached Prophet somewhat hesitantly about his broken sleep, his constant irritability. Although Tom had been there, watching over him while he slept, stopping most of the flashbacks from becoming too terrible, Prophet knew that it couldn't go on like this.

Granted, he wasn't sure exactly how to stop them. Or if he should. If they really were his version of an early-warning system, he had to make sure he paid attention to them.

"Proph, you need to try to sleep again."

"Fuck." He ran his hands through his hair. "I'm okay. I'm better."

"Bullshit."

"I don't want to talk about this. About any of this."

"Come on then, because I'm not asking you to talk." Tom took his hand, led him to the bed. Stripped him down, made him lie on his belly on the bed, and massaged his shoulders. But every time he closed his eyes . . .

"Fuck," he muttered.

"Okay, you're way too tense," Tom muttered. "Let me take care of this."

Prophet knew he was talking about sex, because that was how they took care of each other. It was more complicated than that, of course, but at the core, for them, sex was a way to work through their shit. And so far, it'd been pretty damned successful. "I don't want to have any more flashbacks," he blurted out.

"Is that why you don't want to close your eyes?"

Part of it, but Prophet nodded, because now wasn't the time to expand on it. He was too raw already. He wanted to feel better, not rehash his shit and feel worse.

"Let me help you. You trust me, Proph?"

"With my life."

Tom ran a hand down his back. "In New Orleans, in Etienne's studio . . ."

"Yeah," Prophet murmured. He'd tied Tom down, worked him through his anger. This was slightly different, but the reasoning behind what Tom was suggesting was the same.

At its core, it was about trust. And he did trust Tom.

He just didn't trust himself. But he'd try.

Tom spread his arms and legs and tied him, comfortably. And then he slid the blindfold over Prophet's eyes.

Prophet stiffened. Told himself that he wouldn't freak out.

Because it was Tommy.

Because this was pretty close to the way it would be, all touch and feel and sensation.

No different than closing your eyes.

And really, having Tommy help him with this, unwittingly, was maybe the best kind of therapy. And that worked for a bit to calm him. Tom's tongue helped too, ran from his neck to his spine, and that was great. But he'd known that would be. It was never about not being able to track Tom's movements or worrying that Tom would hurt him.

No, it was that this was how it was going to be, and if that was true, then he didn't want this to be the way he was going to be now. Not now, when he could still see.

There was no more wasting time.

Tom was half on top of Prophet, trying to keep him from hurting his wrists, but it was like trying to ride a bucking bronco. He pleaded, "Proph, calm down. Let me . . . fuck, you're going to hurt yourself."

And take apart the fucking bed, but Tom couldn't care less about that—he only wanted Prophet to stop himself from hurting his own wrists.

Prophet had pulled the knots tight in his struggle.

"I'll cut them, dammit, but you have to stay fucking still." He managed to grab the blindfold and jerk it off. "Proph, look at me."

Prophet did, but his eyes looked unfocused. Panicked. Jesus, he'd been trying to give Prophet a good night, and he'd given him a PTSD flashback instead. He tried everything, but in the end, it took his hand on Prophet's, threading their fingers together, and his weight fully on Prophet's back, to calm him down. They were spread-eagled together when Prophet finally stopped struggling, allowing Tom to safely cut the ropes.

When he freed one of Prophet's wrists, Prophet immediately grabbed the knife and did the other wrist himself. Tom rolled off him at that point, and Prophet let the ropes fall away as he moved from the bed and headed to the bathroom.

Tom followed him.

Prophet was hanging onto the edge of the sink, running the water, but he wasn't bending down to splash water on his face. It was like he was afraid to let go.

"Come on, Proph. Sit and I'll get you a cool cloth."

Finally, Prophet sat on the closed toilet seat and let Tom towel off his face and neck. He moved the cloth to Prophet's shoulders, rubbed and massaged for a while.

"Can a guy get any privacy?" Prophet's voice sounded so goddamned . . . empty. Defeated.

And it chilled Tom as much as it upset him. "No way—not after that shit."

Prophet swallowed hard, but didn't meet Tom's eyes. Tom didn't push. Just massaged and rubbed until Prophet had some color back in his cheeks.

"I fucking hate sharing my pain with you."

"Yeah, well, ditto," Tom said.

"It's different."

"Right. Forgot, you've got the market cornered on that."

Prophet sighed. Looked resigned, so much so that Tom almost let him off the hook. He didn't want Prophet to say anything more, not if it was going to fuck things up between them. But Tom didn't say any of that. Because he wouldn't let it. Wouldn't let anything.

Prophet left the bathroom, went into the bedroom, and pulled on sweats and a T-shirt. Tom dressed too, and found Proph in the kitchen, at the table, staring out the window.

"Every time I sit here, I expect to see Blue pop up," Prophet said. Tom couldn't help but smile. The men were close, and Tom wondered if what Prophet needed to tell him was something Blue already knew. Or something everyone but Tom knew.

He was about to leave Prophet alone so his own anger of being the last to know—true or not—wouldn't take over. It wasn't the time for that now. But he was hit with that goddamned voodoo feeling, the same one he'd gotten when he'd told Prophet to have his eyes checked.

And Prophet was watching him, like he fucking knew. And Tom truly understood, for maybe the first time, how much it sucked to have Prophet know him so damned well. Love and hate, like Prophet said.

And you said you'd take those odds. And he would but . . . "Prophet . . . your eyes?" was all he could say.

"I was thinking it," Prophet said ruefully. "Guess that works."

"Proph . . . really?"

Prophet took a breath, then chickened out and stared at the glass in front of him. Finally, he looked up and Tom said, "You're going blind," at the same time the word *blind* came into Tom's consciousness.

Jesus, Tom had known—it had been vague, yes, and he hadn't dug into it. Because it was like delving into someone's privacy and he didn't do that with Prophet.

He gripped the chair in front of him until his knuckles were white, then realized he was acting just the way Prophet must be afraid of him acting. "Prophet . . ."

Prophet gave him a crooked, boyish smile, and for a second, he was that young SEAL from the photos. He was still young, but there was never a time now when his expression wasn't haunted. But Tom had seen the proof in some of the old photos in the bookcases that, at one point, if even for just a brief time, he'd been carefree.

"It's true, Tom. I never had the freak-out people have when they learn about this, because I've always known it was my sentence. But I'm telling you that it's okay to freak."

"I'm not . . . Jesus." All he could think to do was tug the man to his feet and hug him. And so he did, and Prophet let him. And Prophet's freak-out in the bedroom made sense now. "The blindfold."

"I wear one sometimes. To train myself. You can't cheat with a blindfold on."

Prophet's voice was muffled against his shirt. Tom's hands were on his back, rubbing, holding. When he pulled back, he couldn't help but trace Prophet's cheekbones with his thumbs and stare into those beautiful eyes. "Tell me everything."

"Really? Because half the time, I don't even want to know everything."

"Well, then, that'll be my job." Which was the wrong thing to say. "I just meant . . ."

"I know, T. I know how it starts. Trust me on that." His voice was tight.

"You're not my fucking job, any more than I'm yours." Tom desperately needed Proph to understand that.

CHAPTER NINETEEN ⊙

Prophet couldn't say it. As much as he could say in his mind what was going to happen to his sight—*I'm going blind*—he couldn't say it out loud.

Tom's hard swallow was audible. "You've known. When I told you to see the doctor—"

"I'd been seeing him for ten years already. I went the morning we got back from Amsterdam."

"Is it progressing?"

Prophet turned to him. "It's in the intermediate stage now. I'm starting to get some blurriness. There's no way to know how much I'll lose. Some people stay like I am forever. Some move to losing central vision. Some lose everything, but most lose at least central vision, and with the genetic version I have, that's pretty much a given."

There, it was all out, in one big blurt. He added, "I see the doctor once a month."

There was a pause as Tom took it in, and then said exactly what Prophet didn't want him to say. "So you'll still have vision."

It's not his fault, Proph. He tamped down his temper but wasn't able to keep the edge out of his voice when he said, "Don't give me the glass-half-full bullshit, T. Just don't."

"Who else in your family has this?"

"My father. My grandfather. My great-grandfather. The Drews curse. See, you don't have the market on curses." Prophet knew the next question was coming and steeled for it.

"How bad were they?" Tom asked.

"I don't know. They never stuck around to find out."

He met Tom's eyes. Tom tilted his head and stared at him for a long moment before realization dawned in his eyes. He took in a shuddered breath and muttered, "Fuck," and then, "Don't you fucking think about that, Prophet."

"Aye aye, sir."

Tom was striding toward him, and Prophet's fragile grip on his temper began to fray. He walked out of the bedroom, knowing Tom would follow him. But he needed to put something between them, some large piece of furniture, because he didn't want to fight with him.

He ended up in the living room when Tom said, "Prophet, come on. You can't hide from me."

"Not trying to. Ever stop to think that I've dealt with this for years—my whole life—that I don't want to deal with it with you? I've been through all of this. All the stages of grief. And maybe I'll go through them all again when it happens or maybe I won't, but for now, I'm living exactly the way I always have. One hour at a time and that's always worked for me. Maybe you could figure it out on your own. Keep it to yourself. Talk your feelings out with a therapist. But *I* don't fucking want to hear it."

His voice was calm and controlled, but he wasn't that way inside. No, he was spiraling, the way he'd been from the Lansing flashback, right before LT had called.

It was obvious that Tom didn't know what to say, and no matter what he did say, it would be wrong. Prophet knew that, knew there was no good answer, nothing to fix.

Prophet just had to hope that he'd maintain enough field of vision—enough peripheral—so that he could at least remain independent.

It was all he had.

"Maybe you're not actively trying to kill yourself, but the jobs you take are a slow form of suicide," Tom said, not letting that go.

"And some of them are necessary." Prophet hated resenting that Tom knew him as well as Doc did. He supposed it was transparent enough, but still . . . "We're not going to talk about this anymore."

"Oh yes, we are."

He turned slowly. Tom's hands were fisted too, and this would be a massive brawl if Prophet let it start.

Tom said carefully, "I know how hard this has got to be—"

"Don't you dare give me that pity shit."

"Why would I pity you, Proph? This isn't a death sentence."

Wrong thing to say. And instead of picking Tom up and throwing him against the wall, Prophet picked up the coffee table, letting whatever was on it slide off before throwing *it* against the wall. It broke apart, the wood splitting, leaving a satisfying dent in the wall.

Before he could look for other things to throw, he heard Remy say, "I guess this isn't a great time."

"You're really losing your sight?" Remy asked, and how was it possible the kid was taller than the last time Prophet had seen him, which was maybe three weeks ago? He was sitting at the kitchen table, and Prophet was making him a couple of sandwiches while Tom was on the phone in the other room, trying to get through to Remy's mom. When Prophet glanced over his shoulder at him, Remy offered, "Dude, I couldn't help but hear."

"Yeah, I am." All the fight was drained from him, and there was no reason to take it out on Remy anyway.

"That sucks."

Prophet put the plate down, then ran a hand over Remy's hair. "That too."

"I guess I should've knocked instead of using the key." Remy picked up the sandwich and basically began to inhale it, as if no one had fed him for weeks.

"I gave it to you to use." And if he hadn't been throwing tables, he'd have seen Remy entering the building easily enough. "It's not a problem."

Although Remy running away from New Orleans to upstate New York? Kind of a problem.

He sat down next to Remy, but before he could say anything else, Remy told him, "You're not going to make me go back."

"Remy..."

Remy held up his hand. "No, that wasn't a question. You're not going to make me, and nothing you say will work. And if you try to take me there by force—"

"Force? Where are you getting this shit?"

"I'll keep coming back like a bad penny."

Prophet stared at him, his voice firm, because he needed Remy to believe him. "You're a lot of things, Rem, but a bad penny isn't one of them."

"I want to stay here with you and Tom."

Prophet glanced at him. He was so steadfast in his insistence, but then, just for a second, something akin to fear skittered across Remy's face. "What's wrong?"

"It's just . . . is that going to ruin plans to kill yourself?" he asked seriously, and Prophet saw the fear in the young man's face again, and realized it was more for Prophet than for himself.

"No. That dick already did that." He pointed in Tommy's direction—still on the phone, his expression tight with anger.

"I won't be any trouble. I've got money. I'll pay you back. I'll even stay at a hotel or something and stay out of your way."

Prophet stared at him. "Is that really what you want?"

Remy bravely tried to meet his gaze, but after a second, he hung his head and shrugged. "Not really."

"So try again."

Remy sighed. Looked up. "I want to stay with you and Tom. Dad would've wanted it. I mean, if I can't, I'll go back to Della, but I thought . . . it seemed like you didn't mind talking to me."

Prophet smiled. "I didn't. I don't do much these days that I don't want to do. And I don't do things out of guilt or pity."

"Okay."

Prophet leaned forward, elbows on his knees. "I think I figured out a way to keep you here. Or between here and Della's, depending on where my work and Tom's work takes us."

"Yeah?"

"We'll take care of it, me and Tom, okay? Put your shit in the free bedroom. But first, text your mom, tell her you're fine, because you know she doesn't believe Tom."

Remy sighed. "She's going to send the cops here."

"Trust me—cops don't come here."

"I can go to a lawyer and get emancipated," Remy said as he touched the screen so fast his fingers seemed like blurs. "There. Satisfied?"

"Totally." Prophet stared at him. "And you really want to stay here?"

"Yes."

"So you'll stay here."

Remy opened his mouth and closed it. He obviously hadn't expected it to be so easy. Because it never had been for this kid, or for Prophet or for Tommy and goddammit, someone had to change that shit.

By the time Remy's mom stopped screaming at Tom, Prophet had already cooked half the food in the fridge for Remy and had ordered a couple of pizzas, just to be on the safe side.

Remy reminded Prophet of Blue, the way he ate. Except he could actually out-eat Blue. And he was already as tall as Blue. At sixteen.

"I'm going to need to work overtime to feed you."

Remy grinned and then sobered.

"Hey, it's a joke. It's all right." Because he did not want this kid to feel like a burden—Remy was the furthest thing from it.

"I know you said it was all right. But what about Tom? Is he going to say yes because he feels guilty and shit?"

"About your dad?"

"Yeah. And about being an asshole to you about your eyes," Remy said seriously.

"Ah, Rem, he wasn't. Trust me. And yeah, Tom's got a lot of guilt about your dad."

"From high school?"

"Yeah, that. And then all the shit that went down when Etienne was killed. But he wants you here."

"How do you know?"

"Because," Tom broke in, "he knows me like the back of his hand. It's inconvenient at times, but he's right, Remy."

Remy stared at him. "You're the other one."

"The other one what?" Tom asked, trying to look innocent, even under Prophet's investigatory gaze.

"The other one sending me money every month." Remy shrugged. "It didn't take a rocket scientist to figure it out, so I hope you guys didn't think you were being all stealthy or something."

But Tom turned to Prophet. "*You* were the other one, so don't even start."

"I never told you that."

"You just did."

Remy looked between them. "You two always like this?"

"Yes!" they said in unison.

"Okay. S'cool. I kind of like it." Remy grabbed another sandwich. "Don't stop on my account. Just let me know when the pizza comes."

Tom smiled at Prophet, who smiled back. A quiet moment of peace passed between them, even though the discussion they'd been having was far from over. Everything had suddenly got really complicated . . . and somehow better at the same time. "You could've told me, Proph. We could've just sent it together."

"I saved the money," Remy interjected and pulled out an envelope full of cash. "I figured . . . if I came here and you didn't have to spend any more money on me . . . I could use this for a while and then—"

"That's yours, Rem," Prophet said firmly. "For you to do whatever the hell you want with. And I'll spend my money any way I goddamn please. On you. On him. On whateverthefuck you want."

Tom looked at Remy and shrugged. "He gets like this a lot. Just roll with it."

Remy smiled and went back to eating.

CHAPTER TWENTY ◉

F our days and nights later, Prophet was still sleeping with Tom watching over him. Or not sleeping for very long at all, as the case may be. But Tom would wake him, Prophet would come back to reality, and then he'd stay up with Tom, watching movies. Both of them were also looking through the clippings, trying to pinpoint exactly when John and Sadiq might make their next move, but they didn't talk about it much.

They were both trying to pretend things were normal when they one hundred percent weren't. It was the first time since they'd met that they'd gone without sex when they weren't apart. Because normally, it would've been a constant, clawing need they scratched as often as humanly possible. Tom would've, but Prophet was actively avoiding it, even though it killed him to do so.

There were distractions—Prophet's near-constant nighttime flashbacks, ensuring their need to sleep in shifts, plus there was Remy to take care of, to take him back and forth to the tutor, to make sure none of what Prophet was embroiled in could touch the kid.

But really, they were just damned good excuses, and both he and Tom knew it.

They both knew why, so Tom didn't push him, and that relieved Prophet and made him feel worse all at the same time. Knowing why they weren't having sex and not having sex were two different things entirely.

Now, he checked the monitor he'd activated for Remy's bedroom on the first floor. The building was alarmed, and while he didn't want to invade the teenager's privacy, he needed to make sure he was keeping Remy safe.

"He's sleeping?" Tom asked. He was in the doorway of the living room, and Prophet turned to look over his shoulder.

"Yeah, out like a light. And I got more from the PI today. It shouldn't be much longer."

"Good, because we don't have much longer before his mom calls the police. Which at this point, she's got every right to do." Tom ran a hand through his dark hair, and that small motion somehow made the deep freeze on his sex drive melt, for the first time in what seemed like forever.

But instead of getting up and going over to Tom, taking him to bed, he shifted in his seat and asked, "You're really okay with this? With us bringing Remy to live with us full-time?"

"I'm the one who brought it up," Tom reminded him, and yes, Prophet remembered that discussion on the ride home from New Orleans months earlier. He'd been pondering the possibility, but Tom had given voice to it and from there, the plan moved forward. Neither of them had told Remy, in the event that something went wrong—they didn't want to get his hopes up and knew he could come to them in two years anyway. That he could spend a lot of time with Della in the meantime.

They'd never expected him to show here. Okay, maybe Prophet did, a little.

Tom continued, "Etienne would've wanted this. And while growing up with Della would be great for Remy . . ."

"He can visit her and New Orleans," Prophet said firmly. "With us."

"True. Anyway, there's still a lot to figure out."

Tom wasn't just talking about stuff with Remy. Prophet turned his attention back to the table where the clippings had become commonplace. He didn't even bother to put them away anymore. Remy knew he was working, and he never intruded on this stuff. Give him some art supplies and he spent hours painting and drawing, listening to loud music and generally just being a kid. Which was exactly what he was supposed to do. "He's figuring things out just fine."

"What about us, Proph?"

Tom was still behind him, like he knew Prophet couldn't deal with a face-to-face. And fuck, he knew Tom was talking about his eyes, and their future, because it was all rolled up together now. And goddammit, *that* ball was completely in Tom's court, not his—why couldn't Tom see that?

Because he doesn't want to—not yet. Because it was easier to pretend that all the issues were on Prophet and not on the fact that Tom had to process everything and make some decisions for himself. "I guess we'll figure things out too."

"Easy enough, right?" Tom's voice was light, but there was a slight edge to it.

"There's not much for me to figure out with my sight, Tommy." Prophet bowed his head a little as he heard Tom move forward.

And then Tom was sitting next to him at the table, asking, "So Doc and Phil know? John too?"

"Yeah."

"And me."

"And you," Prophet confirmed. "LT didn't know at first—neither did Dean, until a couple of years ago. I reached out to him for resources. Technology."

And seeing Dean doing what he wanted, on his own terms, gave Prophet hope.

Rescuing him, seeing the panic on his face reminded Prophet that pretending things could be the same, pretending that he was going to be the same man who could do the same things after he'd gone blind, wasn't worth it—it could put everyone associated with him at risk if he even tried to keep working.

Tom asked him now, "What about your team?"

Prophet glanced up at him, admitted, "I need to tell them—but Mal knows. I wasn't ready to talk about it with the others. With Mal . . ." He rubbed his throat. "There's an experimental op. His doc wants to try it. Mal says he will, when he can afford to stay in one place for an extended rehab and recovery. Four months. But that's not really why he's putting it off."

Tom processed that for a long moment, and then his eyebrows raised. "For you?"

Mal would say that all they needed to do was wait until Hook lost his hearing completely and then they'd be their own personal version of See No Evil, Hear No Evil, Speak No Evil. The guy was so fucking twisted . . . and Prophet couldn't deny that, and the way he dealt with Prophet's eyes gave him more than a measure of comfort. "He'll never try it unless there's something for me. And there's not. So I've got to find a way to make him."

"And find a way to tell the others."

"That too."

"Cillian?"

Prophet finally turned to him. "I see a doctor not on EE's payroll. Not on my insurance. But that doesn't mean Cillian doesn't know everything."

Tom nodded. "You coming to bed soon?"

"Yeah."

"Wake me up, okay?"

Prophet didn't even bother pretending. "I will."

Tom rubbed his shoulder, started to walk away. Prophet reached behind him and grabbed Tom's wrist, but he didn't turn to face him again. "When I was captured . . ." he began, "they blindfolded me. For days. I didn't panic. I forced myself to deal with it. To use my other senses. Because I knew, one day, that'd be all I'd have."

"And now every time it goes dark for you, you can't stop panicking," Tom said quietly.

Tom backed up to look at him, and Prophet didn't let go of his wrist. "I know you accept this, Tom. For now. But there's going to come a time—"

"Shut the fuck up."

"Now that I want to talk, I can't?"

"That's right. Because you're wrong."

Prophet didn't push it, let go of Tom's arm. He knew what was going to happen anyway, so why fuck things up for the time they had left. They'd had eight months. And they had more time, but it wasn't going to be enough. Never. But he'd have memories, and he'd finish this job, and then . . .

And then.

CHAPTER TWENTY-ONE ☉

Things had clicked into place rapidly after his talk with Prophet—Phil wanting Prophet to take over EE. Doc's closeness. Prophet's claustrophobia with the casts. And John, who'd betrayed Prophet in more ways than Tom wanted to begin to count.

After a really restless night for both of them, Tom left early in the morning to check in at EE. He'd mentioned to Phil last week that he'd probably need a long leave of absence and Phil hadn't seemed surprised. But his paychecks kept coming in, so he figured actually going in was the right thing to do.

When he pushed through the doors, Natasha greeted him warmly. Asked about Prophet. So did pretty much everyone.

By the time he got to Phil's office, the anger inside of him had built up—probably more at Prophet than Phil, but Phil was no angel in any of this.

Phil's office door was partially open, and he looked up from his desk when Tom—having forced down the urge to barge right in—gave a small knock on the doorjamb.

"Tom, about time you showed." Phil waved him in. "How's Prophet?"

"How's Prophet?" he asked, his voice a dangerously rough tone that even he recognized as a bad sign.

Phil didn't miss it either—he stilled, then pushed his seat back and stood, his palms down on the desk. "What's the problem?"

"I know, Phil—about his sight."

Phil looked pained. "It wasn't my place to tell you."

"And I wouldn't have wanted to hear it from you. Trust me."

"Then we have no issue."

"Oh, we've got a goddamned issue. Because it was one thing for you to force Prophet out because you felt he'd pushed it too far, when that's exactly the reason you hired him in the first place, but a whole other thing to promise a man a soft place to land after he loses his sight and then take that away from him too." He was getting louder and didn't care. "You ripped the fucking rug out from under him. You fucking betrayed him when he needed you most." Phil opened his mouth but Tom put a hand up. "Don't fucking justify it. You took his biggest fear, and you turned it around on him. You betrayed him. You'll never have his trust again."

"Don't you dare put this on me. Who the fuck do you think you are?"

"I'm looking out for Prophet's best interests. You?"

Phil raised his hand and pointed across the desk, punctuating the air with his finger. "Don't you dare question me, boy. I've been there with Prophet for a hell of a lot longer than you, and I'm betting I outlast you."

"You think putting him in charge of EE's going to save him when he can't see?"

"Yeah, I think it'll save him. I also think he can save countless lives with his experience. I won't let him put that to waste."

"You won't let him? You think you can order him to be productive?" Tom asked. "You're fucking with his life. His mind. Like he doesn't have enough of that in the first place."

"What, the search for his long-lost teammate? Such fucking bullshit. He should've let go of that a long time ago, Tom. I thought you'd be able to talk some sense into him." The veins in Phil's neck were standing out.

Tom took a step forward, but a strong hand on his shoulder pulled him back. He turned to swing and saw it was Doc. He put his hand down, and Doc simply led him out of Phil's office and into his empty examining room down the hall. The infirmary was one floor down, along with Doc's office. But this room was for the quick visits and physicals.

Doc closed the door behind him and said, "Go ahead."

"Go ahead, what?"

"Say all the things you can't say to Prophet."

"Yeah, I know you knew about his eyes before me, Doc. Go ahead and gloat about how close you two are," Tom snarked.

Doc sighed. Stared up at the ceiling and muttered what sounded like a prayer before turning his attention to Tom and saying, "I left a job I loved because I knew I wouldn't pass the medical exams to stay a SEAL. I knew I might for a year, if I was lucky, but one good shot to my knee, and I'd be lucky to make it with a cane. And I took stock and knew I didn't want that. So I left. In my fucking prime. I finished med school, and I've made it my job to stop assholes like me from ruining their motherfucking lives by sticking with something long after their bodies can handle the punishment."

Tom was about to answer him—something obnoxious—when he realized . . . "You're pissed you can't do that for Prophet. It's not something you can put off by telling him to stop working."

Doc's jaw clenched. Tom sagged against the exam table. He pulled himself up and sat, hands dangling between his thighs. "He doesn't believe I'm going to stay. Said he knew my first reaction would be acceptance. But once I thought about it—really thought about it . . ."

He wouldn't even say it out loud. Instead, he announced fiercely, "I'm not going to lose him. And *I'm* not going anywhere."

"Good," Doc said. "Now tell me all the things you can't tell Prophet."

"You first," Tom shot back.

"I'm worried he's only going to live for you. That you're the only reason he'll stick around. And while that's a great and powerful thing, it's not enough, Tom. He's got to want to stick around because he's got shit to do."

Doc's words echoed inside Tom's head. "I can't think about this, not until after . . ."

He stopped. Glanced at Doc, who said, "I know about it, Tom. Phil knows some, I know more, but neither of us knows the full extent of what's happening. But it's fucked Prophet up something good. I never thought he'd be able to open up to anyone the way he has to you."

Tom stuck his hands in his pockets, feeling fucking useless. "I don't know what the fuck to do, Doc. When he goes blind, do I keep working here? Will me going on missions freak him out and make him pissed he can't?"

"You can't stop living because you'll be doing things he can't."

"But maybe I can live without doing those things."

"Can you?"

"I think I can. But I don't know about Prophet . . . I don't think *he* can. And that scares the shit out of me."

Judging by Doc's expression, he felt exactly the same way.

Tom ran a hand through his hair and moved on to the reason he'd come to EE to start with today. "How well do you know Proph's old team?"

"I was their Navy doc. I traveled with them."

"They all have PTSD."

"Every sailor, soldier, merc, Marine has it. Including you," Doc informed him bluntly.

"And you?"

Doc cocked a brow. "I'm perfect."

Tom bit back a smile, because out of all of them, he'd actually believe it of Doc. "Is their PTSD bad? Like, could it fuck them up?"

"You *have* met them, yes?"

"They seem pretty normal."

Doc groaned loudly. "It's so fucked up that you say that. Means *you're* so fucked up."

"Doc, this is serious. Did John have PTSD too?"

"Yes." His tone was clipped, like he hated talking about the man. "Now tell me what the fuck these questions are all about."

"Prophet's flashbacks are getting worse."

"How much worse?"

"Nightly. Sometimes more than one. And a lot of them involve John. He thinks he sees John. Talks to him. And then in the morning, I'll find sand on the floor, and it's always in the spot Prophet talks to when he's seeing John."

Doc contemplated all of that for a long moment. "You think Prophet is making John up? Scattering the sand?"

"Do you? Could he be sleepwalking and I'm just not catching it? Because we sleep in shifts, and I know I probably pass out harder than normal from the stress. Christ, I feel like he's going crazy and I'm a short step behind him."

Doc sighed. "PTSD is . . . I can't rule it out. Prophet *could* be sleepwalking. Playing with the sand he's got in that box, putting it where John was in his dream."

"That makes me feel fifty percent better and just as bad." Tom hesitated. "Could he be seeing things?"

"Because of the disease? Or the PTSD?"

"Both. Either."

"The disease? No, it's not like that. He wouldn't hallucinate. He'll just be unable to see one morning."

Jesus. Tom sat heavily in the nearest chair. Maybe for the first time that realization hit him, and hit him hard. And he was only glad he wasn't in front of Prophet when the tears of mourning came.

CHAPTER TWENTY-TWO

W hen he got home hours later, he was a little lighter. Not much, but Doc had taken him out to lunch, and they'd talked, and he'd gone to a movie by himself.

He was actually looking forward to getting back to the apartment, not dreading it. When he let himself in, he knew they were alone just because there was no music blasting. Remy was with the tutor Prophet had hired, so he wouldn't miss anything while he stayed here. They couldn't enroll him in school, but Prophet had sweet-talked his teachers into sending assignments. And Remy was passing tests.

It hadn't even been a week, but already it was like Remy had always been here.

"Hey," Prophet called. He was facing the door instead of away from it, and he had an empty plate next to him—Remy had been encouraging him to eat, taking care of Prophet in a way that Tom found incredibly innocent and mature all at once.

"Hey." He came over and rubbed the back of Prophet's neck. Prophet groaned and bent his head forward, and Tom indulged him.

The clippings were spread out on the table in front of him, a giant puzzle Prophet hadn't quite figured out yet. Tom wondered how many nights over the past decade Prophet had sat alone and pored over his past, letting the memories twine around what should've been purely unemotional work.

He knew for sure that Prophet had been sitting in that spot at least since Tom had left the apartment. The knots in Prophet's shoulders and neck confirmed it.

"Need any help?"

Prophet sighed. "Have at it. After you do that for several hours."

Tom snorted, but he didn't stop while he scanned the newspaper clippings. Prophet had them sorted in chronological order, and Tom thought about what Lansing had mentioned, how Prophet's jobs always took him to places where terrorist attacks took place. That wasn't a coincidence, but maybe the order was wrong.

"There are some spots where you're in a location first and then a small terror attack happens, or a sighting," Tom said now. "Did you ever think that maybe John followed you on your jobs. You said he knows you better than anyone—that he could track you. So, what if he did?"

"And he just happened to have a terror attack up his sleeve for each location?"

"Stranger things have happened. All he'd have to do was make contacts—it's not like your jobs took you to the most law-abiding places."

"So what, he's been framing me for years? While running a terror network." Prophet snorted, then pushed the chair back and stood, forcing Tom to back away before he was run over. Then Prophet didn't move, stood there and stared at the papers, and then he moved away from the table like it was on fire. "Or maybe he was giving me an alibi. Or completely fucking with me."

"Fuck."

Prophet drew in a harsh breath. "Good word for all of it."

"And how does Cillian fit into all of this? He lied to you about John's body . . . that means he knows a lot."

"Which is what Mal's trying to find out."

"When's the last time Cillian was home?"

Prophet thought back. "I think before I went to New Orleans. And he wouldn't leave anything important there for that long. But I haven't been able to get any kind of status report from Mal. He's MIA with me—checking in with King, but giving the barest of reports."

"And Cillian hasn't texted you?"

"No. And yes, I've tried texting him. Nothing."

"I say we go into his apartment and search the place anyway."

Prophet crossed his arms and asked, "For what?" with a smirk.

"So I can trash it?" Tom said hopefully.

"Isn't it enough that you threw the couch out the window?"

"You fucking love that shit," Tom growled. "The jealousy turns you the hell on." Prophet's eyes got that familiar glow. "I was actually hoping we could revisit it. Soon."

"Soon," Tom agreed. For now, that was enough.

Remy came home soon after, and they had dinner together and watched a movie before Remy headed to do some homework and draw.

"He's going to be a fucking terror," Prophet said when they were alone in bed, watching more TV. He was trying to fall asleep, mainly so Tom could actually get some sleep.

"Of course he is. He's on his best behavior, but soon this place is going to be overrun with teenage boys. And girls."

Prophet groaned. "We're going to have to kick Cillian out and make this place bigger."

"And that suits me just fine."

"Figured you wouldn't protest." Domestication was really yanking his chain, telling him that he could have a shot at a family, a normal life—at the same time it was taking away his ability to see any of it.

"Proph, your phone." Tom handed it to him, and he glanced at the caller ID.

Speaking of domestic . . . "Hey, Mom."

Tom's head jerked his way as Judie Drews said, "Baby, how are you?"

Baby. Holy hell. "How're those meds doing?"

"Elijah, you cut the shit, you hear me?"

He tried to wrap his head around how normal she sounded, like the Judie Drews before his father killed himself, before the scheming forced them out of New York and into Texas. It hadn't always been shitty. Maybe it hadn't been the best, but it was better than a lot of his friends' families. "Yes, ma'am."

"Are you okay?"

"I'm fine."

There was a long pause, and she said, "You'd tell me, wouldn't you? You can."

She was talking about his eyes. And it had been years since she'd asked about them. She was really fucking lucid—definitely taking her meds or finally on the right ones. "I know," he lied.

"Good. Listen, I can't stay on long—the girls are waiting for me. We're taking belly dancing lessons."

He groaned. "I could've lived my whole life not knowing that," and she laughed.

"Love you, baby. Talk soon."

He was actually smiling when he hung up. Handed the phone to Tom who sat staring at him. "What?"

Tom gave a small shrug and said, a little hesitantly, "It's just . . . I don't know anything about you or your family. For all I know, you were dropped from the sky."

Prophet pointed. "Ding ding. Dropped in the middle of nowhere and raised by wolves."

Tom rolled his eyes.

"My mom's in a facility. She's been there a long time—mainly because it's the safest place for her."

"Because of your jobs?"

"No." Prophet shook his head. "She's bipolar. And she wasn't taking her meds regularly. Not at all when I was growing up, unless I was there to make sure she took them."

He waited for Tom to say something about his caretaking abilities, but to his credit, Tom only asked, "Did you stay with John because your family was screwed up, or did you do it because of how screwed up John's family was?"

Prophet huffed.

"You don't like me knowing shit about you."

"Give the man a prize. And to answer your question, it was a little from both columns. And you didn't talk about your family."

"No, but you got to live it when you busted into my past."

"When I busted into your past," Prophet repeated, doing his best not to laugh.

"It's not funny."

"I'm not laughing." Inside, he totally was though. "Fucking drama queen."

Tom softened, rubbed Prophet's cheek, and Prophet realized how much he missed the contact. Tom was giving him all the time he needed, the space . . . and sometimes Prophet just wished the guy would push him down and fuck him.

But most of the time, he knew he couldn't. He kept flashing back to the blindfold. And everything else.

"Did John fuck you up with relationships?" Tom asked now.

"I don't know, T. I never really thought about it."

"But he was your first, last, and only one, right?"

"Yeah, he was." Much in the way Remy's dad was Tommy's.

CHAPTER TWENTY-THREE ◉

Prophet was up the next morning at oh dark hundred for a run in the woods and some general training. Remy was locked up tight in the apartment, and Prophet let his footfalls soothe him, the routine lulling him into the zone.

Or he would've let it, if Tommy hadn't been muttering complaints behind him, about how it was too cold for humans to be outside for no good damned reason.

Tom had been the one to insist on going with him, and Prophet knew it was more of a *let's keep track of the crazy man* thing than a burning desire to be in the woods instead of in bed. But Prophet didn't give a shit about Tom's regrets—he wasn't letting him off the hook. The training was too important for either of them to slack off, no matter how exhausted or defeated they might feel. No, that was when you pushed harder, dammit.

And you sound like a drill sergeant. Or a fucking motivational speaker infomercial. "Could you bite back your complaints? You're fucking with my run."

"Your run is fucking with my ability to complain," Tom called back.

Prophet stopped and turned to find Tom stretching out his side. "Cramp?"

Tom rolled his eyes. "No, I always stand like this."

"You're not a morning person."

"We don't even have mornings or nights anymore, Proph. It's all one big blended period of no sleep."

"Do you want to fight?" Prophet asked him, changing his stance. Tom frowned, and Prophet waited until Tom realized that he was talking about sparring and not picking a fight. Hell, it was still a way to get their aggression out under the guise of practice anyway.

"Fine. Gotta be better than running, right?"

"If you say so." Before they started, Prophet showed him some tricks he'd learned during close-quarter battle training, because that was a whole different kind of fighting from what Tommy was probably used to. And then they separated and circled each other.

Prophet's blood was racing—the run got him warm but watching Tom move was a whole different kind of heat. And as much as Prophet tried to ignore his urges, he couldn't. So he simply hadn't followed through on them, but he'd miscalculated the amount of sheer physical contact during a fight. He tried to just keep distance between them, but Tom wasn't letting that happen. Just like he knew what Prophet was trying to do, the bastard. He was like a charging bull, determined to bring Prophet down in his own way. And ignoring every single thing Prophet was trying to teach him.

Every hit Prophet got in went straight to his own dick somehow. Every time Tom touched him was like a jolt of electricity. Prophet wiped his mouth with the back of his hand after Tom caught him on the lip. He tasted blood, and Tom told him not to worry, that it would fucking freeze the way they were.

But they were both sweating. Flushed. Furious and yet . . . not. And then Tom tackled him out of the blue, and Prophet fell with a grunt into the leaves, with Tom on top of him. Smiling.

Prophet shook his head. "You totally did that wrong."

"Uh, who's on top here?"

"You're so fucking deluded, T. You really think this is winning? Do you know how easily I could throw you off and disable you? Kill you?"

"Yeah, I think this is winning," Tom murmured, staring at Prophet's lips—and Prophet realized they were both hard as hell. "And yes, I know how easily you could. I know how fucking fragile it all is. Message received long before I met you."

Prophet shoved Tom off him before this went any further. Because he was picturing Tom naked in the leaves, and it was a good picture because he was naked too and fucking Tom in those leaves. "I'll just take care of all of the shit coming our way myself."

"Good. Because I need sleep. Wake me when you've got John, okay?"

"Ha. Ha."

But then Tom got serious, pointed in Prophet's face—which Prophet of course growled at, and Tom fucking ignored him, saying, "I realize you're planning on fighting all the dragons single-handedly—"

"I'm going to protect you from John, dammit. Show him that he can't fucking mess with you. This is about territory."

Tom narrowed his eyes. "Are you going to piss a circle around me too?"

"If that's what it takes."

Tom rolled his eyes but wisely said nothing else. Because Prophet was going to show him how to defend himself in every single situation possible, dammit, and Tommy was going to learn them and those things would save his life, the way Prophet might not be able to in the future.

It did not matter that Tommy was perfectly capable of saving his own goddamned self, more than anyone else he knew. He was going to show him stuff until he couldn't show him things anymore and then . . .

It was the *and then* that always hit him the hardest. Shouldn't, but did. Fuck, and when it didn't, you couldn't even wish for that because then it would be the *and then* . . .

And then.

"I'm waiting. I get bored easily," Tom mumbled through a yawn.

"No, that's me," Prophet said irritably. "We're done for now."

"You didn't get me up this early—"

"You just said you don't sleep anyway."

"—to teach me shit, then back off."

"Maybe I have nothing to teach. Maybe I'm just crazy like my mother."

There was silence after he admitted that. He stood in the clearing, wanting to take the confession back, but couldn't. Shouldn't.

Tom's heavy arm went around his chest. Pulled Prophet's back to him so they both faced out the same way. "You've got the blind thing already—I think you're probably good without worrying about adding another thing to your repertoire."

Prophet whirled around on him. "You did *not* just make a joke about that."

"I did." Tom grinned. "Besides, the kind of crazy you are? There's no medication for it anyway."

And then he took off at a dead run.

"Oh sure, now you want to run," Prophet called after him. "Just wait till I catch you."

"Counting on it," Tom called back.

Prophet smiled. Finally. And then he chased Tom through the goddamned freezing woods.

CHAPTER TWENTY-FOUR ◉

Tom's phone began to beep at the same time Prophet's did. "It's Remy," he said.

"Mine's Mal. He says, 'Tell the kid to stop pointing a gun at me.'"

"Shit." Tom answered the phone. "He's cool, Remy—Prophet's friend. He didn't know you were there, or he wouldn't have scared you."

Or maybe he was enough of an asshole that he would.

"So I can put down the gun?" Remy asked.

"Yes, no gun. He's fine," Tom emphasized. "We're on our way back now."

"I would've made Mal wait it out with the gun," Prophet said.

"Now you tell me," Tom groaned as he raced with Prophet through the freezing cold morning back to the house. By the time they got inside, Mal was making breakfast for Remy, and Remy was learning sign language.

"Great," Tom muttered. "Uncle Insanity."

Prophet snorted. "See, I'd think you two'd have common ground. All the tattoos and shit. Don't your people bond over that?"

"Your people?" Tom raised his brows. "They're tattoos, not a geographic location."

Mal shot him the finger out of Remy's line of sight, and Prophet nodded approvingly, saying, "See, his response? Much cleaner and to the point."

"I fucking hate you."

Prophet ran a hand down his neck, and Tom fought a shiver. He went to curse at him but caught the look in Prophet's eyes and fucking melted, the way he always did.

Remy laughed, more so when Mal made a gagging sound. Tom shot him the finger back, and Prophet nodded as if to say, *See? Much more efficient.*

"Keeps my mouth free for other things," Tom whispered into Prophet's ear. "Rem, isn't it time to get ready to meet your tutor? I'll drive you."

"Yeah, yeah." Remy pushed away from the table, asking Mal, "Will you be here when I get back?"

Mal nodded yes, and Tom fought a groan. He'd seen Mal's giant duffel bag earlier, but waited until Remy left the room before saying, "I thought you guys weren't supposed to show up near each other at all?"

And Mal's response was a simple shrug, which somehow caused Prophet to start in, his voice at slightly apeshit level. "Cillian's been gone for a while. Like, *gone*, Mal. Won't answer texts or anything."

Mal shrugged again, encouraging the apeshit.

"Mal. Did. You. Kill. Him."

Mal stared at him steadily, then shook his head. Slowly.

"Good."

And then Mal had his iPad and he was typing, not signing. *I don't think I did*, and making sure Tom could see it—and how sweet of Mal to include him in this argument.

As if reading Tom's mind, Mal smirked, and Prophet demanded, "You don't think you did? Okay, what the fuck does that even mean?"

Again, Mal shrugged.

"For the love of Christ, we need to find him."

Why? You miss him? Mal typed.

"Yeah, that's it." Prophet must've caught on to something in Mal's expression to make him stop. "Did something happen?"

Mal shrugged.

Prophet stared at the ceiling, cursing, ignoring Tom's snort. Finally, he looked at Mal and said, "I'm taking Remy to his tutor."

"I said I'd do it," Tom reminded him, because there was no way he was getting stuck with Uncle Insanity of the shrug.

"Yeah, but I figure leaving you two together's torture enough for both of you." Prophet gave them both a mock salute, and Mal, of course, shot him the finger.

Tom shook his head at both men and sat down on the couch. He wanted to bring up John, and the team thinking that Prophet was in denial, but he didn't want to start any problems.

He wondered if Mal knew King had confronted him in Amsterdam—or if he cared. And, to his surprise, Mal took a seat next to him on the couch, his iPad in hand. He stared straight ahead, ramrod tense.

Like, take-out-the-entire-apartment-in-three-seconds tense.

"Want to talk about it?" Tom asked.

Mal turned to him, and instead of the withering look he expected, mouthed, *You saw me—in the back room.*

Yeah, there was no getting rid of that particular image, but instead of telling Mal that, he nodded.

Didn't tell Proph.

Tom shook his head. "Have you really not heard from Cillian?"

Mal studied him, his eyes dark, his gaze penetrating—he typed without looking and Tom glanced at the tablet. *You were right to worry about Cillian, but not in the way that you think.*

"He doesn't want to fuck Prophet?"

Mal shrugged. *He would've, if the opportunity'd presented itself. But no. Cillian's watching Prophet for a different reason.*

"What's that?"

If and when Proph finally gets to the bottom of the John Morse mystery . . . Cillian's the one who's supposed to kill him.

Tom swallowed hard. "Cillian's going to kill Prophet?"

If he fucks things up with John. And I think . . . I think Cillian doesn't want to do what he's been charged with doing. I have no confirmation. But . . .

"So we keep Prophet from John."

And we watch Cillian like a hawk around Prophet, Mal typed. *I can do that. I will do that.*

Something odd burned in the man's eyes. Tom couldn't quite put his finger on it. "You're sure Cillian's going to be back?"

He'll show, Mal assured Tom. *He needs help, and he'll offer it in return.*

"How can you be sure he's on our side?"

Because his own agency's trying to kill him.

"Because the spook's an asshole," Tom practically shouted, then realized that only an asshole who you actually liked could make a man this goddamned miserable. Because he'd been there. But Mal? "I can't believe I'm going to ask this but . . . did you fall for Cillian?"

And when Mal nodded, Tom sat back. "What the fuck is happening?"

No idea, Mal mouthed.

Tom sighed. "Ah, come on. You of all people should be able to fuck without attachments."

Like you?

"That was different."

Why? Prophet's an asshole too.

Dammit. "Okay, so . . . you're involved."

Mal shook his head.

"Did it interfere with the job?"

Mal put his fingers together. *Little bit. But no, not really. I got intel. It's good too.*

"Does Cillian have the same intel?"

Mal shrugged. *He didn't—but his informants did. But Cillian's good, so it's only a matter of time.*

"He's *good*? Ah, Christ, Mal." Tom rubbed his eyes.

Mal looked really off. He was staring straight ahead and judging by his expression, this was way more serious than Tom had originally thought. "What did you find out?"

Coupla things. Locations. I've got maps. And something else more personal.

"I'm scared to ask, but I'm going to do it anyway," Tom muttered.

Mal stared at him. Pointed to his own throat.

"He knows who did that to you?"

Mal nodded.

"I thought . . . I assumed . . . John?"

Mal sagged. Nodded. Typed, *Me too. But . . .*

Tom stood. Moved to face Mal and stared. Yes, calmer was probably the better reaction but fuck . . . "You're sure?"

Mal nodded.

"Did you sleep with him *before* you knew?"

Again, Mal nodded. *Can't tell anyone.*

"Why the fuck not?"

Because we need Cillian. He's actually on our side.

Tom pointed to Mal's scar.

Mal looked down.

"Ah, fuck." He sat back down next to Mal, his hand on the man's back as Mal started to breathe fast. He pushed Mal's head forward between his legs. "Breathe, Mal. Come on—breathe and focus."

Mal nodded and breathed. Tom rubbed his back and neck until Mal sat up, his color slightly better.

"You'll get through this. I won't say anything."

I figured you'd understand.

Tom tilted his head. "How long have you known we were so much alike?"

Mal gave a wry smile and held up a finger. *From day one.*

"And I'm the last to know."

Not always, Mal mouthed.

He hated having secrets from Prophet. But he figured that Cillian almost killing Mal was most likely a misunderstanding because of John, and the fact that it probably was an accident wouldn't matter to Prophet. Not now, anyway, when he was already running hot. And even though Tom wouldn't mind getting his hands around Cillian's throat for many reasons, if they really needed him, then Prophet knowing this could cause some major damage to an ally. And if Mal really did fall for Cillian . . .

It was all a hell of a thing to get through.

"How did you not kill him when you found out?" Tom asked, and Mal's eyes flashed—with an emotion Tom was pretty sure he never thought he'd see on Mal's face. "Love? Really?" And when Mal grimaced but didn't say no, Tom pressed, "Are you sure? Maybe you hadn't been laid in a while and you got confused?"

Mal rolled his eyes.

Tom sighed. "Well, maybe you're suppressing your psychotic urge to kill because you know we need his help? And you'll kill him when all's said and done?"

Mal put his head back against the couch cushions. *It's complicated.*

"Yeah, speaking of, what's the deal with your entire team getting pissed at Prophet?"

Mal mouthed, *Delusional.*

"You think *he's* delusional?"

Mal sighed. Threw his hands up in the air. *There's proof that John's alive and involved in terrorist activities.*

"And that he's trying to have Cillian killed, which, for the record, all of *you* were thinking about doing too," Tom pointed out.

Mal glared at him like Tom was his own conscience. *That's different.*

"Keep telling yourself that."

Mal typed, *He's got a blind spot where John's concerned—always has. And no, that wasn't an intentional pun.*

"Can't help who you fall in love with," Tom murmured.

He didn't love John. Tom's head turned sharply as Mal continued to type. *Not like that. Maybe in the beginning, a little, but really, it was more like two fucked-up friends who looked out for each other. Proph's not easy, but John? He took it to a whole other level. And not the wild kind. With Prophet, it's exciting, but with John, it's exhausting.*

Prophet had pretty much admitted the same thing to Tom. But to hear it from Mal . . . "You can't think Prophet would let John get away."

Guilt's a powerful thing, Mal typed.

"Are you speaking from experience?"

Mal shot him the finger and then mouthed, *Asshole.* Then typed, *I'll fill Prophet in about this*—pointing at his throat—*if and when he needs to know.*

"Yeah, that and the whole fact that you've fallen for Cillian—let's not forget that. And if you don't tell him—soon—I'm going to." Tom shook his head because Mal was mimicking Tom talking with his hand and rolling his eyes. "Okay fine. But Proph's going to ask what we did here alone. And neither of us have any bruises."

Make something up, Mal mouthed.

"It was easier when you pretended to hate me."

Who was pretending? Mal smirked. Tom rolled his eyes, and then Mal typed, *Cillian's going to catch up eventually.*

And Tom couldn't tell if Mal was more worried . . . or if he wanted that to happen.

Something else had gone on between those two, more than the obvious something, to make Mal have fallen like this, but Mal wasn't spilling. And while Tom was glad they had insider info, he was worried.

Worried about Mal the psycho.

Prophet came into the apartment—and it's not like he was trying to sneak in, but he found Mal and Tom with their heads together, deep in conversation. Which was fucking weird.

"What's wrong?" Prophet called over.

Both men turned to look at him. Mal simply stared until finally Tom said, "Mal's pinpointed Sadiq."

"Like, an area?"

"Like a specific compound where he'll be, starting next week," Tom corrected. "I printed out a map."

Mal was holding it. Tom grabbed it impatiently, held it up to Prophet. Near Djibouti, definitely, and very close to the Somali border.

And he saw the flame. "Paper's on fire," he said calmly, and Tom looked down to see Mal, holding a lighter, looking satisfied.

"What the fuck?" Tom started, and Mal laughed with no sound as Tom tried to put the fire out without destroying the paper he needed because it had the goddamned mission plans on it.

Always burn the evidence, Mal signed. Then he stared at Tommy and flicked the lighter, like he was going to light Tommy on fire. *No matter how big it is.*

Prophet ignored Tom's cursing, asked Mal, "Did you find that out from Cillian?"

Cillian's people, Mal signed.

"How are you involved with Cillian's people?" Prophet asked. "And does Cillian know that?"

Long story. And I don't care, Mal signed.

"Where is Cillian?" Prophet practically growled, his patience reaching thin to nonexistent levels.

Which was rewarded with, again, another patented Mal shrug.

"Does Cillian know where Sadiq is?"

Mal shook his head no.

Prophet narrowed his eyes. "And how did you lose Cillian when he's your job?"

Mal mouthed, *I changed the scope of the operation.*

And whether or not Tom understood that, he just tried to look innocent and failed. Fucking miserably. Maybe letting him get in tight with the team hadn't been the best idea, because now he really was just like them.

"You—what do you know?" he asked, pointing at Tom. "Never mind, I'll torture it out of you later."

Tom raised his brows and grinned.

So did Mal.

"Okay, what's going on here?" Prophet demanded.

"What's going on here is that your friend's a sick motherfucker," Tom said. "Is he an assassin?"

"Ask him yourself," Prophet said, and Tom turned to Mal. "You kill people?"

Mal signed something, and Prophet glanced over. "He said, *Not today, but it's still early.*"

Mal held up his fingers like they were a gun and pretended to shoot Tom right between the eyes.

"That's not even fucking funny," Tom told him.

Mal signed again.

"Says it's really fucking funny to him," Prophet translated.

Mal smiled.

"Fuckers. The both of you," Tom muttered.

"Don't shoot the messenger," Prophet said, then sat up and pointed at Mal. "Seriously. Don't."

Mal shrugged and signed.

"What'd he say?"

Prophet's lips twisted into a semi-grin. "Says he doesn't make promises he can't keep."

Tom stormed out of the room and Mal rolled his eyes and signed, *Drama queen.*

CHAPTER TWENTY-FIVE ◉

everal hours later, with freezing rain hitting the windows with a steady *tink-tink-tink*, Prophet had got Remy fed and squared away with homework—and his iPod playing at earsplitting decibels. He reconvened with Tom and Mal around the kitchen table.

Mal had spent time talking to Ren and King, discussing the latest chatter surrounding Sadiq. There wasn't much, which was good. Because terrorists heard the chatter too, and Sadiq got skittish quickly, and often changed his plans at the drop of a hat. According to Ren's intel, Sadiq still planned a week at the compound, where there was a state-of-the-art lab. All the pieces were there.

But they needed a hook to keep Sadiq from pulling an on-camera move rather than being physically at the compound.

"Seems a guy like that's got a lot of power without setting foot where he doesn't want to, so how do we force his hand?" Tom asked.

"By handing him a specialist," Prophet explained. "Sadiq has tried to kidnap other specialists over the years. He needs someone to build the triggers. Like I showed you with the clippings, Sadiq's groups are also responsible for small terror attacks around the world."

"Practice," Tom repeated after Mal mouthed the word.

"They're patient," Prophet added.

"So all this time, Sadiq hasn't gotten a single specialist?"

"No, he hasn't," Prophet said quietly, and flashed back to how close Sadiq had come to grabbing Gary and winced. If it hadn't been for Cillian's interference, Gary might be alive and well . . . and working for Sadiq, happily building nuclear triggers.

We've got them hidden, Mal typed. *First, the CIA helped hide them, and then we re-hid them.*

"Which pissed Lansing off," Prophet added, and Mal nodded, then continued, *We've only lost one. They came for him before we could get there, and he killed himself rather than be taken.*

"Jesus." Tom ran a hand through his hair.

Prophet rubbed his wrists, which had started to ache long before the rain started. "Sadiq's used this time while the big hunt was for Osama. So has John."

"Do you think John'd be this well hidden without the CIA's help?" Tom asked.

Prophet looked grim. "I could hide. With help from terrorists, who knows?"

Mal slid him a look and Prophet held up his hand. "And fuck you and your denial."

Not getting into it now, Mal signed.

"So what is the plan?" Tom pressed.

Mal signed while Prophet translated. *Giving Sadiq what he wants. What he hasn't been able to get since Hal.*

"I thought that Sadiq knows all of you?" Tom asked.

"He does." Fuck, Prophet did not want to go here with Tom. It's not that Tom hadn't gotten a glimpse into how dirty all of this could be, and it's not that he wouldn't understand, but every time he learned something new . . . well, he couldn't unknow it. And that kind of shit changed a man. Might be subtle, but Tom would carry this for the rest of his life, and Prophet felt the guilt sifting inside of him.

"So who's going in to meet with him?" Tom pressed.

Prophet looked at Mal. "We thought about using the most recent specialist, the one we discussed in Amsterdam. He's been found and hidden, but . . ." *But I've never been comfortable with collateral damage, no matter how many times someone tried to train it into me.*

Tom reached out and squeezed his forearm. "We'll figure it out."

Someone must owe us a favor, Mal typed. *Time to collect.*

"Ah, crap," Tom said. "I don't think I want to know any of this."

"Definitely not," Prophet agreed.

"So we're using a random guy who owes you a favor as bait?" Tom shook his head. "You're kidding, Proph, right? You're fucking kidding me."

"Better than dangling an actual specialist out there. We'd be sending in someone trained. We'll just use the newest specialist's background and likeness. No one knows what they look like now. As long as we get a reasonable resemblance . . ."

Mal typed, *We can't use ourselves—they have facial recognition software. Tom's out because of that too. So's the spook.*

"Maybe not," Prophet said. "No proof that Cillian's actually been in the same room as John."

Wouldn't risk it, Mal signed. *Gotta find someone else willing to do this.*

Prophet glanced at Tom. "Dean?"

Tom sighed. "He'd do it. But really, Proph?"

"All he'd have to do is convince them that his blindness doesn't matter. As long as he can talk someone through building a trigger, that's all that's important. And he'll keep his shit together. Because how are they going to think a blind guy's going to be the one anyone would use as a decoy?"

Mal and Tom stared at him, and Prophet shrugged.

It was the perfect plan.

It was also, possibly, a suicide mission, and decidedly too close to Prophet's own truths for comfort.

"Shit." Prophet was staring at the security monitor. Tom glanced at it in time to see a man in a dark suit approaching the building and ringing the bell.

"CIA?" Tom asked.

"No doubt. Hey Mal, hit the buzzer," he called.

"Does this happen often?"

"Never," was Prophet's answer, and that wasn't reassuring. "Trying to keep him out's the worst thing I can do—whoever the fuck he is."

"You think he's here about Lansing?"

"Don't you?" Prophet asked as they went toward the entrance. Mal was already there, waiting by the half-opened door, arms crossed.

"He's a little more . . . psychotic than usual," Tom said quietly.

"How so?"

"He took C-4 to bed with him."

Prophet shrugged. "He's always done that."

"He used it as his pillow," Tom pointed out. "And he slept on the floor in Remy's room."

Prophet cut his eyes to Mal and whistled low under his breath. "Probably a mistake to have him here, but hell, I'm done following their rules."

Done pretending to, Mal mouthed, with a smile that let them know he'd heard the entire conversation while pretending he couldn't. Then he motioned to the door and used his hand to simulate firing a gun.

"No, Mal." Prophet's tone was firm.

Mal signed something.

"Okay, yes, if he tries to kill us, he's fair game. But just talking to us doesn't constitute a threat."

Mal sighed and looked completely disappointed. Tom understood his pain, and it scared the fuck out of him.

He pushed that thought aside to concentrate on the man Mal was letting into the apartment with a nod. The guy was maybe six feet, short-cropped dark hair and an expensive suit. Expensive sunglasses, which he tucked into his jacket pocket, and Tom caught sight of an expensive watch and a shoulder holster he hadn't bothered to hide.

"Can I help you?" Prophet asked.

"I'm Agent John Paul," the man said.

"And you're with the CIA," Prophet added.

"Prophet Drews. Aka Elijah Drews. Currently self-employed," Agent Paul said, before turning to Tom. "Tom Boudreaux. Former FBI. Former Sheriff. Currently on leave from EE, Ltd."

"They're teaching you boys how to run internet searches? How progressive," Prophet drawled.

"And this is?" Agent Paul glanced at Mal, who smiled—psychotically—and made the agent take a step away from him.

Nicely done. Tom would have to try the psycho thing more often.

Luckily, Mal wore a fleece pullover that was zipped up, hiding the scar. Tom thought fast. "He's my cousin, visiting from Paris. He doesn't speak any English."

Tom said something to Mal in French—maybe Cajun French or maybe not, but it didn't matter. Mal nodded and left the room. "I don't think he'll understand much, but there's no reason for him to be here."

Agent Paul frowned, like he wasn't sure he believed Tom, but Tom knew that Mal was the one man on Prophet's team that no one from the CIA could find. Mal was still listed as MIA under his real name, Seamus Dwyer.

"He's a civilian." Prophet's words were firm, as if to force Agent Paul to drop any potential issue he had with Mal leaving, and he managed to sound really bored and calm when he continued with, "Now, how can we help you?"

"The reason I'm here is to look into the death of Agent Lansing."

"Agent Lansing's dead?" Prophet asked, the surprise evident in his voice.

Agent Paul obviously took note of it, nodded slowly. "We thought you knew."

"How? We weren't fucking pen pals."

"You seem upset at the death of a man you had a most contentious relationship with," Agent Paul said.

"Guess what, Agent Paul? The men who've been after *me* might've gotten to *him*. Did you ever stop to think of that? Maybe I'm worried about my own safety. I couldn't give a fuck-all about Lansing, but I need to know more."

"I'm sorry, but that's classified."

"Then why the ever-loving fuck are you here?" Prophet demanded. "Are you taking over his job?"

"Perhaps, yes." Agent Paul straightened up a little. Tom had no doubt the man could do some damage if called upon. "I followed up on your passports and saw you were in Africa during the same time Agent Lansing was."

"You realize he's been tracking my movements for years, right? You're actually surprised?" Prophet asked, just before they heard a brief knock and the sound of the door sliding open.

"Expecting anyone?" Agent Paul asked as Mal strode to the door, thankfully not holding a weapon pointed at anyone. And judging by the look on Mal's face, Tom knew exactly who the fuck was at the door.

Thankfully, Prophet was studying Agent Paul thoroughly and didn't seem to notice. Except that typically, Prophet noticed everything.

Cillian was dressed all in black, his dark hair shorter than Tom had seen it last. He walked into the living room like he owned it, arm extended to Agent Paul, saying, "I'm Mark McDougal. And you are?" in a decidedly American accent.

"Agent Paul."

The men shook hands and Cillian said, "I'm their lawyer. Looks like I arrived just in time."

He pulled out identification that Tom assumed said he was a member of the New York Bar.

Agent Paul glanced at it and then at Prophet. "Do you call a lawyer every time you have company?"

"We saw you coming," Prophet said. "And he lives right below us. Pretty convenient."

"So, catch me up," Cillian said, and Agent Paul repeated his speech about Lansing's death. "Sorry to hear that, but what's that got to do with these two gentlemen?"

Tom still wanted to punch him, for so many reasons, but he had to admit the guy was good. If nothing else, he provided sufficient distraction.

"Agent Lansing was last seen in Prophet and Tom's vicinity."

"I didn't see him," Prophet said mildly. "If I had, that wouldn't make him a very good agent, now would it?"

"I'm assuming Lansing arrived after Prophet and Tom?" Cillian asked.

Agent Paul didn't answer that.

"From what I gather, you're pleasantly inquiring if either Prophet or Tom happened to see anyone suspicious who might have killed Agent Lansing?"

"Listen, asshole—you know exactly what I'm getting at," Agent Paul growled. "I believe one of these men killed Lansing."

"And I'm assuming you have evidence?" Cillian asked.

"There's a long history."

"Witnesses?" Cillian held out his hands. "I'm guessing the answer to both my questions is no, or else these men would be in handcuffs and stamped as property of the CIA."

"I can take them in any time I'd like," Agent Paul informed him. "And they wouldn't be seen from again. Trust me."

"You can try," Cillian said, his tone lighter but somehow more threatening. "We'll be waiting. In the meantime, I'll show you out."

Cillian motioned toward the door, Agent Paul moving grudgingly.

"He'll be back," Prophet muttered when the door closed.

Cillian came back in, a finger to his lips, then said, "You should call me before answering more questions. And stay in the country." He still used his American accent, which made Tom want to punch him hard. Harder than he had before.

Prophet narrowed his eyes at what Cillian said, cut a glance to Mal and then back to Cillian. "We can do that." Then he mouthed to Tom, "Check for bugs."

The four of them searched for listening devices, found two—both Lansing's. Prophet explained to Tom that he could always tell his favorite agent's setup. "After all this time, he hasn't gotten any new tricks. I guess he never needed to. It was all part of his game."

Tom felt a sudden chill. Meanwhile, Cillian and Prophet kept discussing the visit as if they were lawyer and client, including making plans to all go to Cillian's apartment. Meanwhile, Prophet put the bugs out on the deck and closed the door instead.

Cillian did head down to his apartment to check things out—he murmured that he'd text Prophet when it was all clear before glancing at Mal on his way out.

Jesus, the look that passed between Mal and Cillian was palpable, like neither man knew exactly what to do with the other. Like the ice under their feet was thin, so fragile you could almost hear the cracking as they walked.

Cillian went downstairs first. Tom figured Mal would have the good sense to stay up here, and it appeared that was his plan.

But before he and Prophet went to Cillian, Mal mouthed, *The witness?*

And Tom cursed inwardly, because no one had any loyalty anymore when they were paid off. "Guy at the hotel front desk."

Mal sighed, then typed, *That witness needs to disappear. I'll get Hook on it. He'll relocate the guy.*

"There's no other evidence. No footage. I'm sure of it," Tom said.

Blood? Mal mouthed.

"I did it in the bathroom. And I know how to get blood off walls permanently." Tom punctuated that by pointing at Mal.

For the first time, at least in front of Prophet, Mal looked at him and smiled. Signed, and Prophet translated, *That's the most useful thing about you then.*

It was Tom's turn to give him the finger.

CHAPTER TWENTY-SIX ◉

When Prophet and Tom entered his apartment, the first thing Cillian said—in his clipped British tones—was, "I know he's not the son of one of your specialists."

Awesome—that meant Mal had been made before Cillian showed up here, which was probably what Mal'd been hiding from him.

But Mal wasn't hiding anymore, obviously, since he was suddenly in Cillian's apartment, arms crossed, weapon in his hand, waiting at the door.

Prophet glanced at him and shrugged in Cillian's direction. "Good for you. Now what the fuck was that?"

"That would be what you Americans call, saving your ass." And the British accent was replaced by a brogue far thicker than King's.

"How've I survived all these years without you?" Prophet drawled as sarcastically as possible. He willed himself to stay calm, but how long that would work was anyone's guess.

"You killed Lansing," Tom said slowly.

"Give the Cajun a prize." Cillian gave a self-satisfied smile and Prophet saw Tom's fists clench as Cillian added, "I was *supposed* to kill him before you tortured information out of him."

"Really sorry to ruin your plans," Tom said, sounding completely unsorry.

"How the hell did you know where I was?" Prophet demanded.

Cillian said simply, "Don't bother searching your phone for chips."

"Then how did you know?"

"Prophet, I know everything."

Fuck him, Cillian did. "Why kill him?"

"It was either Lansing or you and Tom. Don't you think Lansing would've gone right back and reported it?"

"I was counting on that," Tom shot back.

"Ah, you had a plan?" Cillian rolled his eyes.

"What's your game?" Prophet asked him.

"I'm offering you my services. Directly."

"As in, you were helping me indirectly the whole time?" Prophet asked.

"Yes, I was."

"By lying to me about John?"

"You didn't believe me," Cillian pointed out.

Prophet rammed him, held him against the wall with a forearm across his throat. "Just fucking say it."

Cillian gave a short nod. "If you got too close to John, I was supposed to kill you."

Mal snorted, although he hadn't moved from the wall. Cillian muttered something in his heavy brogue, but Prophet cut him off. "So what changed that you're coming to me offering your services?"

"I left my own agency before they could kill me. They haven't stopped trying. So, as I've suspected, there's a much different reason they want John Morse. And they don't necessarily want him dead, as they've said."

"But they sent you to kill John."

"Interesting conundrum, isn't it?" Cillian's voice was hoarse.

"I want to kill him," Tom said, pointing at Cillian.

"Join the club," Prophet said, pushing his arm against Cillian's neck.

Mal raised his hand to join in the fray, and Cillian's expression hardened.

"So if you were supposed to kill Prophet, you were probably supposed to kill me too," Tom said. "Why am I still standing?"

Cillian turned his attention to Tom. "Because I found out that we're *all* on the chopping block. SB-20 wanted there to be nothing left of anyone who had knowledge of John Morse. Including me."

"So you changed sides because your ass was on the line?" Prophet pressed his arm a little harder against Cillian's throat.

"You know it's not that simple, Prophet. In reality, you should've been dead a long time ago."

"And that's why you're a target—because you couldn't do your damned job."

"You're angry that I didn't kill you? I really don't understand Americans," Cillian shook his head minutely.

"How the fuck can I trust you to work on our side?"

"Do you want me to kill you right now to prove it?" Cillian asked casually. "It's not a problem."

"Yeah, it would be," Prophet told him. "So when did it go from needing to shut me up to needing to protect me?"

"Around the time I received that video of you and Lansing."

Prophet stared at him. "You're the one who sent it to Tom."

Cillian held out his hands, even as Prophet still held his neck. "Now he gets it."

And then Prophet asked the question he wasn't sure he wanted answered, but it needed answering. "How close did I get, Cillian?"

"Close," was all Cillian would say. And Prophet supposed that didn't matter now. Because unless John was in the next room, the *close* of any time earlier than this very minute didn't fucking matter.

"How the fuck am I supposed to trust you? How are any of us supposed to trust you?"

Cillian sighed. "The same way you've been for the past two and a half years. All of that wasn't a game, Prophet. We're both good liars, but it's probably best we don't lie to ourselves any more, yes?"

"Why would you risk your job for me?" Because Prophet really wanted to hear this goddamned slick answer.

"The video," Cillian said simply. Prophet took a moment to process, stared until Cillian said, "I saw it, Prophet. My organization showed it to me as a way to convince me of your guilt. It did exactly the opposite."

Prophet pulled his arm away and took a couple of steps back, but Cillian didn't move. "So you've been on my side the entire time?"

"I've wanted to kill John the entire time. And Sadiq. And, of course, Lansing, and I finally got to carry that one out. That counts as protecting you, yes?" Cillian asked. "I know the information about Sadiq. No thanks to Mal."

Mal snorted and bowed.

"What Sadiq's planning, it's either a warm-up, or it's meant to throw all of us—and the CIA—off the scent," Cillian said now. "I think we have to force his hand. Put someone in his path that he can't pass up. Make him think this is the big score."

"Yeah, we've already gone there and figured that out. Do you have someone in mind?" Prophet asked. "Because it's pretty hard to fake a specialist, and we've all been made."

"I have two men in mind. One, Sadiq doesn't know at all—he's the man who'll be taking the goods to Sadiq. As for the specialist . . ." Cillian held up a finger, then went to his slightly opened bedroom door and said, "It's time."

The door opened and Gary walked out.

Gary.

Dead Gary. "What the hell?" Prophet asked.

Tom pointed to Cillian. "Can I kill him now?"

"Yes," Prophet said, and Tom raised his weapon at Cillian and held it there.

"I'm never saving you again," Cillian told Tom.

"No, because you'll be dead," Tom reasoned.

"Prophet, please, I'm okay." Gary sounded so different, no longer the bratty kid. Guess a kidnapping and an exploding helo did that to a guy.

Prophet took a step toward him. And another. Touched Gary's shoulder, wanting to reassure himself that he was real. Swallowed hard and couldn't say a word.

"I'm so sorry, Prophet," Gary said.

Prophet cleared his throat, managed, "No. I failed you. I'm—"

"Failed me? I fucking sold you out to a terrorist, along with myself. For something I didn't understand." Gary's voice was rough with emotion. "You saved me. Cared enough about me and Mom—and Dad too—to keep us safe and hidden for years. And I fucked it up."

As much as Prophet hated having to owe Cillian, he reached out and pushed Tom's arm—the one holding the gun—down. Tom resisted at first, but acquiesced after a few seconds. Prophet didn't take his eyes off Gary, like he was afraid the kid would disappear if he looked away.

"Where have you been?" he asked Gary now.

"All over. Cillian moved me to different safe houses with friends of his."

"No one from SB-20," Cillian added.

Prophet kept his attention focused on Gary. "I don't know what Cillian told you, but there's no way I'm letting you voluntarily go back into this." His words were slow and deliberate, more for Cillian's benefit than anything.

"You have to let me make up for what I did."

"If I had to go back and make up for all the shit I did in my twenties . . ."

"Aren't you?" Cillian asked mildly. Prophet leaned over and pulled Tom's arm back up to point the gun at Cillian.

Tom smiled.

Cillian didn't.

Prophet turned back to Gary. "You barely made it out the first time. I'm not letting you, because you have nothing to make up for."

"Perhaps we can discuss this over dinner," Cillian suggested. "Be more civilized."

"Literally over your dead body," Tom said, and there was something in his voice that made Prophet turn to watch him.

Because, for half a second, Tom was one hundred percent serious. Like his eyes snapped fire. Tom'd never hidden his jealousy over Cillian, but this look had nothing to do with texts and couches.

Tom pointed at Cillian with his free hand. Nodded. Cillian's jaw clenched at the silent exchange and then Tom put the gun down.

Prophet urged, "Tom, we'll talk about that later. Just take Gary into the other room, okay?" And Tom did as he asked, leading Gary into the kitchen. Prophet turned his attention back to Cillian, his teeth clenched. "You let me think I got him killed."

"I had no choice. If you didn't believe it, you'd have gone running off trying to liberate him. Guilt has no place in this mission, Prophet. And you're leaving your guts spilled everywhere you go lately."

Prophet narrowed his eyes. In a quick second, Cillian was re-pinned against the wall, with Prophet holding a knife to his throat.

If Cillian so much as swallowed, the blade would nick him. "Let me explain something to you, you fucking Irish asshole spook. I know things. I know what you fucking did. You all think I'm some naive asshole living in denial, but that shit suits my purpose. So don't think I won't kill you if I need to. Or even if I want to. And right now, I really goddamn want to."

A hand was on Prophet's shoulder. He didn't turn around, but he knew it wasn't Tommy. "You really want to save him, Mal?"

A single, quick squeeze on Prophet's shoulder was the answer. *Yes.* And whatever the reason, this was Mal's battle to fight, and Prophet assumed he'd learn why soon enough.

"Fine," Prophet managed. "You're going to make sure he helps us through this. If he gets out of line . . ."

Another squeeze for yes.

Cillian wasn't watching him any longer. No, his stare was over Prophet's shoulder, on Mal.

"Who knows that Gary's alive?" Prophet asked.

Cillian glanced at Prophet again. "Besides the people in this room?"

"You didn't tell your boss about Gary? No wonder they didn't like you much," Prophet muttered.

"Surprisingly, this job's not a popularity contest," Cillian snarked.

Prophet glanced over at Mal. "Just one shot. I'll just maim him."

CHAPTER TWENTY-SEVEN

They left Cillian alone downstairs with Gary—mainly because it was far safer for Gary to be hidden by Cillian at this point, despite his status with his old organization.

Now, back inside his apartment, Prophet sat at the kitchen table as Mal called the other members of the team and filled them in.

They all sat there for several minutes, everyone trying to absorb the consequences.

Remy can't stay here, Mal mouthed after he'd signed something to Ren and King. Hook was unavailable at the moment, taking care of the only witness who'd seen Prophet, Tom, and Lansing together.

"He's fine for now," Prophet said.

No way. Mal shook his head emphatically. *Even if Gary's not here, which I'm betting he's not anymore. I'll take Remy to Doc's and stay there with him until we move out.*

Prophet looked at Tom, who nodded and said, "I think that's the safest option."

"Okay, fine. I'm going to go have another talk with Cillian in a bit though."

I'll go pick Remy up. I'll grab his things later on, Mal signed.

Prophet translated for Tom, then pointed to the clock. "Yeah, he's coming out of tutoring now—one of us is always there to pick him up." He rattled off the address for Mal.

When Mal was gone, shutting the heavy door behind him, he turned to Tom. "So . . ."

Tom stared at him. Innocent-looking bastard.

"Don't, Tommy."

"I didn't do anything."

"You're about to lie to me."

"Now you're psychic? I thought it was only your cock."

"It's very perceptive."

"I'm open to it."

"God, that was terrible." But Prophet gave a small grin anyway. "Look, I know you don't trust Cillian but—"

"I'm happy for Gary," Tom said roughly. "But I'm not throwing Cillian a parade, all right?"

"Fair enough."

"Are you really going to use Cillian's friend?"

"We don't have a lot of options. I know Mick and Blue would help, but I don't want to risk them. Blue's too well known. With my luck, Blue's stolen from—or for—Sadiq."

"But Cillian's got a motive."

Prophet nodded. "Yeah, to stay alive."

Tom saw the battle in Prophet's eyes. "Gary should be allowed to make his own decisions. For the first time in his life, he knows the score. He's in on it. He's had months to come to terms with it."

"He wants revenge," Prophet countered. "He feels bad for what he did. That's not a reason to risk *your* life. He's *my* job. My promise."

"He's a grown man, ready to avenge his father," Tom pointed out. "Neither of us would let anything get in our way."

"Fuck you." Prophet walked away, and Tom punched the wall lightly with the side of his fist. Because fighting with each other was the last thing either of them needed now. Things were fracturing at a time when solidarity was a necessity, not a luxury.

But Tom also wasn't backing down from his stance on Gary and what was ultimately his decision.

That didn't mean Prophet didn't need support. So Tom went and found him. "I've got your back, Proph. You know that. Part of that's helping you through this. You can't take it all on yourself. You tried that—it's coming back to bite you."

"This talk is very inspirational," Prophet said sarcastically.

And yes, the tension between Mal and Cillian wasn't the only tension in this apartment. Sex was their go-to stress reliever, the way they dealt with anger—at others and toward each other—and it'd been too long for them. And it was showing.

But after what happened the last time, he didn't want to force Prophet into anything—he wanted Prophet to give in.

"You have no idea what you're asking me to do, Tom. I made a promise to his father. How can I go back on that after . . ."

"You tell Gary everything—explain it all to him and let him decide. Hal couldn't fault you for that."

"Gary knows."

"Then tell him again, until you both feel better."

That was easier said than done, but Prophet knew Tom was right—he had to talk to Gary tonight, one-on-one, and deal with this head-on. Time was running out, and they had a really small window of time to get to Sadiq.

And as much as he hated to admit it, using Gary was the best way in. That didn't mean they couldn't trick Sadiq another way.

Tom spoke quietly. "I don't think Cillian knows."

Tom was talking about his eyes—not wanting to say it out loud. The man was way more superstitious than he let on. "Good. If I get to the point where I'm compromising anything, you'll be the first to know."

"I'm not worried about that." Tom's smile was tight. "So you and Cillian had the same kind of jobs."

"Ironic, right?" Knowing for sure Cillian had him in his sights as opposed to merely suspecting it made Prophet think about Hal.

"I understand the jobs in theory, but I have a hard time wrapping my head around it," Tom admitted. "I know these people can be dangerous if they've been compromised. But . . . what if they've been captured and you rescue them? Is that possible? What happens then?"

He'd like to be able to tell Tom that yes, the specialists were rescued and lived happily ever after. But it didn't work like that. "It seems like that should work—if the guy's been through hell and he's lived through it, he should be allowed to live. But the theory is, if you buckled once under torture, you'd do it again. You're an easy target."

Prophet grimaced. "And it's like, well, he already told them what he knows. What's the point in killing him? But he knows shit that another terrorist can use. He's a target. Always will be. Sometimes, you could tell that they'd tried to kill themselves before. Sometimes it was a relief."

"Is that what you did for Phil?"

"No. And I stopped doing it on my own jobs too. I focused more on the ones I could save, them and their families."

"How many others are there?" Tom asked.

"Five," Prophet said. "I rescued a kid of one of the specialists right before I went to the hurricane. The dad wanted to get away from the CIA."

"So you facilitated that."

"Actually, I delivered Kasey to the CIA," he said wryly. "Then I went to see a man about a hurricane. King and Ren stepped in when things calmed down for Kasey and took care of the relocation last month."

"So they took them right out from under the CIA?"

"Yes." Kasey had called for Prophet a couple of times, and Tom knew that.

Tom met his eyes. "Good. Fuck them."

"Who taught you interrogation methods?" Prophet asked finally.

"Ollie," Tom said. He swore he saw a hint of wince on Prophet's face, but when he double-checked, his expression was placid. "He said that everyone should know them, how to use them and how to live through them."

"He was right." Prophet tapped his head. "It's all about what's up here. Providing your body doesn't give out."

"You've withstood a hell of a lot."

Prophet smiled. "So have you. Some of it from my moody ass."

"We'll get there, Proph. Not always going to be smooth sailing. Gotta tell you shit you don't want to hear and vice versa. Or else we've got nothing. And I know we don't have nothing."

Prophet gave him a hell of a lot of credit for putting that out there. "We have a hell of a lot, Tommy."

"And we'll have more when this is over."

"Right. You'll have your tattoo shop. And I'll . . . fuck, I don't know. I thought I couldn't see beyond this shit with John, but I think I'm too scared to look. Suppose there's nothing there?"

"Of course there's something there. You just never looked very hard."

"Yeah?" Prophet challenged. "Since you know me so well, why's that?"

"Hurts too much to see what you're missing," Tom said simply, and when Prophet just stared at him, he continued, "We're not twenty, and we were never indestructible. And the thought of staying here, watching Remy prepare to go take on the world someday . . . it's nice."

Prophet couldn't disagree at all. He'd wanted normal, convinced himself he'd never have it, so he'd moved on. But that normal, a different kind of normal, was right here with him. "I don't know if I can give that kind of life up completely."

"It's not worth it, Proph. Even if your eyes weren't fucked up."

"Fucked up?" Prophet repeated.

"It would be too much. I'd be telling you the same thing—that you should get out. You did more good in the past fifteen years than most do in a lifetime. You need to get out while you can still sleep at night. Or get back to sleeping at night."

Prophet knew he was right. "Thanks, Tommy."

"I don't want to lose you to this." He pressed his fingers to the side of Prophet's head. "Whatever's happening in there, let it out."

"That's the problem. I don't want to let it out. I want it gone."

"It will be."

"Suppose it's not?"

"I'm not going anywhere, Proph. If you are . . . I can't stop that. I can try to convince you, but ultimately, it's your decision. But I'm staying."

Prophet wasn't sure why that sentiment wasn't as comforting as it should be. "I'm going to talk to Gary."

"You're not going near Cillian without me." Tom's tone was fiercely protective. "And we're not calling ahead—no reason not to surprise the fuck out of him."

Prophet raised his brows but didn't say a word, just followed behind his self-appointed bodyguard and let him slam on the door.

"Open up, Cillian—you know who it is."

"Some identification would be nice," Cillian called, and Tom grabbed his weapon and pointed it at the peephole, saying, "I'll show you ID," and that's when Prophet stepped in, pushed Tom aside and used a key.

When he slid the door open, a surprised Cillian stood blinking. "You had a key made of my door?"

"Yes," Prophet said. "And the key to my apartment's right in your kitchen."

Cillian tilted his head, conceding that he'd been caught. "I'm guessing you're here to see Gary?"

"Is he still around?"

"For the moment. I don't plan on housing him here any longer than the next few hours. And then he'll be safe."

"I need to talk to him. Alone."

Cillian sighed. "Sometimes, you're entirely too noble for your own good."

Prophet took that as a come on down, so he did, with Tom on his heels. Cillian was by the door. "Gary's in the bedroom—he's expecting you. Tom, let's have tea and discuss interrogation techniques."

"I'd rather use them on you," Tom growled.

Prophet hurried to see Gary, because he didn't have much time before Tom started swinging.

CHAPTER TWENTY-EIGHT ◉

Gary was lying on Cillian's bed, watching TV, with the posture of a man who'd been doing that too long. His feet were moving with nervous energy, and he didn't look surprised to see Prophet coming in.

He got up off the bed and stuck his hands in his pockets. "I asked Cillian to call you, but he said he had a feeling you'd come by."

"He was right," was all Prophet said.

Gary had filled out more—he'd been training while he'd been staying in Cillian's safe houses. He looked older, slightly haunted . . . but he also seemed calm. He wasn't the same angry kid Prophet had known for so long.

"None of this was your fault, Prophet."

"Gary, I . . ."

"No, listen, I pieced together what happened based on Sadiq's story. I was able to figure out what the lies were pretty easily."

"I shot your father," Prophet told him bluntly. "Sadiq wasn't lying about that."

"I know, Prophet." Gary looked sad, more for Prophet than anything else, but he also looked strong. "Dad knew the risks."

"It's not the same, knowing and having it happen." Prophet tore his gaze away from Gary for a second to sweep a glance around the room. The heavy curtains were pulled so no one could get a view in . . . the bedroom a mirror of Prophet's, so much so, he could almost picture John sitting on the windowsill, shaking his head.

Gary broke his reverie. "Prophet, I can't imagine what you've been through. I only had a taste and I'm . . ." He shuddered at the memories of being held by Sadiq. "I was an idiot to approach him, to think you were anything less than honorable."

"I promised your father that I'd keep you safe at all costs. And right before he died, he looked me in the eye and he said, 'Remember.' And I did. I do."

"But it's not your decision alone anymore. Dad would understand that. He'd want me to do the right thing. He didn't live in fear, so why should I?"

Prophet had no answer for that.

"If I don't make it, that's not on you—that's on Sadiq," Gary said firmly, and Christ, the kid had grown up a hell of a lot in the past months. "Just let me try."

How could he not? "If you're sure . . . I know trying to stop you will just make things worse. So we'll plan and make sure you're as safe as you can be."

Gary brightened. "Good. I'd do it anyway, but your okay makes it better."

Prophet left Gary in the bedroom and went out to talk to Cillian and have him share the plan he'd obviously worked out.

When he entered the living room, Tommy was pacing the floor and Cillian was uncharacteristically quiet. Both men turned toward him, and Cillian looked more than a little relieved.

"Are we settled?" Cillian asked.

"As much as I don't want him to do it . . . I won't take this away from him," Prophet said. From behind Cillian, Tom gave him a nod and a smile. "Let's go over the plan. I don't want to do it in front of Gary."

Cillian motioned for the men to follow him to the next floor. He had cameras set up, the same way Prophet did, and they had a clear view of the windows outside the room Gary was in, the entire building's perimeter, the front door of Cillian's . . . and Gary himself. Cillian adjusted it so they could just see from his calves down, and that made Prophet feel better. He hated thinking about the fact that Gary'd been kept like an animal in a cage, watched over constantly, whether or not it was for his own good.

"Do you forgive him, Prophet?" Cillian asked out of nowhere.

"Forgive him?"

"He set you up. If it wasn't for him . . ." Cillian trailed off. "He almost set off a chain of unstoppable events."

Prophet ran his hands through his hair. "It's amazing how much you can push out of your mind. That's not the way I feel about what happened. It's not an issue."

Cillian stared at him, then shook his head. "You never fail to surprise me, Prophet."

And then Tom growled. Prophet smiled. "Let's get on with it."

Cillian nodded. "It's quite simple. I find that tends to work best. I'll have my guy make the initial contact tonight. He'll meet with Sadiq's people. Next week, when Sadiq's at the compound, my guy will bring Gary to him. And from there, we can expect Sadiq to keep both men, even though that won't be part of the initial deal. We'll be close by. And we'll wait, give Gary some time to make Sadiq comfortable."

"How do we know Gary's safe once he gets in there?" Tom asked. "Sadiq's going to be suspicious that he's back."

"Sure. But he's also not going to be able to turn away someone who can build him the triggers he's been waiting for."

"So Gary will start building the triggers," Prophet said.

"Right. He'll also be wearing a transmitter so we can keep track of him." Cillian's eyes trailed over to the screen showing the front door where Mal was coming in. Finally he tore his eyes away and said, "Perhaps you should text your teammate so he doesn't worry."

Prophet was already on it, and they watched Mal getting the text, staring into the camera, and then heading up to Prophet's apartment.

"Suppose they find the transmitter?" Tom asked.

"It's hidden," Cillian told them. "Bottom of his foot, between his toes."

"Like an implant?" Tom asked.

"Yes," Cillian said, as though it was the most natural thing in the world. Which, really, it was. Prophet had seen it work well many times. "There's a second in the scar from his appendectomy."

"If they scan him?" Tom continued, obviously fascinated by the technology.

"It turns off," Cillian confirmed. "Specially made for this. And it's implanted sideways, with a special foam coating, so if you try to feel it, you'll get an edge that feels pretty similar to scar tissue."

Cillian lifted up his sleeve to show a still-healing scar. "Before I cut it out, I wore it for five years. And trust me, I've been scanned by every criminal and terrorist I've come in close contact with. So Gary's not going anywhere without us knowing about it. He's ready for this—he'll build the triggers, leave out something crucial. And we'll disassemble anyway when we're done."

Prophet nodded. "And then we come in and kill Sadiq, plus the other men in the organization who are there. Leave John in the wind."

"And then we go after John," Tom added.

"With no mercy," Cillian said.

"And your friend who's selling Gary to Sadiq?" Prophet asked. "He'll going into hiding?"

"I'll make sure he gets paid, and we'll keep him open as a good source for John to use in the future, when we make our next move."

Prophet shook his head slowly. "You don't think John will realize that the guy was part of this?"

Cillian gave a slight smile and looked at the now-empty hallway. "I don't know what people believe anymore."

CHAPTER TWENTY-NINE ◉

After another restless night where Prophet attempted to sleep and Tom stayed up to watch over him, the two of them barely touching, Prophet pushed himself up sometime after sunrise.

Tom was sleeping peacefully, and Prophet took a long moment to stare, to try to memorize his features, like he'd been doing more and more lately.

Finally, he went into the bathroom to get ready for a run. He wouldn't wake Tom up for it. Even though they seemed far apart, and space seemed like the last thing they needed, they actually did need some physical distance between them.

He brushed his teeth. Pissed. Washed up. Toweled his face dry, and when he went to hang it up, his vision blurred, more his left eye than his right, but fuck, this was really fucking happening.

He forced himself to remain calm, blinked, but the blur was still there. He couldn't judge how long it'd been—maybe it was the same pattern as it had been every other time it'd happened, but it felt like fucking forever. He splashed his face again, rinsing his eyes, hoping maybe something just got in there—dust or whatever the fuck—but it didn't help.

He reached into the medicine cabinet and pulled out the drops. Put them in, blinked and waited. Stared at the picture on the wall—a still from a trip to Lourdes that Dean had given him years ago, telling Prophet that whatever his religion, whatever he believed in exactly didn't matter. It was only important that he believed.

"I believe and it's not doing any fucking good," he muttered now. Heard the guy's words echo in his mind.

We can't question why something's been planned for us. We can only figure out how to use it to the best of our ability.

He stared at the blurred black and white and swallowed back the lump in his throat. Dr. Salen had explained to him that the blurring would come and go, and then, one day, it wouldn't leave. And blurry was still better than no frontal vision, but it wasn't a long trip from blurred to blind.

He closed his eyes and put his palms up to them, pressed a little and tried to stave off the panic. His breath was coming out harsher than he expected and he cursed, probably a little too loudly. Or maybe Tom had been standing there for a while and he hadn't known, but Tommy said quietly behind him, "Proph, what's wrong?"

"I can't . . ." He reached for Tommy's hand and thankfully, Tommy grabbed for his, grabbed him actually too, and held him close.

"I'm here, okay. Just fucking breathe, Proph. It's okay."

But it wasn't. Couldn't be. And even when his vision came back, just like that, a curtain pulled back so he could see Tommy's handsome face, it didn't take away the underlying panic that had been there the entire time he'd been with Tom, the thing he couldn't quite put his finger on.

Now, he could. "Listen to me, all right, Tommy? Just fucking listen. Because no one thinks it's too much in the beginning. It doesn't happen overnight. But the only way I'm going to be able to live with it—and live with myself—is to know that if you can't do it anymore, you'll walk the fuck away. You have to fucking promise me that. I can't do this if you don't."

And there it was—Prophet's biggest fear, one of the last walls, crumbling down. All Tom could do was wrap his arms tightly around Prophet and murmur his name.

"You have to fucking promise me," was all Prophet murmured against his neck.

And even though it broke his goddamned heart to do so, he said, "I promise, Prophet. I swear to you, I would walk away before I let it get like that between us."

"I'd fucking die if I made someone live that way."

"I know. That's the only reason I made that promise."

"Good." Prophet put a hand on his cheek. "We've got other shit to do, while I still can."

That wasn't pity for himself—that was simple truth. And the thought of finishing up what had been haunting this man for ten years plus made his need to help even stronger. "Let's get rid of those fucking ghosts once and for all, Proph. We tried burying them, but that never works. So how about we just set them free?"

"And let them go to the light, Carol Anne?"

"And just like that, you're a goddamned bastard again." But Tom was smiling as he said it.

CHAPTER THIRTY ◉

After Tom made him the promise, Prophet went for a run. Alone. Tom offered, but did so like he knew Prophet would say no.

Now, as his feet pounded the dirt along the wooded trails, AC/DC blasting in his ears, everything settled.

All the secrets . . . they're almost all out there.

And you're about to let your father . . . your grandfather . . . win. And you're nothing like them.

That stopped him in his tracks. Literally. He stood there, his breathing hard in the cold, and for the first time he truly knew that he wasn't like the other Drews men. He'd never been. And God, he'd been a fucking asshole to deny himself and Tommy what they both needed to get through this.

He raced back to the apartment, took the stairs two at a time and pulled his phone out of his pocket, prepared to leave it aside.

Until he noticed the recent call he'd missed. He listened to the message from Doc telling him what he'd been waiting to hear.

And yeah, he definitely believed in signs.

He didn't bother to shower—Tom had said he'd lift weights while Prophet was out, so he must be sweating too, probably about to get into the shower. Prophet burst into the bedroom, and Tom stared at him, a little suspicious, but curious too. And hopeful.

"You're wearing too many clothes," Prophet told him.

Tom smiled, that fucking smirky, *I knew it* smile, as he stripped, and yeah, Prophet was going to wipe it right off him. Replace it with something even better.

"Bed. Against the pillows," he said and Tom complied leisurely while Prophet went into his dresser drawer and pulled out what he needed: cuffs, rope, and lube.

He threw the lube onto Tom's belly and proceeded to cuff one of Tom's wrists to the headboard. Although he'd taught Tom how to break out of cuffs, so he also roped his wrist to keep him in place. He wanted Tom to know he wasn't fucking moving until Prophet was done.

He wasn't maudlin, but neither one of them could fully predict what would happen next on their search for Sadiq and John. He wasn't going out with regrets—not about Tom. Not when this heat between them was the most healing thing either of them had experienced. It was ridiculous to punish himself because of his freak-out the last time they'd started to have sex.

No one ever lived a good full life when they fully sacrificed what was good for them.

And this? Tom stretched out, piercings on display . . . this was good.

Tom glanced up at him, still smirking but also more unsure. And that was exactly what Prophet wanted.

"Touch yourself," he commanded as he grabbed the lube and put some on his finger.

Tom stared at what he was doing, even as he reached his free hand down to stroke himself. He fingered the piercings in between strokes. Groaned because Prophet was staring at him.

"Spread your legs wider," Prophet ordered, moving in between them, circling Tom's hole. Teasing. Pressing. "You like that, baby?"

Tom nodded vigorously, grunted when Prophet entered him with a lubed middle finger and pressed his gland.

"Good. Keep stroking yourself. Don't come though," Prophet warned as he added two more fingers, knowing how much Tom enjoyed the burn, the twist of pain.

Tom's hips came off the bed, trying to force Prophet to his rhythm. But Prophet wasn't having it.

"You'd do anything for me right now," Prophet confirmed.

Tom nodded, but his eyes were beginning to go unfocused.

Prophet pinched Tom's nipples, pulled at the rings. He wanted to leave Tom strung out and boneless. He owed that to Tommy . . . to himself.

He moved away from Tom, who gave a moan of protest. He closed the shades, shut the door, turned off the light.

He heard Tom's sharp intake of breath as he stripped off his own shirt and shorts and moved back toward the bed, his hands resting on Tommy's thighs as he knelt between them on the mattress. It was really dark in the room as he explored Tom's body bit by bit. Tom's breaths guided him. This *wouldn't* change. That was the most reassuring thing right now.

This wouldn't change. And that made the next thing he did much easier.

He closed his eyes against the darkness. His tongue found every single tattoo. He traced them with his tongue and fingers and teeth, nipping and sucking Tommy's skin. Cataloging the small scars, the entire map of Tommy's body. He knew it well, but there was more to learn.

Always more to learn.

And when Tom was frenzied, begging him to come, Prophet pinned him, the back of Tom's thighs against his chest, Tom's calves over his shoulder. Prophet's hands played along Tom's chest, tugging his nipples, feeling how stiff and swollen they were.

"Yeah, Proph . . . like that," Tom groaned. Prophet twisted them harder and Tom's cock leaked. Prophet's cock rubbed along Tom's ass.

Then he lubed up his cock, quickly, because hell, it'd been too long for him too. And as much as he wanted to come immediately, he wanted to savor what was about to happen.

"Tommy?"

"Please, Proph . . ."

"Tests came back." As he spoke, he pushed inside of Tom, breaching the tight heat without a condom for the first time.

Tom gasped. Bucked. Tried to push Prophet in deeper, faster. "Holy fuck, Proph . . . feels . . . it's incredible. Hurry. Want you all the way in."

"Fucking greedy."

"Slut for you," Tom readily agreed, and they both stopped for a long moment when Prophet bottomed out inside of him.

And then Prophet was on his elbows as he plowed into Tom. His mouth was everywhere—Tom's jawline, his neck, licking his biceps, his armpit—and that made Tom jolt. "Fuck yeah. Fuck . . . Proph . . ."

Prophet grinned, because he loved finding new kinks of Tom's. He licked Tom's armpit again, kissed it, buried his face in it while Tom came hard between their bodies.

"Son of a bitch," Tom groaned.

Prophet realized his hands were shaking. Tom's legs were trembling. And then Tom begged again, and Prophet rode Tom harder than he ever had—like he knew he wouldn't last long with the new sensation of skin to skin . . . and from the way Tom teased him with dirty talk, he didn't want Prophet to.

"Come on, Proph. Want to feel you filling me. Give me everything. Come inside of me, right fucking now."

Prophet wasn't sure when Tom had taken over the reins, but his body responded to Tom's commands like it had no choice. He came hard, shooting inside Tommy, his entire body shuddering with a climax that seemed never-ending.

Tom held Prophet through his orgasm, the feeling of the man coming inside him an indescribable power. As Prophet's head came to a rest on Tom's chest, his legs dropped off Prophet's shoulders to tighten around his waist, and he rubbed the back of Prophet's neck.

After several minutes, Prophet half pulled out of him as he began to lick Tom's chest and belly where he'd spilled between them.

"Proph . . . Jesus." His free hand threaded in Prophet's hair, still restrained and yet still somehow controlling the situation, moving Prophet so he could clean him up everywhere. Moving him down lower, holding his head in place and forcing him to deep-throat his cock. Prophet whimpered, which made Tom's balls tighten, and yeah, he was more than half-hard again.

It'd been too long. And he wasn't giving up the chance to be inside Prophet bare. But he forced Prophet to keep his mouth working. "That's it, Proph—get me hard. And then I'm going to fuck you. You'll feel it for days."

Prophet moaned around his cock. Tom took his hand away, telling him, "Don't you dare stop."

Prophet didn't, kept up a slow steady rhythm until Tom was ready. Leisurely, he let himself out of the cuffs and the ropes, because really? Did Prophet think he hadn't studied Naval knots?

He wrapped a hand around the back of Prophet's neck and shifted over. "Come on, Proph. On your hands and knees. Keep your eyes closed."

Prophet drew in a sharp, surprised breath.

"Yeah, I figured you had them closed, baby. Keep them that way. Trust me."

Prophet obviously did, because he followed directions. When he was in position, Tom spread his cheeks, tonguing his hole, driving Prophet wild. He could keep Prophet on edge for a long time like this, but no, his cock was demanding equal time.

He carefully lubed himself up . . . thought for just a second about taking the piercings out, then discarded that notion. They were smooth barbells . . . and Prophet would now get the full benefit of them.

He eased inside of Prophet so carefully. The sensation drove Prophet to rest on his elbows until finally Tom pushed Prophet's face down into the pillow, listening to the man's breathing, having the sex they were supposed to have . . .

They were making up for the last time. And if Tom had his way, they'd never need to make up for it again.

And Prophet was rock hard, ready to come again. "You need to come again this soon, Proph? Maybe I shouldn't let you."

"Tommy." A hoarse, needy cry. A push back against his cock. Pain mingled with the ultimate pleasures as his piercings caressed Prophet so intimately. There wasn't an ounce of fear in Prophet's body, but it was strung as tight as a bow. "Been . . . so long. Before this . . . please . . ."

Jesus, for Prophet to be ready again this soon . . . "You've been punishing yourself by not coming?"

"Yes."

"No wonder . . . you were . . . such a bastard." Tom's words were punctuated by his thrusts, hard, purposeful, wonderfully skin to skin, no barriers between them. "Not happening again. Never . . . again."

"Maybe," Prophet managed.

"Try it. I will turn you over the nearest piece of furniture—and I don't care where we are and who's around—and I'll fuck you until you can't walk."

"Do it now, Tommy," Prophet groaned.

And Tom did.

Feeling Tom coming inside of him was the most amazing thing. He'd known it would be, to actually have it happen, to feel the throb of the man's dick with no barrier . . .

No more barriers. He'd make sure of it.

And then Tom reached down and stroked him several times with hard, firm strokes until he came again, a tight, hot climax that made him babble incoherently.

Finally, after what seemed like days on his knees, Tom was pulling him down to him. Tom's hands came up to twine in his hair. Prophet's cheek was on his chest, Tom's heartbeat pounding a crazy rhythm in his ear.

"So fucking good, Proph," Tom murmured.

Prophet realized his eyes were still closed. He opened them cautiously—it was still so dark.

This is what it'll be like.

"It was never like this, Tommy. Not with anyone."

Tom reached up and stroked his cheek with his knuckles.

"And yeah, I've fucked some partners. I've fucked a lot of other people too, but the partners were never my partners for long. It just didn't work."

"So you figured sleeping with me was a good way to get rid of me."

"No. I knew sleeping with you was the worst thing I could do."

Tom laughed. "There's a compliment in there somewhere."

"Well, look at us now."

"Yeah. Together. Home."

Home. Fuck. Prophet had never been one of those guys who was all, *I'm too wild to be domesticated.* But he liked his place. He liked being with someone.

And when he blurted all of that out, he heard the laughter in Tom's voice when he said, "Yeah, I can see that about you—but the domesticated part? I'm never letting you do my laundry. Again."

"I didn't know the red towel was in there," Prophet protested.

"You did it on purpose to get out of doing laundry."

"Maybe. But it worked."

"Fucking impossible."

Tom flipped him onto his back suddenly. Prophet braced himself for . . . something. And then Tom told him, seriously, "What if I'd never found you, Proph? Where the fuck would I be?"

He sounded so serious. So worried.

"But I'm here, Tom. You did."

"We both came so damned close to not being here." Prophet couldn't deny the truth in that. "No matter what, I'd never regret this."

"Me neither, Tommy."

Because, as much as they didn't want anything to happen, both men were, at heart, painful realists.

"So you can make me promise, you shit—and I did promise you—but if you think your losing your sight is going to make me leave you, you're so fucking wrong. And I'll spend the rest of my days proving it to you."

Prophet's breath came in harsh gasps.

"I know there are things you're holding back. I don't know what they are, but I know you have to. And I trust you. You need to know that."

"I know, Tommy." He touched Tom's cheek. "I'd never betray you. It's just you now."

"Just you." Tom closed his eyes for just a second, soothed by the warm rub of Prophet's palm, then opened them. "I love you. Who the fuck else could compete?"

Prophet pulled back for a second. Repeated, "Who the fuck else could compete?" with his hand on Tom's heart.

CHAPTER THIRTY-ONE ◉

Whatever Mal was hiding was bugging the shit out of Prophet. Especially because the tension between Mal and Cillian was so goddamned thick . . .

If he didn't know better, he'd swear that somehow Cillian was into Mal. He was still an arrogant ass, but he was also just slightly lovesick when he looked at Mal. And Mal, like Tom said, was slightly more psychotic and protective . . . but Cillian knew that.

Which meant, at some point, Mal had broken cover. For whatever reason. And Mal would only do that with very good reason.

But he'd been so wrapped up in his eyes, in the John shit, in what was happening with Tom, that he hadn't delved deeply enough into it.

So when Mal came to him to go over the plans, to deal with every possible scenario, the way they'd been taught in the military, Prophet first slid the maps to the side of the table and stared at Mal.

Typical Mal, he rolled his eyes and mouthed, *What's up?*

"I figure if you knew about Gary, you'd have told me."

Mal signed, *I wouldn't leave you hanging about that. Wouldn't leave you hanging at all, Proph.*

"But something's up with you and Cillian—so what the fuck happened between you two?"

Mal shrugged.

"You're not getting away with that shit."

Mal made a circle with the fingers on one hand and slid a finger on the other through it, the universal sign for fucking.

"I knew that."

There's more than one way to get fucked, Mal signed. *And I'm not talking about it now. It's under control. Obviously.*

Prophet shook his head slowly. "I don't feel in control."

But I am in control—of myself and of Cillian, okay? You need to trust me and spend time dealing with your own denial.

"Do you think I didn't know you believed John slit your throat?"

Mal blinked, surprised, and that wasn't an easy thing to do to the man.

"I get it. You were protecting me. But come on, fucker, you're withholding intel. Then and now."

Mal sat back. Signed, *And where do you think I learned that from? Remember that time in boot camp when—*

"Enough." Prophet held up his hand. "You think I can't recognize this bait-and-switch crap? I invented throwing people off the track. Mal, what happened with Cillian?"

He was facing Mal, pointing at him, a dangerous move. Because Mal looked ready to spit fire.

Not now, Prophet. Maybe not ever.

"But Tom knows."

Why would I tell that voodoo asshole?

Why indeed.

Tom came home to an empty apartment. He'd known Prophet was meeting with Mal, and he saw some coffee cups on the table but no sign of either man. But the alarms had been turned on, so he figured they'd gone out to train.

Tom had come back from a run in the woods—training with Prophet drove him crazy at times, but that didn't mean he didn't respect what Prophet was teaching him. So he'd practice it on his own, learn to apply the situational awareness he'd been born with to his training. To differentiate the different types of danger feelings he sometimes got.

He wanted to help Prophet—even more now. The stronger he got, the stronger Prophet would be.

If Prophet decided tomorrow that he couldn't do this job with Sadiq or with John, Tom would go with the team and let Prophet sit it out. If he was totally honest with himself, he wished that Prophet would.

After Tom showered, he pulled on sweats and a T-shirt and went to see what there was for dinner. Trying to retain a sense of normalcy when, in less than forty-eight hours they'd be on a plane to East Africa, face-to-face with a terrorist who'd tried to kill him.

It was then that Prophet slammed into the house. Tom turned in time to see the look on his face and knew what he was in for.

His cock immediately got hard. Whenever Prophet got aggressive, when Prophet got mad and Tom wasn't the source, Prophet took it out on him. And Tom loved every goddamned minute of it. He surrendered to Prophet, let him wear himself out on Tom's body, because it gave Tom what he wanted . . . and it gave them both what they needed.

First, though, Prophet stopped at the doorway to the kitchen, his eyes dark. "We need to talk."

"Hi to you too."

"You knew . . . about Mal."

"Knew that Mal was a psychopathic asshole? Yes," he said confidently, even as Prophet began to stalk him. And Prophet's stalking was a beautiful thing to be sure, with just the right amount of menace to get Tom hard.

"You knew about Mal and Cillian, Tommy."

Tom took a breath and wondered exactly how much Prophet knew . . . or if this was a fishing expedition. "Mal told me."

"You saw him fucking Cillian in the back room."

"It was dark."

Prophet got closer. "You saw them fucking."

Tom was pinned. "If I say yes, what do I get?"

"Get?"

"Yeah."

Prophet's mouth quirked. "You'll get what you need."

"Here's a hint—I knew."

"Here's a hint for you—I'd have given you what you wanted even if you didn't admit it." Prophet pushed his chest against Tom's, until Tom hit the kitchen wall. Prophet kissed him as he tore at Tom's shirt. He heard a tear and groaned into Prophet's mouth. Ripped Prophet's shirt off just as hard and a shudder ran through Prophet. He went for Prophet's jeans, but Prophet grabbed his wrists and yanked his hands away. He backed off, spun Tom to face the wall and held his wrists behind his back. With a hand wound in Tom's hair, he pulled him off the wall and marched him into the living room and over to the couch, the poor, abused couch that wasn't Cillian's. And he pushed Tom over the back.

Tom braced his hands on the cushion as Prophet took his pants down. His fingers dug into the fabric when Prophet's hands separated his ass cheeks and he tongued along his crack, speared his hole, ate him without mercy, leaving Tom to hump the couch.

"If you come now, I swear I'll spank you," Prophet threatened, in a tone that told Tom that he wanted Tom to come right fucking now.

The orgasm pumped from him, leaving his legs weak and his cock still hard. Prophet didn't wait, slapped his ass four times in quick succession, leaving Tom gasping.

"More, Tommy?"

"Yes. Please . . ."

"Fuck. You beg so well for what you need."

And Tom knew Prophet needed this as well. He pushed his ass out to catch the brunt of Prophet's smacks, his skin hot and tingling, the pain coursing through his body and turning to the pleasure immediately. He was floating. Flying. Ready to come again when Prophet pushed inside of him, his cock stretching Tom.

"Tommy." Prophet's voice was a raw gasp, a plea as Tom contracted around his cock, forcing him over the edge, needing to take him there.

He was sweat slicked, could barely move. Prophet was helping him onto the couch, wrapping him in a blanket. Kissing his cheek, murmuring how amazing he was . . . how perfect . . . how glad he was that Tom walked into his life.

Tom heard it all as he floated down to earth. Prophet's words anchored him, and he realized he was clinging to Prophet, his arms around the man in a death grip. But Prophet didn't seem to mind, remained next to him, comforting him.

When Prophet went to get up, Tom tried to pull him back down.

"Let me, Tommy," he said, and he only left for a few moments, coming back with a wet washcloth and towel. He cleaned them both up, then settled in again next to Tom. "Hey."

Tom glanced up—he was still in that blissed-out place, but for Prophet, he brought himself back into focus. "Things okay?"

"Yeah, they are. But I know you and Mal are hiding something. I also know it's not something that would fuck with this mission—Mal wouldn't do that to me. Neither would you."

No, Tom wouldn't. And sure, what had happened between Mal and Cillian could absolutely fuck with the mission . . . if Mal didn't have such a tight leash on Cillian, so to speak. If they all didn't need one another to survive. But if Cillian decided to bail, to throw Prophet under the bus . . .

Then again, he'd been protecting Prophet long before Mal came into Cillian's orbit. That's what Tom held on to now. Cillian was as protective as Prophet. And maybe that was something for Mal to hang on to as well.

CHAPTER THIRTY-TWO ◉

As much as Prophet didn't want to work with Cillian, he knew that they all needed one another. There was no other way out of it.

And they all still thought the intel was on target. Mal was playing the part of one of the informants—literally pretending to be one of Cillian's informants to Cillian's former boss, Trent. So Mal basically held Cillian's life in his hands.

"Getting anything on the voodoo-meter?" he asked Tom now from the couch in their living room.

"About Cillian? I wish," Tom muttered. "So fucking tense around here."

After several hours of training, Prophet wasn't feeling all that tense. His training was as much to keep his mind settled as it was in preparation for the physical parts of the upcoming mission.

He and Tom were back on track—and he was really fucking grateful for that.

They were set to leave in the morning, had a private plane at the ready, thanks to Cillian's friend—aka, the guy pretending to sell Gary. Prophet would board with Tom, Mal, and Cillian in a few hours, that way anyone surveilling the plane tomorrow wouldn't see anything out of order.

Last night, Tom had told him that he'd always known that most of the shit shown in spy movies was exaggerated, but in another way, it absolutely didn't go far enough to show the length spies went to in order to keep their covers.

"It's a house of cards, but it's all we've got," Prophet had explained. Every second he trained, he pictured the mission, step-by-step from the time the plane touched down onward. He'd seen the plans of the compound, but that wasn't one hundred percent foolproof. Gary would attempt to signal yes or no, but if that was too risky, they'd deal with it once he finished his end of the job.

"Do you think we'll get lucky?" Tom asked now.

Prophet shifted on the cushions. "As in . . . do I think John will be there? No. I don't think he and Sadiq are ever in the same country at the same time."

"Dammit. Proph—" Tom touched his arm, and Prophet jerked around to look at the security monitors—and at the man who'd managed to bypass all the alarms and was now at Cillian's door with a drawn weapon.

"Back me up, Tom—and text Cillian," he said, stood and grabbed his own weapon from the table where he'd taken to keeping it over the past weeks. He slid the door open when Tom motioned that the man had gone into Cillian's apartment and held up the phone.

"He knows."

"Good. Stay here and run a check of the perimeters."

Tom didn't argue, began punching buttons as Proph slid down the bannister and listened at the partially open door to Cillian's apartment.

There was dead silence, which made Prophet's hackles rise, and then there was the sound of a silenced gunshot. He eased the door open and entered to the left with his weapon drawn . . . and saw Cillian standing over a dead man.

"Who is he?" Prophet grunted.

"My former boss at SB-20," Cillian said casually.

"Did you know he was coming?"

"Perhaps. I figured it was better to get rid of him before he tried to follow us."

"And telling me that was going to happen when?"

"This part?" Cillian motioned to the dead man. "This isn't your problem. Trent was always my problem, the way John is your problem."

Prophet couldn't argue. And there'd been no indication that Trent had fucked anything up with the Sadiq intel, but Trent's agent was following in Cillian's footsteps, and there was no way Prophet was letting anyone take down Sadiq or John but him and his team. Mal had been feeding the SB-20 agent who'd taken Cillian's place with the wrong intel—successfully—for the past week. And Hook was helping to reroute messages to Sadiq so the terrorist wouldn't have a reason to veer from his own plan.

Now, Cillian told him, "It was only a matter of time before Sadiq went down. He's good, but we're better."

Prophet shook his head. He didn't tell Cillian that he felt like they were getting as far as they were with Sadiq because John was pulling away, leaving him out to dry. Yeah, probably other men couldn't have gotten as far as Mal and Prophet had, but . . .

"You don't look convinced."

"This shit?" He pointed at Trent. "This is messy. I don't like messy where I fucking live. Especially with Remy. So you're going to have to get the fuck out of here once this is all over."

"Once this is all over, I'll have the same number of people trying to kill me as you will. Actually, fewer, since the last time I checked, you're wanted in far more countries. And several states."

Prophet narrowed his eyes at Cillian. "Get rid of him. We leave in an hour, just in case there are more where he came from."

"I think that's an excellent plan."

"Where's Gary?"

"Safe," Cillian said. "Not here."

"Good." Prophet walked away, but just as he got to the door, Cillian said, "You need me."

Prophet whipped around to him, closing the space between them, stepping over Trent to crowd Cillian. "That's where you're wrong—I don't need anyone to do what I need to. Everyone wants to be involved. It'll make *them* feel better. But I know John best. I'm the only one who should be making sacrifices here."

"Maybe your friends feel you've made enough."

"Where does that leave you, Cillian?"

"You're still alive, Prophet. Long after you weren't supposed to be."

Prophet considered that. "Whatever you did to Mal, I'm going to find out after we take down Sadiq. And then you might not be alive much longer."

"Threats, Prophet? After all we've been through."

"Promises. And I'm really goddamned good at promises."

CHAPTER THIRTY-THREE ◉

After a long, tense overnight on the plane, they were all restless and far too much in their own minds—a dangerous thing for the warriors Tom was surrounded with. And he had no doubt that's what they were. Seeing them together like this, ready for the job, made him understand the training they'd received . . . and how Prophet was trying to take him over and above the FBI and EE training he'd had.

It was something to be seen, rather than described. It was in the way Prophet moved once the flight was underway, how Mal's signs became hand gestures that were concise and easily understood.

It was in the way Cillian held himself, almost ramrod straight, staring straight ahead . . . and still, Tom knew he missed nothing that went on around him on the flight.

Gary was in his seat, and occasionally Prophet would sit with him. At one point, there was laughter, which had to be a good sign. Cillian's friend, Louis, had a copilot, a woman named Sally who was former military. She would stay with the plane until it was time for them to leave, and she had backup waiting for her at the airport.

After nearly fifteen hours in the air, Prophet sat next to him. "How're you doing?"

Tom stared at him. "What aren't you telling me?"

"We can't land with this plane—Gary and Louis will, but not the rest of us."

"Is that a new development?"

"No."

Tom absorbed what Prophet said. "Told you, it's been a while."

"I know. So we go together. Tandem chutes." Prophet squeezed his knee. "Good way to get into the game."

Tom took a deep breath. "I really fucking hope so."

Mal and Cillian had their own harnesses, and Tom was to be strapped into a tandem one with Prophet.

Prophet, who sat down after he buckled himself in, patted his thighs, and in his best Cajun drawl instructed Tom, "Come sit on my lap, *bébé*."

Tom rolled his eyes at the man, but did as he requested, letting Prophet secure their harness.

"Trust me, I'm a good ride," Prophet murmured.

Tom glanced over his shoulder. "That thing going to poke me the whole way down?"

"I'd imagine so, yes," Prophet said calmly.

Together, they stood and shuffled toward the door. Cillian and Mal were already waiting there, standing so close to each other . . . but still so separate. Tom had observed them during the trip, mainly because he'd noted Prophet's eyes on them.

Of course, Cillian and Mal had noticed that too, so the whole thing was . . . weird. And maybe it would've been funny if they hadn't been about to put themselves directly into Sadiq's path. And jump out of a plane.

Then Mal jerked the door open, letting in an overwhelmingly loud burst of deafening sound that brought Tom right back to his early days at the academy. He swallowed hard, his body strumming with anticipation as he looked out into the darkness.

Mal nodded to them one last time, then turned to look at Cillian. Something passed between them, something so goddamned palpable that Tom even felt Prophet jerk back slightly. Tom caught sight of Mal's smile as his head turned to face the open door. For a moment, Mal was still, framed in the doorway . . . and then he jumped and vanished. Seconds later, Cillian was in the same position, following Mal into the eerie darkness that was streaked with white clouds, disappearing immediately.

And then he and Prophet walked together to the edge of the door. He wasn't supposed to do anything at all to hinder the free fall, just stretch his arms and legs out once they went over the edge and flipped, and then Prophet would mirror him. Which felt so completely right.

Prophet murmured against his ear, counting down.

On one, Tom breathed and crossed his arms to his chest, fingers touching his shoulders.

On two, they crouched together, and three came fast on the heels of that. There wasn't time to think, just let his body jump with the force of Prophet's behind it, pushing him out and at the same time, balancing their weight. They had to act like one.

Which, hell, wasn't hard at all.

It was a slow-motion leap into the nothingness, and, for a moment, it was like they were frozen. But then their bodies pushed forward into a weightless front flip that disoriented the fuck out of him. The darkness didn't help. He let Prophet guide them and after what seemed like a long moment but was no doubt mere seconds, they were horizontal. Prophet tapped on his shoulder, reminding him to spread his arms and legs out, so he did. And that's when the pulse-pounding, almost painfully euphoric adrenaline hit his bloodstream.

He stretched his arms and legs out as the wind battered upward against him. They hung for what seemed like minutes but was, in reality, maybe half a second before they accelerated down fast. But they weren't hurtling. Not yet.

The wind buoyed them even as their bodies slammed down against its force. It was so goddamned loud that it was impossible to hear anything at all . . . and at the same time, strangely peaceful.

It was almost too much sensation—the build of pressure, flying in a blind hurtle . . . like an orgasm denied, the pleasure building to an almost unbearable level.

When Prophet pulled the chute, there was a dizzying, dramatic slowdown, the force of it yanked them upward hard. It was slightly disorienting, and that was the part he remembered most in training, one of the danger zones where you could lose it. But Prophet was there and Tom wasn't lost. Not anymore.

The chute spiraled as Prophet steered toward their makeshift LZ. The dizziness returned and Tom's ears popped. The view was jaw-dropping, especially because it appeared they were making their descent directly into a black hole of nothing. Which, of course, they basically were . . . but Prophet kept them on course, until Tom saw the lights that Cillian or Mal must've put down on the ground, and then a wide patch of ground appeared, hurtling up toward them. It happened so goddamned fast—one minute hovering, the next, hitting the ground at what seemed like one hundred miles an hour but definitely wasn't—before coming to a complete, heart-pounding stop. The chute leveled and their boots slid in the dirt, both of them stumble-walking forward with the weight of their own bodies.

As Prophet unbuckled them from the harness, Tom smiled, his mind still somewhere in that blissed-out place. Prophet hung onto his biceps, checking to make sure he was all right and laughing. "Sick motherfucker."

"Oh yeah."

Tom still hadn't come down from the free fall, not until they arrived at the airstrip where Sadiq's men would take custody of Gary. Prophet liberated a vehicle to get them from the LZ, but they'd abandoned it a mile back in favor of quietly edging toward their target. And that's when Tom fully came back down to earth, just in time to watch the plane land on the private airstrip, to be surrounded by Sadiq's guards. In the dark, Gary and Louis exited, Gary in handcuffs.

He and Prophet were belly down in the bushes, rifles aimed at Sadiq's guards, whose posture made them look menacing. But none of them had weapons drawn on Gary. On Cillian's man, yes. Both were patted down, and then there was a brief argument when Louis tried to leave. Just as Cillian had promised, that wasn't allowed to happen. Louis was handcuffed and, alongside Gary, guided into a waiting car.

He and Prophet had already decided it was better to simply track Gary and make sure he was headed to the compound they'd been given intel on. After lying in silence for two hours, letting Sally turn the plane around and head to the airport, Prophet checked in with Cillian.

There was a crackle in his earpiece, and he heard Cillian's voice saying, "We're at the location—Gary's chip is functioning perfectly. They're on their way to the compound."

So he and Prophet would head to the compound and wait for the next phase of the plan. They went back to the stolen car and drove through the back roads, stopping several miles outside of the compound, just out of range of potential monitors. They moved closer, found a sheltered spot to wait out the next hours, which would, by their best estimates, turn into at least a full day.

Once settled, Tom stared off toward the lights they could still see, even through the thickly wired fence around the compound. "And now we just wait for the signs."

"It's always about signs, Tommy." Prophet was turned on his side, facing toward him and the lights. "This is really going to happen."

Tom knew what he meant. It was always a reality, but now, it was close enough to touch. Questions were getting answered. And men would die. "I want to protect you. From everything."

Prophet smiled, said, "Me too," without a trace of sarcasm.

And that was all Tom needed to hear to get him through the rest of this mission.

King and Ren were close by, ready to help. Mal would remain with Cillian on the west end of the compound. Tom didn't think that was the best idea, but Mal hadn't fought it, and neither had Cillian. So for the next twenty-four hours, he and Prophet lay in a foxhole-like ditch on the north outskirts of the compound, monitoring movements and looking for signs of Sadiq.

They'd been prepared for Gary to be unable to give them the signs they needed—in which case, Prophet readied him to look for other signs: sudden movements of guards, more cars entering or exiting the compound . . . and of course, Tom's voodoo was a sign all its own.

"Anything hinky, tell me," Prophet had warned. And Tom would've, but aside from nerves, he'd felt nothing but calm and ready. And then, just hours past the projected time, Gary managed to get them two signals—one, that the layout was exactly as they'd studied it on the plans, and two, that he'd started building the triggers.

Tom breathed, letting the relief of those messages wash over him. "I really don't know how you do this—the waiting."

Prophet turned to him, his face serious. "I know you trust me."

"With my life."

"Keep that in mind." With that, Prophet pulled out the listening device in Tom's ear, then took out his own, took both of them and buried them in the dirt. He turned off the sat phone that connected them to Mal and Cillian and disconnected the wires inside.

And then Prophet leaned in and murmured in Tom's ear.

CHAPTER THIRTY-FOUR ◉

Three hours later, the click of a gun made Prophet stiffen. He didn't have time to look at Tom before a hood was put over his head and the muzzle of the gun was stuck into his neck.

Right before the capture, he'd been sitting in basically total darkness with Tom by his side, the way he'd done last night too. But this . . . of course it was different. The stuff of all his goddamned nightmares.

If you let it be.

One of his captors yanked him up, out of the hole, then forced him to kneel.

Prophet reached for the gun, grabbed it, and slammed his attacker to the ground. He was tackled by several more men.

"You want your friend to live?" one of them asked, and Prophet stilled. He heard sounds of a semi-struggle, Tom trying to gain a little leverage and not succeeding, based on the sharp commands from the other guards.

He was half-dragged along for several feet before he was dumped inside the trunk of a car. Alone. The trunk slammed, and he forced his breathing steady. Shifted to see if he could hear anything that was happening in the car itself.

They were keeping Tom with them, which meant they thought Prophet was the bigger threat. At one time, Prophet might've agreed.

He was being driven in circles. Even though he knew where the compound was, they were trying to disorient him, throw his concentration off. Make him worry.

Classic mindfuck.

Finally, he was roughly grabbed out of the trunk. His ankles were chained, and he was prodded to shuffle along blindly. The temperature change told him they were inside. The floor was concrete, not dirt . . . and it was quiet, save for the hum of computer monitors that would no doubt show security footage of the perimeter around the compound. And then a door opened, and he was shoved through. He smelled chemicals, heard hushed voices, and then silence.

He was forced to his knees, heard a barked, "Down," and Tom's grunt as he hit the ground maybe ten feet from him. He'd kept his eyes closed against the roughness of the bag once he'd realized he wasn't going to see any light through it anyway, and now he focused on the conversations around him. Pictured the room from the floor plan he'd studied.

Tom had gone silent next to him, tension ricocheting off him as they both listened and waited.

Judging by the low murmur he'd heard before, Gary was in the middle of the room, surrounded by Sadiq's men and other scientists who were helping him. Three scientists, three guards next to them. Gary. Sadiq. A guard outside each of the three doors.

Then the hood was pulled roughly from his head. He blinked under the florescent lights, his vision blurring slightly. But he'd know Sadiq anywhere. It didn't matter that this was the first time being in the man's physical presence.

"Welcome." Sadiq opened his arms and Prophet scanned the room, made out a blur that looked to be Gary. In his peripheral vision, he could see Tom glaring at Sadiq.

"You think I don't know?" Sadiq smiled. Turned to Gary and motioned to the innocuous metal that was the start of the triggers. Gary didn't move, which forced an impatient Sadiq forward to grab the trigger himself.

He turned back to Prophet and Tom, shifting the trigger from palm to palm. "I know the rest of your team's out there. You don't think I have men on them, ready to pull the trigger, so to speak?"

"I try not to worry about what you think," Prophet said calmly. His wrists were lashed tightly behind him, and the guards had jerked them viciously. He'd need casts again—he knew that. But right now, he had bigger concerns.

"I'm just watching your other friends for now. And this man next to you, he's risking his life again. For you. Are you worth it?"

"More than you'll ever be," Tom muttered.

"So you're sticking with him, then? Not taking a way out?" Sadiq asked.

"Like you're going to let me walk out of here?"

"Stranger things have happened. What's happening with Prophet is karma, pure and simple. An eye for an eye," Sadiq said, and Prophet closed his eyes for a second at the blow of irony.

"I'm staying with him," Tom said, and Prophet's eyes opened again.

"Then you'll both die." Sadiq's words were casually cold, which made them harsher than if he'd snarled them.

Prophet forced himself not to react, to hear Tom's words . . . to know he'd let Tom do for him what he'd do for Tom.

He blinked again and his vision cleared.

Sadiq turned to point to Gary, telling Prophet, "Your friend here sold you right back out. Almost the second he came in here. He's been a good boy. And we've been watching you the whole time."

"He's not my friend—he's a job," Prophet snarled. "And good for you."

"Your best friend knows you as well as you know him. Did you really think I didn't know this was a setup? That John didn't know from the start?"

To hear John's name out of Sadiq's mouth made a red-hot anger shoot through him. Of course, Sadiq noticed. He turned back to Gary. "You're going to keep working."

"Gary . . ." Prophet shook his head, tilted it to the left slightly.

Gary stared at him. Blinked. "There was never any other choice, Prophet. If you weren't smart enough to know that," Gary said, and Tom spat on the floor in front of him.

Sadiq smiled again, opened his mouth to speak . . . and stumbled forward. The trigger dropped from his hand, hitting the floor and breaking apart as Sadiq went to his knees, his eyes on level with Prophet's.

It was Prophet's turn to smile.

Prophet's "Go" was a quiet command but a command nonetheless. As the guards moved to help Sadiq, Gary used the chaos to come around to Tom and Prophet and cut their bindings.

"Stay down, Gary," Prophet ordered, then nodded in Tom's direction. Tom lunged for the nearest guard, slammed him to the ground, grabbed his weapon. Two clean shots to the head—and Prophet was doing the same to the other guards.

They were frantically trying to help Sadiq, rather than being worried about defending themselves. Their lives were over, no matter what.

Tom heard shots echoing from other parts of the building. He wasn't surprised when Mal kicked the door in several moments later, surveyed the scene, and nodded in approval. He motioned toward the scientists who'd been working with Gary over the last couple of days. There were three of them, two men and one woman.

Tom walked over to them and smiled. Nodded, as if in sympathy, and they visibly relaxed.

He took them out in rapid succession—single bullets to the brain—without question. They'd been traced as working with Sadiq for years, which meant they weren't unwilling hostages. They were in the unique position of somehow knowing both too much and still having no real information that could help in the search for John, given the way Sadiq compartmentalized. Since there was no way to bring them back home without hindering their own safe escape, no time to remain here to interrogate them, they had to die.

"We're ready for the video," Prophet told Mal. He glanced up at the cameras that Ren controlled at this point. "Let's get into place."

He and Tom moved out of the way. Cillian's man came in with his machine gun and sprayed bullets around the already dead bodies. That's where Ren would pick the feed up. Gary remained hunched over in the corner, in a protective ball until Louis grabbed Gary, who tried to fight. His arm went around Gary's throat, dragging him along with his gun pointed at the door.

"Cut," Prophet said. He looked behind at the room one last time, then walked over to Sadiq splayed on the floor. "Poison on the trigger worked like a charm. But just in case . . ." He pulled his weapon out and put two bullets into Sadiq's head.

Tom nodded approvingly. "We're almost there."

Prophet's expression softened slightly. "Almost, Tommy. Almost."

Sally landed the plane just outside the compound—a risky move but the safest for the team. Driving back after what had happened was a suicide run.

Most who saw that tape wouldn't understand what had happened. But John would know that one man couldn't have taken down a compound.

Prophet sighed in relief as the plane leveled off and shot steadily through the sky. After half an hour in the air, he stood to survey the others, and saw Cillian stand as well.

Cillian'd been furious back at the compound—he hadn't hidden that in his expression—and all Prophet could see for those first moments after the dust settled was Mal, unwilling or unable, to pull his eyes from the spook.

Because Cillian had been the only one left out of the alteration to the plan. And that had been Mal's suggestion, Prophet whispering it to Tom for the first time in the foxhole, when he'd explained that they were going to force their own capture.

A show of force was one thing, but Prophet wanted to be closer to Gary when things went down. And so the poison on the trigger was something Gary himself had suggested, an easy way to incapacitate Sadiq, providing no one else touched the trigger in the mere seconds Gary had between brushing the poison on the metal and Sadiq picking it up to show it off to Prophet. It was, as he'd taught Tom, all about quick, nearly undetectable movements. Nods. Head tilts.

It was all about the signs.

"You did it," he told Tom now, who was sprawled in the seat.

"We did it," Tom corrected, brushed a hand over Prophet's thigh and smiled.

And then Cillian was strolling over to them, with Mal following. Tom stood at that point, and Prophet waited for Cillian to speak.

Cillian glared at him first, though. "I hope I've passed your test."

Prophet stared at him for a long time while Cillian—and Tom and Mal—stared at him. "We still have shit to discuss, Cillian. But for this? Yeah, you passed."

"I would never compromise Gary," Cillian said tightly. "Or either of you. Not after spending all this time saving both of your asses . . ." He shifted his gaze from Prophet to Tom before turning it on Mal. "I had your back on this one."

Mal just nodded. And it looked like both men wanted to say more, and hell, Prophet wasn't getting in the middle of that shit, so he stood up and guided Tom with him over to where Gary sat.

Gary saw them coming, stood. He had dark circles under his eyes, but Prophet knew he was all jazzed up, would have trouble coming down enough to sleep.

Prophet clapped Gary on the shoulder. "You did it." Gary hugged him, and it was like Prophet was holding that little kid again. Like he'd gone back in time. "Sadiq's gone."

Gary nodded against his shoulder.

"I'm still going to watch out for you. Now, more than ever," Prophet informed him.

"I figured." Gary stared at him. "Are you going to use me for the next part, or kill me off?"

Tom snorted. Prophet pinched the bridge of his nose and said, "Jesus, Gary—it's called witness protection, not killing you off. And I don't know yet."

"Thank you, for letting me do this much. It meant . . . everything."

Prophet clapped him on the shoulder, his throat too tight to say anything else.

But all of them now had a bigger bounty on their heads than they'd ever had with the CIA . . . or any other agency. John, and the men who'd stood behind Sadiq had them in their sights, and that was a sick kind of glue that held them together indefinitely.

CHAPTER THIRTY-FIVE ◉

Three weeks later

Tom walked into the apartment and heard Prophet telling someone to shut the fuck up.

Sounds about right.

He dropped his bag and heard the window in the bedroom close. He took his jacket and boots off so he wouldn't track snow everywhere and then he padded to the bedroom, only to find Prophet sitting on the bed, shivering.

Tom glanced toward the window, assuming that Prophet must've closed it. He saw the sand, in the same spot he'd found it last time, by the window. At times, Prophet did move during his flashback dreams. More often than not, he dropped off the side of the bed like that was a cover from gunfire, or he threw himself over Tom's body to protect him.

But to go to the box, grab sand, and drop it on the floor . . .

"Hey, Proph," he said quietly.

Prophet looked up and for a moment, Tom knew Prophet wasn't seeing him. Not clearly. So Tom waited, watched as Prophet pulled himself out of the flashback—what was left of it—and then sighed.

"Hey, T."

"You okay?"

He nodded. Then shook his head. He was holding something tightly in his hand and Tom came over and knelt in front of him, rubbing his own hand over Prophet's fist.

"What's this?"

Prophet opened his hand and showed Tom the sand, staring at it like he was really confused.

"You've done this before with your John flashbacks," Tom started. "I come in here and find sand on the floor by the window, and I put it back in your box on the dresser. I figured that's where it came from, that it must relate to some memory of him."

Prophet glanced down at his hand again and then back at Tom. "I . . . the sand's from by the window. Every time I have a John flashback, I find it by the window."

Tom stilled. "You don't remember getting it out of the box and bringing it over to where you think John is sitting?"

Prophet looked confused. "I don't think . . . no. I mean, there's sand in that box, Tom. Not a lot. And that's a memento, but it has nothing to do with John. The first time I found sand on the floor I figured . . . yeah, maybe in a flashback I fucked up and threw sand there. But . . ."

Tom got up and looked in the box. He didn't want to invade Prophet's privacy, but Prophet didn't object. At the bottom, he found a small jar, full of sand. Filled to the top and corked. And lots of loose sand inside the box.

No way could it have all fit inside the jar. Never.

Calmly, he drew his weapon and sidled up to the window. But the fire escape a couple of feet down was empty. There was a light dusting of snow over it, which could've covered footprints by this point, since it was coming down pretty hard.

He opened the latch and looked to see if there were any signs of forced entry. Nothing.

And then he ran his finger over the black outer moldings and stilled again. Because the paint was wet.

"Tom?"

"Are you sure it's John you're seeing?"

"Yeah."

"Bet your life sure?"

"Why?"

He turned and showed Prophet the black on his fingers. "I don't think you're dreaming these visits, Proph. Not all of them."

Prophet didn't stop to listen to Tom—he was out the apartment in his bare feet, taking the stairs two at a time, shoving open the heavy front door and cruising the alleyway. The snow on his bare feet didn't bother him because he was so fucking numb already.

He looked up at the side of the building, traced the route John would've had to take back down. Prophet could do it in thirty seconds. Less if he jumped the last few feet.

Someone who practiced could do it in less. Or move up to the roof to get out of sight.

"Proph." Tom was behind him, weapon drawn, holding Prophet's boots.

Prophet turned to him, "He never wears tags, Tom."

Tom furrowed his brow for a second, then said, "Because they're in the truck."

"He wouldn't know that. Or maybe he does and figures that he wouldn't have time to get the tags back into the truck." Prophet ran a hand through his now-wet hair. He glanced at the dumpster at the end of the alleyway, a shared one for a couple of stores around the corner. Now, he double-timed it there, opened it and looked in.

Nothing but garbage. No place for a guy to hide himself, but . . .

Then he looked behind the dumpster. Stuck his hand back there and felt around and pulled out a plastic bag. If you weren't looking for it, you'd never see it.

His hand shook as he opened it and pulled out a desert BDU jacket. With a name badge sewn onto it.

Morse.

"He was wearing it that day," Prophet said quietly.

"How can you be sure?"

Prophet fingered the hole in the collar. "My bullet. I almost hit him after I killed Hal. Not on purpose, but it nicked his neck. I saw blood and he brushed it off, joked about a new fashion statement."

He slid down the brick wall, clutching the material.

Tom bent down to him. "Proph, we can't stay here."

"You think he's still close?"

"Don't you?"

Prophet looked around. "No. He wouldn't risk that."

But would he come back if Prophet left the jacket where he'd found it? Would he come back into Prophet's apartment where Tom and Remy and Mal were? Where Cillian was. Where Doc might be. And no, fuck it, no, however easy that might be . . . it was his home.

He wasn't going to let John insert himself into his flashbacks anymore . . . but trying to take him down during one was too risky. No, this needed to happen on a level playing field.

Tom was looking at him strangely, and it was only then he realized he'd been humming.

"It's been a long time since I've heard you hum that song," Tom said quietly.

The song from the video. The song that reminded him of John. *If I ever . . .*

Wordlessly, he shoved the uniform jacket back into the bag and slid it under his arm. He grabbed Tom and kissed him—hard, sinking against him for a long moment. Tom's hand brushed the back of his neck, and then Prophet let Tom wind his arm around him and they walked that way—with Tom supporting him—back to their apartment.

Explore more of
SE Jakes's *Hell or High Water* series at:
riptidepublishing.com/titles/series/hell-or-high-water

Get ready for adventure with the
Havoc Motorcycle Club!
riptidepublishing.com/titles/running-wild

Dear Reader,

Thank you for reading SE Jakes' *Daylight Again*!

We know your time is precious and you have many, many entertainment options, so it means a lot that you've chosen to spend your time reading. We really hope you enjoyed it.

We'd be honored if you'd consider posting a review—good or bad—on sites like **Amazon, Barnes & Noble, Kobo, Goodreads, Twitter, Facebook, Tumblr,** and your blog or website. We'd also be honored if you told your friends and family about this book. Word of mouth is a book's lifeblood!

For more information on upcoming releases, author interviews, blog tours, contests, giveaways, and more, please sign up for our weekly, spam-free newsletter and visit us around the web:

Newsletter: tinyurl.com/RiptideSignup
Twitter: twitter.com/RiptideBooks
Facebook: facebook.com/RiptidePublishing
Goodreads: tinyurl.com/RiptideOnGoodreads
Tumblr: riptidepublishing.tumblr.com

Thank you so much for Reading the Rainbow!

RiptidePublishing.com

ACKNOWLEDGMENTS ◉

I am so incredibly lucky to be able to write stories I love, and for all the help and support I get along the way.

For Sarah Frantz, who simply gets me. For Rachel Haimowitz for all the opportunities she's given me. For LC Chase and the gorgeous covers and layouts. For Keturah Jenkins, who is always on top of creating amazing book tours and other opportunities for my books. For everyone at Riptide for making my publishing experience insanely wonderful.

A special thanks to those who keep my online spaces under control when I go into the writing cave: Andrea, LisaT, Susan, and Shawnie. Thanks for managing the havoc so well. And thanks to all the readers I've met and the friends I've made in the ASK SEJ Goodreads Group and the Dirty Deeds Facebook Group and on Tumblr and Twitter—thanks for being so crazy right along with me. And thanks to all of you who have taken this ride with Prophet and Tommy so far, for having faith that their series will end happily ever after. I promise we'll all come out of this in the end—bruised, put together with duct-tape . . . but smiling.

Last, but never least, for my family. For everything, always.

ALSO BY SE JAKES

Havoc Motorcycle Club
Running Wild

Hell or High Water (EE, Ltd.) Series
Catch a Ghost
Long Time Gone
Not Fade Away
If I Ever (Coming soon)

Men of Honor Series
Bound by Honor
Bound by Law
Ties That Bind
Bound by Danger
Bound for Keeps (EE, Ltd.)
Bound to Break

Standalone
Free Falling (EE, Ltd.)

Dirty Deeds Series (EE, Ltd.) Series
Dirty Deeds

ABOUT THE AUTHOR

SE Jakes writes m/m romance. She believes in happy endings and fighting for what you want in both fiction and real life. She lives in New York with her family and most days, she can be found happily writing (in bed). No really . . .

SE Jakes is the pen name of *New York Times* best-selling author Stephanie Tyler (and half of Sydney Croft).

You can contact her the following ways:

Email: authorsejakes@gmail.com

Website: sejakes.com

Tumblr: sejakes.tumblr.com

Facebook: Facebook.com/SEJakes

Twitter: Twitter.com/authorsejakes

Instagram: instagram.com/authorsejakes

Goodreads Group: Ask SE Jakes

Truth be told, the best way to contact her is by email or in blog comments. She spends most of her time writing but she loves to hear from readers!

Enjoy more stories like
Daylight Again
at RiptidePublishing.com!

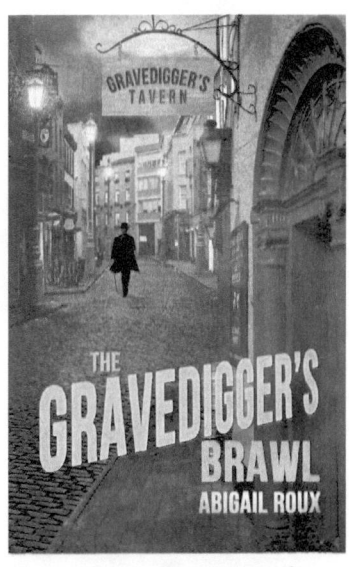

Gravedigger's Brawl
ISBN: 978-1-937551-53-7

Falling Sky
ISBN: 978-1-62649-040-6

Earn Bonus Bucks!

Earn 1 Bonus Buck for each dollar you spend. Find out how at
RiptidePublishing.com/news/bonus-bucks.

Win Free Ebooks for a Year!

Pre-order coming soon titles directly through our site and you'll
receive one entry into a drawing to win free books for a year! Get
the details at RiptidePublishing.com/contests.